THRIFT STORE TROLLS

A Flea Market Magic Novel

NEW YORK TIMES BESTSELLING AUTHOR

SHAWNTELLE MADISON

VALKYRIE
RISING
PRESS

eBook ISBN-13: 978-1-7344510-0-9

Print ISBN-13: 978-1-7344510-1-6

Natalya Christmas Artwork Copyright: Kate Sherron

Editing: N-Squared Edits, MK Books Editing

www.valkyrierisingpress.com

This book is dedicated to the readers who couldn't get enough of Natalya and wanted to hoard holiday cheer one more time.

CHAPTER 1

"Now you might believe you don't need a machete for a business conference," I said calmly to my mate, "but some would say they're a necessary tool for outdoor survival."

Thorn Grantham's blond eyebrow rose and he cocked his usual handsome grin. "Really, Nat? For a conference at the Holiday Inn in Montana?"

I pursed my lips while my gaze swept over the three suitcases I stacked against one of the bedroom walls. A part of me knew my help bordered on excessive—I did have obsessive-compulsive disorder—but the last time Thorn took a trip to California, he managed to sneak past me with only a single gym bag.

This time, I got up early to intercept him.

Try leaving the house without a first-aid kit this time, pal.

"Last I heard, the city of Helena doesn't have any jungles," Thorn said.

"Zombie outbreak?" I asked.

"Nope."

"Sirens tempting men to their deaths?"

"Montana doesn't have a coastline, babe."

I folded my arms. Fine.

Thorn reached for me, and I slid into the warmth of his arms. His heartbeat—strong and steady—thrummed against my cheek. *Now this is what bliss feels like.* Just me and my mate existing. Loving.

He rested his lips against the top of my head and murmured words I couldn't make out.

I leaned back. "What did you say?"

Mischief danced in his hazel eyes. "When I get back, you'll find out."

"If you keep this up, I might not be here when you return."

"Uh huh." He winked and let me go. To my dismay he took one suitcase and placed the other two in a pile near the closet.

If he ran out of tighty-whities, it wasn't my fault.

We strolled hand-in-hand through our cottage from our bedroom to the front door. The sun had yet to rise and bring with it June's relentless heat.

At the doorway, Thorn drew me into his arms again and his lips pressed against mine. Our kiss deepened and my toes curled from the delicious rush that flowed through me. He gently leaned me against the wall to push the long length of his body to mine.

"You sure you want to leave?" I murmured.

"Yeah, I gotta go." He kissed my nose. "I'll be back in a week."

"Be careful out there. It's been quiet for too long around here."

"Quiet is good. You'll be fine, Mrs. Grantham."

If Thorn believed everything was right with the world, maybe I should believe, too.

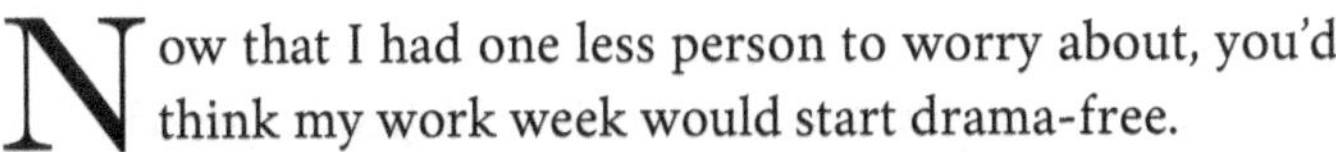

Now that I had one less person to worry about, you'd think my work week would start drama-free.

What a hopeful fool I am this morning.

"Okay, either someone brought a sack lunch straight from hell or our janitor necromancer has a dead minion who followed him to work," I snapped.

I scanned the expansive flea market floor, moving from one face in the crowd to the next. Not one of my four co-workers smelled like the culprit. Just another early morning at The Bend of the River Flea Market, also known as The Bends to the locals in South Toms River, New Jersey. The human shoppers, who didn't hear my quip, browsed our wares and didn't know about the supernatural world or the mystical objects that were sold on these shelves.

"It doesn't smell that bad, Natalya," a blonde next to me said.

I threw Erica a raised eyebrow. As a werewolf like me, her nose worked just as well as mine did. Maybe the cloud of designer perfume around her kept the funk at bay, but I could damn well smell it. And it stank to high heaven.

Saturday mornings never fared well for me. At eight-thirty in the morning, we had a sizable crowd hungry to rifle through the latest shipments to The Bends. My boss Bill should've been here complaining about the stench and ordering us to handle it. Naturally, the goblin was nowhere to be seen.

Looked like I'd get to have all the fun. As usual.

Since I couldn't trust the cleanliness habits of my fellow employees, I followed the one thing I could: my nose, which led me through a set of wooden doors into the business office.

If I found one of the janitor's zombie minions shuffling around the desks, he wouldn't get an invite to the company picnic this year.

The back office was empty. No Bill either. Maybe my boss was hiding somewhere. Didn't matter as I was on the hunt. Everything in the office was as I'd left it after the workday ended yesterday. The stack of invoices was in an ideal pile, the chairs arranged perfectly behind the desks, and even the merchandise we needed to prep for sale stood at attention.

Except for the old, beige steamer trunk on the floor.

It reeked.

Other than the foul stench emanating from within, the faded trunk was a thing of beauty with polished brass hinges and intricate clamps. The edges were slightly marred from where perhaps a dockworker long in its past had knocked it about. Under the fog of death, the saltiness of the sea still lingered.

I circled the luggage, noticing two strange things. There were strange carvings along the trunk's backside. The etchings were so tiny the human eye would've assumed they were scratches and nicks. There was also a palm-sized stone next to the trunk with the same markings. Nothing else was amiss.

Until that sucker shifted to the right. No warning, just a hard push on its own—from inside. I peered over the trunk's side to look at the front again. Something poked out. A large digit, hooked by a sharp talon and black and mottled with blue spots on the skin, tore a fist-sized hole through the leather near the seam. A four-fingered hand emerged. At least I thought it was a hand.

What in the ever-living hell?

The necrotic claws flexed along the edge, perhaps attempting to create a bigger hole. The stench of rotten eggs burned by eyes and twitched my nose. I hadn't smelled anything that foul since my aunt Vera tossed out six-month-old cabbage that somehow hid in the back of her basement refrigerator.

I took a step back.

Another quarter of claws crept through the gap that the first had formed. Now I had two potential escapees. The first then snaked out of the hole, revealing a long gray arm, the skin dry and scaly. Together, they reached about until one of the talons found the lock along the front.

Then the trunk shook with a hard thump.

A third set of claws came out to join the first two. Were all three attached to one body, or did I have multiple foes to face?

Hell to the no.

With a gentle push—this stuff wasn't mine—I tipped over the trunk onto its side.

"Get back in there!" I grunted.

Another thump from inside the trunk knocked me on my ass. The concrete floor in this room wasn't forgiving. The trunk jerked to the left on the floor. I plucked the fire extinguisher off the far wall, ready to kick some ass.

Now, to be honest, this wasn't the first magical mishap to go down at The Bends. Most problems though came from backfiring fairy wands to jock-itch-inducing jewelry. Cruise trunks containing monsters trying to break out was madness at a whole new level. Poised over the gray appendage, ready to knock that puppy back in, I bent back to do the yo-heave-ho when the customer service bell rang.

Under most circumstances, pretty much all of them, the bell would've had me scrambling like a werewolf caught butt-naked in human-form at dawn. Today, I had no choice but to ignore it. Damn it all to hell, I wasn't the only warm body working here.

Mid-swing that annoying shrill filled the air again.

Anxiety shot up my spine and smacked the back of my head.

Let it go, Nat.

I hit the arm hard with the fire extinguisher, and the luggage jumped. The second fist swung at me, hard and fast, but I dodged with a leap to the right. My body's shift pushed me toward the third set of claws, which seized the chance to slam me against the wall. Office supplies stacked on the shelves rained down on me. More work for me to do, huh?

A growl rumbled in my chest. The wolf within urged me into a full-out fight. No more obsessive-compulsive tendencies for the day. No more high heels. To hell with my clean blouse and pencil skirt. I advanced on the trunk, grabbing the fire extinguisher on the way.

The shrill ring of the buzzer entered my haze.

Don't answer it. Time to get medieval on the monster in the box.

Buzz. Buzz. Buzz.

I stormed out of the back office, fire extinguisher in hand, ready to knock out whoever thought it was a fun idea to do an Irish Line Dance on the buzzer, only to find a group of gaping nuns and a wide-eyed Erica.

"Oh, Jesus," I whispered and hid what I held behind my back.

"Indeed, Ms. Stravinsky," one sister, the shortest, chirped.

Erica plastered her charm on high with her debutante grin. "The Sisters of Divine Grace wanted the antique cross that came in two weeks ago."

Ugh. If there was a hell for goblins, Bill had a first-class ticket. In truth, that antique cross was a broken T-shaped torture device from the Spanish Inquisition.

"And?" I managed. The need to be polite was pivotal here. If you crossed the "SDG," as they were known in South Toms River, their gang-like mentality would mean ruin and dirty looks during the Christmas season.

"We'd like the cross loaded into our truck please," the woman said, her smile crisp and unwelcoming.

"Of course—" A loud crash from the back office made everyone look past me with concern, but I didn't miss a beat. "—we'll have a staff member load it up for you once we process payment."

The sound of glass breaking forced my jaw shut so tight the back of my teeth sang. "Will that be cash, check, or charge?"

"Is there a problem?" one of the nuns asked. Fear blossomed in the sweat of the tallest one who peered at me with suspicion.

One of the clerks, a fire witch named Millicent, paused from checking out another customer at the register and gave me the look. The should-I-stop-what-I'm-doing-and-make-a run-for-it look? I wouldn't be hearing a *Braveheart* rallying cry from her anytime soon.

"I need to see about a trunk," I said as I backed away. "Ms. Holden will assist you with payment while our staff prepares your cross. It will be a lovely addition to Sunday Mass, I'm sure."

The moment the sisters turned around, I hightailed it to the back office. What was left of it.

Holy shit.

One desk was toppled on its side, pens and paperclips scattered across the floor. I stepped over a broken stapler to inspect the new panes of glass we planned to use to replace a broken display case window, now shattered to glittery bits. And finally the coup de grâce, that stinky escapee smashed the box of week-old donuts Bill had left out for his employees. The dry jelly donuts bled their gooey centers all over the floor like a ravaged strawberry field.

There was no trunk or stone, but a revolting trail of grayish goo oozed from the center of the room to the busted-out double dock doors.

The odor was so bad that I pulled my collar over my nose as I drew closer to where the trunk had sat. Fear pulsed through me. Something magical, something strange that I never encountered until now, had been here.

From behind me, the doors to the main floor opened.

"So, Nat—" Erica stopped cold. "What happened?"

I pointed toward what was left of the dock doors. "Our merchandise just made a run for it."

CHAPTER 2

After five hundred dollars' worth of haunted merchandise slithered away, the morning didn't go well.

"We need to close the store and go after it," I said.

"We should wait for Bill," Erica said firmly. All the while, the expression on her face was stern but her blue-green-eyed gaze was planted to the ground. I snuck a quick glance at her. Erica Holden was perfect in so many ways. Compared to my chestnut-brown hair, her blonde curls shined like she was in a shampoo commercial with flawless lighting. Even with a back straightened in frustration and her head turned from mine, she was still painfully pretty. I had to remind myself that, nearly six months before, we fought on a starry New Year's Eve night for the rank of alpha female and I was the one who'd won. I was the one who'd snatched her dreams away. All her aspirations for an arranged marriage with the love of my life, Thorn Grantham, came to an end when I won the right to lead the pack.

The topic of he-who-shall-not-be-named never came

up during her training as assistant manager nor as we worked day-to-day together. It was simple in my opinion: Erica loved power and that power came with the position of alpha female. If she truly loved him, nothing I did that night would've come between them. As a werewolf who barely scratched her back the right way, I didn't make the best alpha female and my leadership skills were quite lacking.

Which made moments like this one awkward as hell.

"We can't let whatever escaped the trunk to roam wild." I took a step toward her. "If that thing gets recorded on someone's phone, it's gonna be more than the next viral video star. Everybody in the public will wind up in our business, and we'll have a lot more than Bill rubbing our fur the wrong way. When magical problems arise in New York City, the magical community sends warlocks to take out the trash." I drove my point home. "Would you like to know what warlocks do to people like us? Would you like to know how they use us for their dark magic?"

Erica stiffened. Her mouth briefly opened, but she sealed her lips just as quickly.

"You want a bunch of spellcasters sniffing our butts?" I asked again.

Erica didn't dare look me in the face, but her crossed arms and tight upper lip told me she didn't want to be involved in matters involving the magical world.

"Unlike you," she bit out, "I'm not equipped to handle this. I'm not a werewolf spellcaster."

There it was.

Werewolves weren't allowed to cast spells. According to the Code, or the rules governing werewolf behavior, we didn't dally in magic like witches, warlocks, and wizards. Though there was a reason for this, I still disobeyed the rules and went to Russia to learn Old Magic. No one could've stopped me from protecting or helping my family, and yet the knowledge I'd learned was both forbidden and unforgettable.

Thorn made me promise to never cast a spell again unless my life was at risk, and I crossed my heart to keep that promise.

"You must think I'm tossing around magic like I'm seasoning chicken." I held in a laugh. "It doesn't work like that, sweetheart. Spellcasting requires a currency I'm not willing to pay. So you and I are going outside and some-how, someway, we're dragging that thing back in here and putting a For Sale sign on it."

Her jaw twitched. "Fine."

She went to the overturned desk. I groaned when she reached inside the drawer for her purse. What good would that do? Then Erica smirked as she plucked a .45 from her expensive handbag and placed the gun into an ankle holster on her leg.

Huh. The woman who brought sushi for her lunches was packing heat? How plucky of her. And daring as well. The Code of conduct for werewolves also forbade us from using guns. Guess we were both rule-breakers.

She saw my confused expression and blurted, "I have a Prada handbag. You can never be too careful in a neigh-borhood like this one."

I snorted. "Yeah, those old ladies with antique fetishes and tourists with their fanny packs are such a threat. The danger is crazy real."

Except now, with that thing out there, it actually was.

Instead of closing the store, I put a college student in charge. That was a safer bet than the chain-smoking fire witch who set the counter on fire a few months ago.

Erica and I left through the new gap in the dock doors and crossed through the parking lot. The overcast sky threatened to bring rain and make our hunt even more somber. Thank goodness, there weren't any shoppers in our outdoor area. During this time of the year, we sold more merchandise on the rows of tables out here.

"If you can't do magic, how do you plan to defend your-self?" Erica asked.

"My *gun* is in my car. I can't take mine to work." I didn't carry a gun per se, but rather a magical weapon I'd acquired over the past year.

On the way to my Nissan Altima, I caught a faint whiff of copper. My gaze scanned our surroundings. The Bends was a large, old building nestled between a parking lot and another flea market. There wasn't much to see. South Toms River was basically a small town.

The strong, metallic scent of human blood drew us to the edge of the parking lot between The Bends and the neighboring flea market.

We found a glistening pool of crimson and nothing more next to a beat up, black pickup truck.

"It's human blood," Erica remarked.

"It's fresh, too," I murmured.

She glanced at the busy four-lane road not far from us. The trail we needed to follow was clear. Whatever we were after had headed straight into town.

"Looks like it had its first meal. Would you rather go back and wait for Bill?" I gestured in the direction we came from.

"Wait for Bill?" She scoffed. "Yeah, right. Are you sure you want to be pack leader?"

I frowned as Erica broke into a run down the Garden State Parkway.

～

By the time I fetched my handy magical blade from the back of my car, the mid-morning sunlight was nearly gone. Humidity dampened the air and signs of an incoming rain shower increased with each southward step we took. The rising heat made the hunt miserable.

No more than twenty feet away to our left, cars zipped past us on two lanes heading southbound on the Parkway. Clusters of trees gave us cover, but they also offered hiding spots for our prey. Not surprisingly, Erica took point. I was the better tracker between the two of us, but we'd get along better if I let her lead for now. Besides, fighting over who'd be attacked first was a waste of time.

The goblin blade hummed in my hand. Usually as active as a fork sitting on the dinner table, the goblin blade twitched, as if it sensed something supernatural lurking nearby. The weird weapon ended up in my possession during a trip to save my dad from the werewolf Russian mafia in Atlantic City. While cornering a conniving goblin hellbent on capturing my mate and me, I took the silver blade he tried to cut me with—not knowing that the goblin blade transformed into a new weapon based on the nearest supernatural threat to the owner's proximity. All the attempts I made to return the goblin's toy failed.

I guessed it was mine now.

The trail took us southwest past the subdivisions. Past the little league fields and playgrounds with perfectly good morsels of humans for the creature to eat. Then the houses disappeared, and our path became all too familiar once we crossed Double Trouble Road and came to a stop at the end of a long driveway.

"This place looks familiar," Erica whispered.

"It should. It's my old house."

CHAPTER 3

Before I'd fought Erica and moved in with Thorn at his house across town, I'd lived here alone as the pariah of the South Toms River Pack.

I had memories here—most of them good—but right now unease tickled the back of my neck. Normally, the forest surrounding my two-story cottage offered a wall of protection from the judgmental outside world, but with that creature potentially stalking my hallways, I felt thrown off.

"Any idea why it came here?" A hint of suspicion lined Erica's words.

"You have to be kidding me." My sigh was heavy with sarcasm. "I dunno. Especially since the last crazed monster meeting I held was at my mom's house."

Erica rolled her eyes. After she pulled her gun from her ankle holster, she hurried down the driveway and I followed. As we approached the house, the shadows along the trees grew ten-fold. The cottage, with its bright red shutters and whitewashed wood, seemed more like an evil witch's hideout from a fairytale than a regular home.

I scanned the area from the tree line to the house's roof. Branches swayed about with a growing wind. The squirrels and rabbits that freely roamed during the day had already sought shelter from the storm. While I checked for danger, I tried to push away the obvious doubt eating at me.

Erica had a right to be suspicious. Something weird showed up at The Bends, and while that wasn't all that usual, it could have gone anywhere but went straight to my former house. Not the place where I currently resided, rather the place I *used* to live. Had an old enemy sent me a gift? After everything that had happened over the past year, the likelihood that I had a cushy spot on someone's Shit List was quite high.

As we got closer to the house, the knife's hilt grew warmer against my palm. My heartbeat sped up. With each step, anxiety bled into my senses, making it harder to focus on what I had to do.

Erica glanced at me. "You all right, Natalya?"

My face grew warm with embarrassment as I nodded. Hiding fear among fellow pack members was near to impossible. The wolf within me whined, but I didn't so much as speak. I came here to handle business and I planned to do it. I tossed her the keys to the door. Erica fumbled with the lock then paused. Her head tilted to the right. Did she hear something from inside?

Then I heard the faint scratching on the porch roof overhead.

The wooden hilt in my hand elongated, extending until the wood became marble and the metal blade darkened from silver to black. Within moments, the weapon grew to match my five-foot-eight height. Tiny letters, like the ones I'd seen on the trunk, were carved into the stone.

Not good.

Every time this damn blade transformed, it told me what I was about to face. A broad sword or a battle-axe I could handle, but when the goblin blade morphed into a weapon like the one I now held, I had no idea what kind of madness I was about to step into.

For all I knew, the lance's strange writing read, *"Run, stupid!"*

The scratching wasn't far away now. The closest thing I could compare the noise to was fingernails dragging something heavy across the porch roof…

Claws appeared first.

But they were much bigger than what I'd seen sticking out of the trunk.

Erica twisted toward the movement, her gun drawn, but neither of us had time to react before a pungent mass flew between us. With a wet plop, the creature landed on the porch stairs.

My face contorted with disgust.

What I'd seen earlier had been no arm, but the legs of a beast with a serpentine body, a rooster's head, and black, bat-like wings. The hands from earlier were in the place where I expected to see feet. Its scaly, green torso shined from a putrid, bubbling fluid covering its skin. The creature, now the size of a Great Dane, hissed at us from its hooked orange beak.

"Oh, gross!" Erica shot first and asked questions later.

Bullets pelleted the creature, but the few that reached their target didn't keep it from rushing me. My lance went up in time to deflect its attack, the blade stabbing deep in its midsection. *Gotcha.* It squawked and bounded away, crashing across the porch and through the living room window.

I headed for the front door, but Erica grabbed my arm.

"Are you crazy? We need to call for help against th-th-that thing. Those bullets did nothing."

"That thing is a *basilisk*." Only once in my life had I seen one, and that was in a picture book. Unlike the harpies and other malevolent creatures I'd gotten up close and personal with, the basilisk was very rare. Legendary.

"I don't give a *fuck* if it's a chicken or a snake. It's not natural." Her normally refined composure collapsed as she jerked her gun toward the house. "If we can't get help from those warlocks, then we need the pack. What about the Stravinskys?" She paused briefly. "What about Thorn?"

Did she really just utter my husband's name? "He left town this morning on pack business. He's not available, but I could call my family—"

A crash inside the house told me the basilisk was wrecking the place. *My* place. If it so much as broke a single ... *Screw waiting.* I yanked my arm free and kicked down the door.

With the curtains drawn, the inside of my house was dark except for a few slivers of light reaching across the floors. My eyes adjusted to the dark to see that the living room, where the basilisk had entered, was trashed. The intruder's escape path was evident from the scratches across the wood floor, the gouges it ripped into the couch as it scampered over the furniture, and finally, to the wall where it crashed into my storage boxes filled with fragile collectibles.

Rage built in my stomach when I spotted massive dents in the boxes. "That motherf—"

"Quiet!" Erica picked up a lamp and crept toward the stairwell, following a slimy path. "We need to sneak up on it."

"Don't you have more bullets?" I hissed.

Her head whipped in my direction to give me a dark

look. "I haven't been caught breaking the Code's firearms rule yet, but I'm smart enough to not carry a bunch of extra clips around."

"Then I should take point." Reluctantly, she let me go up the staircase first. A few times on the way up, I had to grip the banister to keep myself from slipping. Gooey shit covered everything.

By the time I reached the top of the steps, most of the determination that fed me on the bottom floor disappeared. The stench was overwhelming—practically to the point that I couldn't track my prey by scent.

Where is it?

We crept along the hallway. Two bedroom doors were open. The wet trail ended along both.

So where could it go next?

The dead silence ended as we were thrown to the floor from above. That sneaky bat-chicken-whatever-the-hell-it-was clung to the ceiling and dropped down on us ninja-style.

I rolled out from under it, jumping up to swing the lance. Only to have it clank against the wall. Could you tell I often used these things?

The basilisk continued to pin a now-growling and snapping Erica against the floor, the claws from its four hands digging at her torso.

I swung the magical lance around—correctly, this time—and repeatedly stabbed that son-of-a-bitch like my life depended on it. "Get off her!"

The basilisk's squawk turned into an ear-piercing shriek when one of my jabs pierced between its black wings and went deep. It whipped its long tail in my direc-tion, forcing me back.

With a hard twist to the right, Erica slammed the lamp across the injured basilisk's rooster head and sent it careening into my old bedroom. It landed on my bed, bleeding from its wounds and seeping goo on the sheets and floor.

I jumped over Erica and rushed it. *Hold tight to the lance, Nat. Time to end this.*

The lance's obsidian blade slid straight through the basilisk's body into the wall, effectually impaling it. For now, anyway. It reached for me, clawing and biting at the pole. The flapping of its wings made it hard to hear anything else.

Then it slid forward along the pole, edging toward me. Its nimble fingers got closer and closer.

"Erica!" I gasped. If I moved back, I'd free it.

She slowly got up, holding her bleeding stomach. Was she hurt badly? With each step she took toward me, her steps grew steadier. "I'm here."

"Pin it," I grunted, jerking my head to the dresser on the other side of the room. Using her shoulder, she shoved the dresser across the floor until it held the basilisk in place.

"I'm moving!" I warned her. I stabbed it again and again. I got in more stabs than the chicken kabobs got at my aunt's house during Stravinsky family barbecues.

The basilisk grew silent. When it finally moved no more, I stumbled away.

"Is it really dead?" Erica asked.

"Good question." I advanced on the carcass, ready to do a few more hits for good measure, but the basilisk melted into a rotten puddle that smelled like wet trash decaying under the sun.

"It's gone," I said.

Erica sagged against the dresser and panted.

"Will you be all right?" I approached her to check the wounds, but she shied away.

"It's just a few scratches." She shrugged, but I could

smell her pain along with her pride that wouldn't let her show weakness. Especially not to me.

There were so many horrible things she'd done to me in the past—beatings, verbal abuse—but the pain I'd experienced should be her burden and not mine. I let her be and fetched her a towel.

By the time I caught my breath, it took everything I had, including popping a few anti-anxiety pills, to stop myself from *really* looking at the sad state of my former home. I hid my collection—my shameful hoard of Christmas collectibles—in this house and sooner or later I'd have to survey the damage.

At least Erica and I were alive. The rest could be dealt with in time.

I opened the bedroom window to air out the room and spotted someone standing outside.

Bill. Of course, our boss's smug goblin showed up after we made chicken noodle soup out of that monster. The cavalry had arrived. Conveniently late, I might add.

"Holy shit," he marveled as he looked around. "I hope you got good insurance, Nat."

To humans, Bill was just a tall, thin man with wire-framed glasses. But I'd seen goblins for real, and they were quite ugly and reeked of magic with a bitter tang of iron. The invisibility spell he used was quite welcomed.

"Good insurance?" I snapped. "I bet The Bends has no plans to compensate me for the damages."

Bill was the kind of guy who scrambled for dropped change off the flea market floor. I wouldn't see a damn penny for what the basilisk did to my house. I took in the disaster that was once my bedroom. My old bed smelled like snake shit. My whole house smelled like snake shit. Which meant there was no way in hell I could sleep tonight at the new house I shared with Thorn until every inch of my old house was wiped clean of this slimy crap.

Atomically pissed now, I began to clean while Erica slowly healed. As I tossed soiled linens out my bedroom window, Bill joined us.

He tsked at the sight. Erica continued to sit against the dresser as if she was glued to it.

"So, what are we taking back to The Bends again?" she murmured. Even her voice sounded tired.

She had a good point there. The trunk had disappeared when the basilisk bolted from The Bends, and now the trunk, the stone, and the creature were gone.

"I don't know." I turned to Bill. "What do you know about the steamer trunk or the basilisk we found inside?"

He shrugged. "Nothing, Nat. It showed up on the dock this morning. Probably part of a delivery from a wholesaler."

I sighed. Of course, he didn't know where it came from. Nothing he'd bought before, though, had ever attacked us like this. "What about the person who owned the black truck? I'm pretty sure that was the basilisk's lunch."

"That's what took me so long to get here. I had to take care of that mess," Bill replied. "Some guy just passing through town."

Bill's nonchalant attitude forced a growl from my throat. "How do you know he didn't have a family?"

Bill stiffened. "I said I took care of it, Nat. Unless you're willing to cast a spell. Perhaps call in a favor?"

"Not happening." He knew very well I'd learned a thing or two, and I wasn't willing to pay the price to do werewolf magic.

Some prices are worth paying, my Grandma Lasovskaya always said. She'd saved my life using werewolf magic, but I'd seen the cost and it wasn't worth it. Now that we had each other again, I intended to live as long as possible with Thorn. No spell would take him away from me.

I paused in the middle of working as my unease grew again. The basilisk had known where I *lived*.

Someone placed a target on my back.

"You don't know where it came from or why that thing went to my old house?" I asked.

Bill shrugged and pushed his glasses higher on his nose. The smile on his seemingly innocent, pale face sent a chill up my spine. "That's the crazy thing about dark magic, Natalya. You might think you've dodged the worst of it, but what goes around always comes back around for more."

If this was just the beginning of what was coming for me, I was scared senseless of what might be next.

CHAPTER 4

Three hours later, my bedroom and the slime trail down to the front door had been wiped, scrubbed, and decontaminated. The only stench here now was lemon-fresh goodness.

I dreaded checking on my collection. Just thinking about what I hid away here—exactly 523 Christmas, Hanukkah, Kwanzaa, and even Festivus holiday decorations—stirred my stomach in ways that threatened to make me lose my lunch. Living in another house with Thorn let me pretend I was normal. At first, I'd carried over a few boxes to my new place and stored them in corners, but over time I'd brought them back here so Thorn and I could build a home together.

A home without the old Natalya.

With a storm cloud of trepidation following me, I ventured into the living room and surveyed the damage. Two boxes were crushed while several stacks were knocked over. I scrambled to rearrange the containers, seeking out the comfort the neat lines offered. Even with the basilisk tainting the air with its funk, I still caught the faint scent of nutmeg and cinnamon. That was a good sign. Not so much a good omen for the crushed boxes. I opened them gingerly and cringed to see broken sets of holiday cheer lawn figurines and soiled Santa Loves Mrs. Claus teacups.

I'd have to throw them all away.

In the second box, hope sprang within me to see a single unmarred maroon box.

"Of course, you'd make it." I carefully pulled out a plastic-wrapped wooden figure. My beautiful Christmas nutcracker was quite the sturdy soldier in his red and green attire. The colorful glass jewels on his hat still shined in the dim room. With relief, I wrapped him back up in his plastic bag and stowed him away in another box.

That nutcracker fulfilled the promise he made when I lived here. All I had to do was gaze at him and recall the promise of a perfect holiday filled with a Christmas tree and family. Thank God, I had my family back, but if I *needed* him again, he would be here waiting for me.

Still safe and sound.

Time to finish cleaning up.

In between a few naps, Erica watched me without a word. She appeared paler though.

I offered her water, but she declined. As I put my cleaning supplies away in the closet, she crept down the stairs.

"Feeling better?" I asked.

"Not really, but a good night's sleep might help."

I nodded. What else could I say as I turned off all the lights and we plodded out. I whipped out my phone to call my younger brother Alex, but she declined a ride with a shake of her head and trotted down the road.

I called after her again, but she didn't answer. Guess we'd seen too much of each other today anyway. Twenty minutes later, Alex showed up, bleary-eyed, but conscious enough to drive.

My brother wasn't alone. I chuckled a little.

Seeing my sister-in-law Karey in the passenger seat almost made me double over with laughter, but I planted a smirk on my face instead. Looks like his wood nymph wife was far more vigilant about his self-care than he was. I climbed into the backseat. On the other side, my nine-month-old niece Sveta snoozed away in her car seat.

"Thanks for the ride," I said softly.

I could've called for a cab—hell, as the South Toms River alpha female, any of the pack members would've offered me a ride, but seeing my younger brother brought me peace.

The drive home was quiet with only the sounds of soft rock coming out of my brother's expensive speakers. After he'd traded in his shiny blue truck for a family-friendly Ford Taurus, he still managed to cram two thousand dollars of audio equipment inside. Go figure. The boy still had his toys.

Instead of dropping me off at the edge of the cottage property, they drove me all the way up to the house.

"Go check inside," Karey murmured to Alex with a nudge.

"I'll be fine—" I tried to get out of the car, but she turned around and grasped my arm. Her pale skin glistened as if morning dew formed droplets on the surface.

"No." Karey's light blue eyes shined with an unnatural glint. "There are whispers among the people of the forest. The brownies visiting the ShopRite were restless."

Was their wariness from the absorbent prices the place had?

"What's going on?" I asked.

Alex took my keys and checked out the house while

Karey spoke. "The forest folk feel a great shift is coming. These shifts come in waves. The first wave arrived today. Be careful, Sister Wolf."

I opened my mouth to ask her more questions, but she released me and turned around—ending the conversation for now. I hurried into the house. Rest now, questions later.

As I bid my brother goodbye and locked up the house, my stomach quivered. Why did all this shit have to go down on my watch as the South Toms River Pack alpha female?

~

When Thorn left the house on business, restless nights and I became besties. We spent hours searching for that one middle piece in those thousand-piece puzzles. Sometimes we partied together while I baked sugar cookies and listened to soft jazz that soothed my nerves.

I even tried to craft a fly fishing lure. You see, over the past couple of months, Thorn and I had made plans for a weekend trip to Maine. Just the two of us, our supplies, and a box of hand sanitizers. Not that I knew how to fly fish, Thorn would have to teach me, but what mattered was that it was just me and him.

So far, every time we crossed out a date on the calendar, another pack issue popped up and forced us to change plans.

Pensive nights like these were also a reminder of when I didn't live alone at the old cottage and my best friend from childhood kept me company. It was about this time, three in the morning, that Agatha McClure—or Aggie as her good friends called her—stomped on the flowers outside of my house and tried to see if I was inside. Naturally, I'd thought she was an intruder, but she was just passing through and needed a place to stay. If I closed my eyes, I could imagine how she looked that day: a tall redhead holding a small bag in hand.

Even though she was rich and outspoken, Aggie hadn't judged me when she walked into my small house and spied my mental illness piled up against the walls. She only reached out to me with concern and not incrimination. When I asked about her plans, all she'd said was, "I'm moving out west to Vegas."

But Aggie never jumped on the next Greyhound to Sin City. She stayed by my side and shoved me, kicking and screaming as I was, from my role as the local pack pariah to alpha female.

She should still be back in my cottage, living and thriving, but Thorn told me she'd disappeared while I was out of town. She'd left no note or sign she'd been taken against her will. Only an empty bedroom and her personal belongings where she'd left them.

Maybe she'd boarded that Greyhound bus after all and was now living it up in Las Vegas. My heart though knew the truth: something had gone wrong while I was away.

And now I had no clues to uncover the truth.

I turned up the music louder. John Coltrane's soulful saxophone played "Body and Soul" and tugged me away to happier times.

CHAPTER 5

The next morning, I woke up to stiff limbs and the strange taste of plastic in my mouth. Maybe I'd accidentally swallowed some of that basilisk goo. Eww.

Thorn's side of our bed was cold, but his scent lingered, giving me a smile that would last me for the rest of the day. As I got up, stretching and grimacing, I ran my nose over his pillow and giggled like I had no common sense.

That's what a good man can do for a woman, I thought.

Briefly, Erica came to mind and I swatted the thought away as I walked across my bedroom to my closet. Erica and Thorn weren't an item anymore—but I did wonder how she fared. Did she fully recover after the basilisk attack?

I browsed through the blouses in my closet. The task felt fruitless since I typically wore the same set of clothes to reduce anxiety, but I decided to forgo my usual uniform.

See? Personal growth achieved.

From the dresser I shared with Thorn, I retrieved a

casual cuff-sleeve blouse and a pair of business slacks. After I slipped the clothes on, a nagging crept up my spine. These clothes didn't feel right: the top was gray instead of white and the slacks weren't tailored like my skirts. But as my gaze swept over my reflection in the mirror, the look of determination on my face said otherwise. If I wanted to be the pack's alpha female, I had to be flexible. Even if I wanted to rip off this top and see how fast I could drop-kick it into the hamper.

After I grabbed a quick breakfast of some oatmeal and hot tea, I left the house and made my way to work.

Nothing seemed amiss as I sped down the Garden State Parkway. Sunday mornings should always be so calm. Fluffy clouds shaped like balloon animals stretched across a magnificent blue sky. I could practically extend my head out of the window and let the warm breeze bring the promise of summer barbecues with my family.

Yet as I scanned the familiar buildings lining my path to work, from the ShopRite to the fairy-owned bakery, something tickled the back of my neck. Nothing seemed unusual when I passed the local day care or Archie's Burgers, but my sister-in-law warned me a shift was coming. What shift had she meant? And who would I have to ask for answers?

I pulled my car into the parking lot at The Bends. Sure enough, the Sunday morning die-hards already clustered outside the doors for their flea market fix. Two witches, a cyclops couple, and a kobold draped under the heavy glamour of a middle-aged lady in a loud floral-print dress formed a lopsided line.

When one of the witches spotted me heading for the back door, an eagerness glinted in her eyes. I could practically read the "hurry it up, lady" in the way she shifted from one foot to the other.

With the customers' eyes boring a hole through my back, I hurried to the far end of the store, passing our awning-covered tables. The tables were bare, but in a couple of minutes, Quinton would haul goods out for shoppers to browse. Usually the back door was clear, but this time, new items cluttered the path to the door.

All of them were trunks like the one I encountered yesterday.

None of them stank to high hell, but I gave them a wide berth nonetheless.

Once inside the shop, I dropped off my purse in the business office. My nose told me Erica had yet to arrive. Matter of fact, the lack of noise on the shopping floor outside the large set of wooden doors meant I'd arrived first. As usual.

I glanced at my watch. It was 8:20 am. Most of the time, I arrived appallingly early, well before Erica came and began prepping the cash registers. Tumbleweeds could've swept the floor better than my underlings.

I swallowed a curse as I calculated how quickly I could carry out the newest merchandise, catalog the goods, and toss them into the proper displays. I could make it. Just had to focus on what the customers would buy. I dashed into the back office and searched through boxes until I spotted a crate with the wands. Witches with deep pockets came first. They loved a personalized selection. Working at The Bends for several years taught me a few things about magic outside of the werewolf realm. Witches bought wands based on the type of wood, some preferring mahogany over cherry while others were tempted by birch, and that wood type also had to match with a water, wind, earth, or fire witch. You just couldn't have a water witch casting off spells with an earth witch's wand—that's how geysers happened.

Hammer be damned, I wrenched the box open, snagged a handful of goodies, and raced to the display. We already had pre-labeled tags for miscellaneous wands, which made my job faster and easier.

With the witches taken care of, I considered the other clients lined up. Kobolds and other fairy folk tended to meander without something specific in mind, but once they spotted any enchanted clothes, they riffled through our racks until they filled their baskets. They hoarded the stuff—you wouldn't catch me wearing someone's sweaty, let alone charmed, hand-me-downs on a good day—but to each their own.

Now the cyclops were another matter. How long had it been since I'd seen one? Let alone a couple. I shrugged and let it go. Stressing about satisfying every customer was a bad habit I used to have.

My co-workers' enthusiasm for their job was yet another concern. I needed them here and on-time. First, Millicent, Erica, and another werewolf clerk named Melissa, sauntered in at exactly 8:30.

"Hey, Nat," Millicent chirped. A cloud of cigarette smoke trailed after her and clung to her purple braided hair. I watched her walk past the door to take her place behind the counter. My hands were full of some amethyst bookends the cyclops pair might fancy. My last Hail Mary before the morning rush.

Was anyone gonna open the door?

With an amused expression, Erica intercepted me and hurried toward the entrance to unlock the doors. "We're all late because a double-wide truck blocked southbound traffic on the Expressway."

"Really?" I replied. "Were they hauling a house?"

Did a tornado drop the house on the fire witch before she got here?

Customers flooded into the store. Far more than I spotted when I arrived. In a manner much more efficient than our co-workers, Erica managed to speak and usher in our customers at the same time. "No, they were unloading this…shack across the street into the empty lot."

If I had ears on the top of my head, they would've perked up.

"You mean Baker's empty lot with half-dead trees?" I wondered. "For the last twenty years, the mosquitos got more action outta that place than any people."

Erica shrugged and flipped her hair behind her ear. "Where one man finds trash, another finds treasure."

As much as I wanted to check out the new tenants, I had other matters to worry about. The witches headed to the wand display case, and as I predicted the kobolds made a beeline to a rack full of enchanted capes. The cyclops couple made a surprise decision and overlooked the book-ends in favor of examining the new selection of Haunted Heather figurines. Every time a cyclops touched one, the antique groaned until the one-eyed customer had a chorus of tiny statuettes going strong.

With all the customers occupied, I settled into my morning routine. Somebody had to run this circus until the clowns went home.

Eventually, lunchtime came. Time passed too quickly—which meant I still loved this job no matter how crazy things progressed. I glanced up from doing data entry in the back office to see Erica eating her sushi lunch. My growling stomach told me her meal was fresh tuna delicately wrapped with vegetables and a hint of wasabi.

How sensible and healthy.

Silence floated between us. Soon enough, I couldn't take it anymore.

"You healed up from yesterday?" I asked.

She nodded. "I won't be wearing a two-piece any time soon, but I'm fine."

More silence. More sushi. The *click-click* noises from her chopsticks bounced off the walls. I had a lunch packed, but I couldn't get excited about the chicken salad sandwiches I'd prepared.

"You're not going to say anything about what we saw?" Erica finally murmured. "Or why it was at *your* house?"

"Honestly, I wish I knew why the basilisk targeted me. Only one thing is certain. Whoever is behind the trunks knows who I am and where I used to live. How come it didn't go to my new house with Thorn?"

At the mention of Thorn's name, she rose from the lunch table and threw away her empty can of diet soda.

I continued. "Last night, Alex and Karey took me home. While Alex checked the house, Karey told me a *shift* of some kind was coming. You know anything about that?"

She shrugged. "If that trunk hadn't shown up, I would've told you it was just another day in South Toms River."

"Just another day," I whispered. What I wouldn't give for a couple of dull days. *Oh, monotony, how I missed thee.*

Erica headed to the double doors. "By the way, Quinton asked about the trunks near the back door. He's not supposed to touch them, right?"

"Yup, I secured them with locks. Leave them be until Bill shows up," I grumbled. "And that goblin better have the answers."

~

Bill never showed up for work. That goblin gnawed my last nerve raw. I stayed past my shift—even lingering to my dinner time around six o'clock. The decadent aromas from grilled burgers, fresh-cut fries, and pecan pie wafted from Archie's Burgers down the road, but I remained strong until I clocked out and my stomach gladly led the way out of The Bends.

The wolf within needed to be fed.

Archie's Burgers was only three blocks away, so I walked up the street and scoped out the construction Erica mentioned. Over the past nine hours, the folks on the other side of the Parkway had been quite busy. They cleared a cluster of imposing oak trees. A concrete mixer, still parked off to the side, poured out fresh concrete for a meager parking lot capable of holding around ten cars. Guess they weren't planning on a deluge any time soon. Next to the makeshift parking lot, stood the building—if you could call it that. Erica was being generous when she called it a shack. I tilted my head as I studied it and tried not to stare too hard—"Don't be rude," my mother would say—but the shingles on the exterior were barely nailed on and, worse yet, they were crooked.

The store's front wasn't any prettier. The truck that hauled the building here had torn giant gouges through the grassy lawn. My gaze jumped from the butchered lawn to the lopsided stone path leading from the parking lot to the building. Hope they had plans for landscaping.

I tried to peer through the four dirty, tinted windows in the front, but I couldn't make out the interior. The whole place screamed don't-bother-shopping-here.

I walked faster. The exterior was subpar, but as I imagined what the place held within, a familiar tingle danced down my spine.

Did they have something I wanted? was the question.

Once I had my fill of being nosy, I pushed the new business from my mind and headed to Archie's. The restaurant had been here since I'd been born. One werewolf owner passed it to another and Archie's burned meat the best. A fine char on the outside while the inside was nice and juicy.

If I could drool in public, I would.

I walked inside and assessed the place. Most of the red booths were empty—the dinner rush had already passed. I had many memories here, many of them peppered with good and bad.

Most of them bad, but I wasn't the pack outcast anymore.

To order your chow at Archie's, you went up to an order window and then one of the waitresses brought your food to your table. After a long day of working, I looked forward to someone taking care of me for once. Even if I paid them for it.

I approached the order window and a familiar face appeared.

"Hey, Natalya, you're eating later than usual," Jake the cashier said.

I forced myself to meet his eyes. "Early summer crowds."

Jake was about my age, twenty-five or so, with a friendly smile and blond hair that never fit under his black and red striped hat.

"The usual?" Jake asked.

I grinned to see he'd already written my order on the ticket.

"Yep. Double cheeseburger and fries."

"Kill it with fire," he yelled to the back. He shoved the ticket in the order shelf.

From the back I caught the grunt of Harold, the owner of Archie's and the cook. I rarely peeked back there anymore. It was like seeing how the Wizard of Oz worked behind the curtain. Most of the time, I feared microorganisms lurked in my food, but Harold had a sparkling kitchen—and his stove probably had a nuclear reactor hidden inside. Nothing under five microns was coming out of there.

I paid for my meal and snagged my usual booth in the back. A few werewolves from the local mill were heading out as a family of five ambled inside. As I sat, the new werewolf customers nodded my way with respect. I returned the gesture.

Eight minutes passed and then Jake's younger sister Misty brought out my food on a tray. Months ago, she would've slapped the food on the table. This time, she placed the tray carefully in front of me, added a pile of napkins, and small packets of wet wipes. (That was my idea. Greasy food needed something with more spunk than a paper napkin that'd just fall apart.)

"Thanks, Misty."

"Sure." She lingered next to me.

I wolfed down three piping hot fries before I couldn't take it anymore. Manners be damned.

"Can I help you with anything?" I asked, my hand clenching another fry.

"I usually go to Thorn with this problem, but he's out of town."

"Ah." I put down the fry. Thorn had sheltered me from pack business for months. As the alpha female, however, I couldn't avoid it forever.

"Well," she began as she folded her arms across her chest, "my boyfriend Josh is acting out again."

My eyebrow rose. "Acting out again?"

"It's a long story, but Josh has always thought of Thorn as his big brother."

That sounded natural since Thorn's younger brother Will was the same age as Josh.

Misty continued. "Every time Thorn leaves town, my boyfriend gets jealous and too protective. I don't understand why he needs his alpha nearby to reassure him."

As if on cue, the dude in question popped into view across the street. He was rather cute in his gray Coldplay T-shirt and jeans, leaning against his dark purple Honda Fit like Jake in the movie *Sixteen Candles*, but Misty didn't appear smitten. An annoyed grimace filled the dark-haired, young woman's face.

"Is he waiting to pick you up tonight?" I asked.

"He's been there for the last two hours. When I don't come out exactly at ten, he gives me the silent treatment."

Oh, hell no. I was a control freak, but even I had my limits.

"First, I'll talk to him. Second, why do you put up with his bullshit?" I took in my food—the fries still begged for me to snarf them down and the burger was temptation all wrapped up like a gift, but I had pack business to settle.

As Misty followed me to the door, she said, "He's a really good guy—"

"—but *only* when Thorn is around? Not good enough. Stay inside."

I marched across the street, my chin held high. I wrangled employees all day, how much harder could it be to tell a possessive boyfriend to take a chill pill?

The minute he saw me approach, Josh stood bone straight. Good. But then he had the nerve to sidestep around me so he could keep an eye on Misty through the window.

"What are you doing, Josh?" I might as well get to the point.

"Hey, Natalya." Respectfully, he kept his chin low, but I

could smell the black-pepper scented guilt floating out of his pores.

I gestured toward Archie's. "You didn't answer my question."

"Gettin' some fresh air."

I scoffed. He better not waste my time—I had eating to get to. "Standing around and watching your girlfriend work isn't right. To be honest, you're in creepy stalker mode. Not cool, Josh."

He stiffened, but he didn't speak. A hint of anger touched his features, but the feeling disappeared as quickly as it came.

"Look, I know you're concerned for Misty," I added, "but her older brother is inside. Would Jake let anybody hurt her?"

"None of you know what's coming," he said under his breath. "I can feel something in the air."

The hair on the back of my head stood at attention. I narrowed my eyes. "What do you mean?"

"My old man used to talk about this gut feeling he'd have whenever something bad was about to happen to the pack."

I took a step closer to him to hear him clearly.

"Now I know what he's talking about," he added. "For the past couple of days, I've felt really weird."

I sucked in a breath. Did Josh's family know a bit of Old Magic? Not powerful spells to be conjured with words, but an uncanny intuition touched werewolves, too.

"Everything's fine." I angled myself to block his view again. "Going with your gut is good and all, but you're taking it too far. Misty doesn't like it, and neither do I."

I opened his car door for him. "Go home and give her some space. If she wants you around, she'll call you when her shift is over—"

"What's that?" Josh interrupted, his voice hollow.

From where Josh and I stood, we spotted a small crowd standing next to Archie's side entrance. Misty, Jake, and a few customers surrounded something on the ground.

It was another trunk with a black stone next to it.

And those damn fools just popped the trunk open.

CHAPTER 6

Not one but two basilisks sprang from the trunk, squawking and flapping their dark wings. Immediately, one of them swiped at the crowd with its claws, and my stomach dropped.

"Get in the car!" I yelled to Josh, but my command was ignored as Josh bolted toward the diner.

Across the street, Jake fell back into Harold and Misty. I scanned the area to see if anyone—or, specifically, any creature—fled on foot. Someone left a present behind, and regardless of whether it was for me or the werewolves working at Archie's, my duty was to uncover the culprit.

A cluster of trees to my left rustled. The wind blew east toward the coast, effectively blocking any scent from within the woods. I shifted to give chase until the harsh sound of broken glass tugged me back to Archie's. One of the basilisks entered the restaurant through a window. A single human woman fled out the front. Shit. Hopefully, she could be convinced that someone laced her post-work latte with LSD.

I pointed down the road. "Go that way!"

She pulled out her phone and ran, which meant the cops would be coming soon.

I didn't have the goblin blade with me, so I'd have to improvise. Josh's car door was open. A quick scan of the interior didn't reveal much, but I spied a crowbar on the floor of the backseat. Perfect. I snatched it, right as a basilisk jumped onto the top of the Honda Fit. Its talons scraped the roof with a hair-raising screech. The whole car shuddered under its weight and the creature's stench, which I now knew far too well, flooded the interior. I wrenched the door shut.

Inside the restaurant, I spotted two werewolves along with Josh and Misty, protecting a few kids. Damn, I'd forgotten about the family inside. And they were all looking to me for help as their alpha female.

The basilisk's claws made a *clickity-clack* racket as it traipsed across the car's roof toward the back. Once it spotted me through the rear window, it scratched at the glass, its disgusting goo drenching the surface. My whole body tensed. My grip on the crowbar tightened. What I wouldn't give to have that lance. If that bastard wanted a fight, I'd give it one. Fractures formed on the glass—it wouldn't hold much longer—and a massive crack snaked across the surface. The wolf under my skin yipped, hungry for the confrontation to come. Finally, the glass shattered, raining shards and slime into the backseat. I reached back with my new friend Mr. Crowbar. The moment the chicken-snake poked its head inside, I gave its head a good *thwack*. Not once, but three times without letting up. Stunned, the basilisk wobbled and crashed to the opposite side of the car.

It wouldn't be down for long.

I heaved open the dented-in door and scrambled to Archie's. Gotta move fast. The cops had to be on the way, thanks to that human chick. All hell broke loose inside the burger joint. Armed with a butcher's knife, Jake clung to the basilisk's back. The duo crashed into the booths along the wall, fissures driving up through the plaster. The basilisk shrieked and flung him off. Misty and Josh, still holding their chairs, pushed the kids toward the nearest door, but the basilisk regrouped and jumped into the way, its massive bat wings blocking any escape route.

Rage bubbled in my gut. If that bastard touched them, I'd never forgive myself. I leapt through the broken window, crowbar ready, but the distance was too great. The basilisk's hooked beak snapped the nearest chair into bits, its claws reached for Misty's head.

No. No. No!

The words to end this madness jumped to the tip of my tongue. All I had to do was speak them and draw fire from within. Or I could pull every drop of water from its body and dry it to a crisp. But the words refused to come and I was left with one option: I chucked the crowbar. With a hard *thunk*, the metal bar hit the chicken-snake in the head and clattered behind the tables.

And now I'm empty-handed and it's looking at me like I'm dinner.

With its attention on me, I turned heel and bolted to the kitchen. I had a much better selection of sharp toys in there. I scanned the far wall past the dishwasher and prep table. I snagged a Rösle portable propane cooking torch. The moment I turned to face my adversary, the basilisk got a mouthful of fire courtesy of the cooking torch and PAM cooking spray.

"Chew on this!" I yelled.

A screech filled the air and the basilisk flailed, its skin bubbling and burning and rooster feathers catching flame, filling the room with a rancid odor of burnt bat. I scurried around the beast, leaping out of the way when its burning tail swiped at me. Thank heavens, it missed. Once out of the kitchen, I slammed the door shut and Harold slid a booth in the way to block it.

One trapped and dying. One more to go.

The dining room was empty. The family had thankfully escaped and the parents stood outside with their children close. Josh and Misty raced to the front.

The fire alarm in the kitchen blared, smothering the sounds of the screaming basilisk.

"Did you see the other one?" I asked them.

"No, it's gone and the trunk, too," Misty said.

Damn it.

"We can track it," I replied. "They leave a grease trail for miles."

The faint wail of the police siren grew louder. Time's up. Someone had to go after the damn thing, and yet what the hell could we tell the humans? Would they believe a bunch of mythological creatures crashed the joint?

Crashed.

I glanced at Josh. "Get in your car. For real this time."

~

Five minutes later, Jake and I raced out of The Bends parking lot in my Altima. We drove past Archie's in time to see the back end of Josh's Honda Fit poking out from a crumbling wall.

"I hope you have insurance," I muttered.

Jake sighed. "You think State Farm will believe all that damage came from a car?"

"He shoved that sucker in there pretty good," I replied. "I'd say he was going at least forty miles per hour."

I navigated the Altima along Dover Road with the

window cracked so I could follow the second basilisk's scent. Like last time, that slimy creature made a beeline for my old house.

I glanced at Jake. His breath was labored, and a nasty cut carved up his side. It was the same place Erica got hit.

"How you holding up?" I asked, reaching into my glove compartment for some napkins. As hard as I tried to ignore the trail of blood dripping into my seats, my mind conjured hours of scrubbing and sanitizing. Could blood be removed from cotton? Would I be too busy hours from now to do anything?

No, not now, Nat.

I swatted the errant thought away and focused on driving scarcely enough over the speed limit as to not draw any attention from the cops. By the time we pulled up the long driveway, Jake had paled considerably. When I stopped right next to the door, he reached for the door handle.

I grabbed his shoulder. "Don't think about it, pal."

"It took over five of us to wrangle that thing," he rasped. "What are you going to do?"

I got out of the car, popped the trunk, and pulled out the goblin lance. I couldn't help but grin as I hefted the weapon. "Don't worry. This blade is great for pest control problems. Just need to shove this thing down its throat a couple of times."

As I unlocked the front door, I caught Jake saying, "I hope to God roaches and rats never get that big."

CHAPTER 7

I never imagined that I'd ever learn how hard it was to wash basilisk sludge from my hair, but here I was. My house didn't fare any better than the last time, but at least I had enough experience that I could dispatch that chicken-snake son-of-a-bitch much more efficiently. How many folks could say they were pros at killing basilisks? It was something to be proud of, really.

After the attack at Archie's and another seven minutes I spent chasing basilisk number two through my old house, I was exhausted but relieved when Misty came to pick up Jake. As she planned to patch up his wounds at home, I patched up my house, toiling away at the gunk on the walls and debris from my old life.

Not long after finishing, my dad texted me about a pack meeting at their house. I hadn't given the call to meet—another werewolf who always rubbed my fur the wrong way jumped at the opportunity to lead: Rex. We grew up together, and before I dated Thorn, my parents even considered him an ideal match for me.

But Rex was never meant to be alpha and he hated

living in Thorn's shadow. I suspected he wouldn't want to stay there forever.

As I parked behind a bunch of cars next to my parents' Colonial-style home, dread soured my stomach. Car after car filled the street. A few pack members arrived earlier, and if there were this many of us gathered, word had to be spreading about the magical what-the-fuckery going down in South Toms River. Rex probably convened early so I'd show up late and lose face. Any chance to rub my nose in it, I guessed. After I took my role as alpha female, I thought I was done proving myself to him.

With my shoulders straightened and my hands free from sweat, I marched up to the house and went inside. Dinner time passed two hours ago, but the mouthwatering scent of Mom's slow-cooked *borscht* still filled the house. Layer after layer of beets, cabbage, and pepper coursed through my nostrils. I could practically hear the stew bubbling in the pot from memory.

My mother, an elementary schoolteacher, was a master of meat. Not that she couldn't bake, sauté, or slice food to perfection as well, but mom crafted roasts and whole chickens with the finesse of a well-trained chef. The Stravinsky clan, along with other pack members, filled the living room, kitchen, and dining room. Every seat, sofa, and chair was taken so I waited in the foyer, my gaze sweeping over the room until I spied an older woman sitting on the sofa on the far side of the living room.

Grandma Lasovskaya's whole face lit up as soon as she saw me. Other werewolves nodded my way, but I merely blurted out a hello until I knelt to greet my grandmother eye-to-eye.

"After I heard what happened, I was worried about you." Her face was wrinkled with time, but her speckled brown eyes had depth. She'd seen the world change over the centuries, even witnessing the construction of St. Basil's Cathedral in Moscow.

"Nobody pushes a Lasovskaya girl around," I replied with pride.

Her warm hand brushed against my face. "Be mindful..."

Her words lingered in the air between us and I understood her warning.

No Old Magic.

I nodded and rose to head into the kitchen. My mother's domain was where I found Jake, Rex, Uncle Boris, and my father.

Jake glanced up. "Hey, Nat. What kept you?"

I was going to tell them I was too busy with decontamination but didn't bother.

"Looks like I missed the memo." I shot Rex a death glare and he returned a small shrug. And he called himself a werewolf, more like a jackass. When I was younger, I'd thought Rex was quite the catch. I'd call Thorn a child of summer with hazel eyes and untamed blond hair while Rex was the opposite—the temptation of winter with dark eyes and hair. Underneath the veneer of his strong chin and well-sculpted mouth, he was cold and bitter.

"You didn't miss much." My dad nodded my way. He accepted another plate of food from my mom. "We're waiting for Alex's wife. Her family wants to meet us."

Uncle Boris stood, offering me a place at the four-seater table. A heavy wave of his pepper-scented aftershave made me grimace. *Ladies, beware.* I teased him about the smell last week and he replied, "A month ago in Atlantic City I got four phone numbers."

Rex didn't so much as twitch. I glanced around the room. A thin fog of anxiousness touched us all. My fair-haired mother stirred her soup, her gaze fixed on some point outside the window over the stove. I didn't dare interrupt her. My father filled the most space in the room with his barrel chest and thick arms, yet he slowly scratched his bald head—a sign of agitation. Jake hunched over in his seat but tried to appear positive.

"Are there any decisions waiting for my approval?" I directed the question to Rex.

"Nothing you need to worry about," he said smoothly.

A trickle of anger pulsed through me. "The minute Thorn left, you couldn't wait to piss in my yard."

He merely flashed me his classic smug expression in response.

"Whoever is behind the trunks isn't done wreaking havoc," I said stiffly. "We need to work together."

He sighed. "An alpha leads. What have *you done?*"

Tension filled my shoulders.

"Does Thorn know what's gone down?" His jaw twitched.

"I'm calling him later tonight."

"And he'll roll in and save the day, right?" he chuffed. "Got any ideas before we all die?"

My mouth opened then shut again.

You know he's doing this to outmaneuver you, I reminded myself.

We stared at each other while I swallowed any retorts and counted to ten. I reached eight when noise from arriving guests doused the flames.

"Looks like the nymphs are here." I got up before I shoved my dad's bowl of *borscht* down Rex's throat so he could choke on it. "I'll greet our guests while you massage your ego."

I entered the living room with Rex not far behind. Erica and her father Oliver had arrived, as well as Alex, Karey, and her family. Everyone tried to fit into an already packed house. I counted four nymphs total, including my sister-in-law. Karey smiled at me, while Grace and Dione, her fair-haired and freckled nymph sisters waved my way.

The loud werewolves in the room grew silent. My eyes briefly connected with Oliver Holden, but his sharp glare made me clench my fists. He was just as handsome and brusque as his daughter, but he rarely made appearances anymore.

Back before I became alpha female, the pack had financial debts to pay and Oliver had promised to help—if Thorn took Erica as his mate. She was a natural fit for the role, but Thorn loved me and the deal went south. Recently, Oliver's great fortune tumbled into the trash, too. Without his money, his strut around town had lost its swagger.

I turned to my family and ignored Oliver. "Glad you could make it."

I reached for my niece to hold her, but my mom snuck past me and snatched Sveta to take the baby to the kitchen. I chuckled. My alpha privileges couldn't keep a grandma from her grandchild.

Karey spoke up. "Before we could meet, my aunt had business to settle in the forest."

She gestured toward the short, middle-aged woman with dark-green eyes and salt-and-pepper hair. Her hand-made floral print dress made her stand out among the other nymphs in their casual clothes. "This is my aunt Mevelyn. You've met my sisters Grace and Dione before."

"Yes, I remember them from your wedding." I was introduced to a gang of nymphs that day.

Karey's features darkened. "I heard about what happened at Archie's. Are you okay?"

"The pups had quite a fright, but we'll be fine," I replied. "I'm more worried about the aftermath. If we cause too much trouble around here, humans will catch on, never mind that spellcasters will come snooping around to clean up the mess."

"True, I—" Karey began to say before Mevelyn touched her shoulder.

"I have much to say and there's work to be done," her aunt whispered.

"Of course, Auntie." Karey stepped back.

I motioned for one of the wolves lounging on the couch to stand for our guest, but Mevelyn declined the offer. She surveyed the room first then she told everyone about what Karey had already told me: that a rare shift was coming.

She continued. "We found the source of the shift. The Great Northern Fairy Path is changing. It's gradually moving south, and it will arrive here soon, bringing chaos and death."

The gaze of every werewolf in the room flitted to me to gauge my reaction. I took a deep breath and stilled my heart. We had yet to hear concrete repercussions. "And what happens when a fairy path shifts? I've heard of them, but I thought they were pseudoscience."

Karey chuckled. "Some things the humans got right. Other things not so much."

Mevelyn added, "If I see one more crazy *Ancient Aliens* episode—"

Karey then said, "What you need to understand is there are places in the world where powerful beings dwell. Dong Hwi the Dark One in Asia. The Eternal Night Wanderer near Kamchatka in Siberia. Some of these legendary creatures are benign and stay put, while others follow a set pattern—a migration of sorts. Those who follow a fairy path are very dangerous and should be avoided at all costs."

The werewolves murmured among themselves until my hand rose a little. They quieted.

Wow, that really worked. I needed to remember that.

Karey continued. "These slumbering gods and demi-gods affect the land around them, either bestowing strength, riches, or damnation."

The concern in the room ended abruptly as Oliver laughed. No one joined in until Rex let out a guffaw. Erica snorted until our gazes connected.

"Erica, let's go," Oliver said with distaste. "I don't see why I need to stay here." He made his way toward the door. "I've got better things to do. The pack should worry about our personal business instead of this stupid fairy shit."

Karey advanced on him fast. She barely met his chest, but he backed away.

"That stupid fairy shit could get you and your family killed. Don't you forget that," she snapped. "We all have to understand what we're up against."

"She Who Always Walks the Path is coming," Mevelyn whispered.

Behind Mevelyn, Rex's eyes rolled so hard you'd think he'd suffered a concussion. Jeez.

Mevelyn continued, unfazed. "Her path hasn't changed for the last two thousand years. We *must* know if other powerful beings are proceeding her. Those *leeches* are dangerous."

"She Who Always Walks what...*the Back Road*? What kind of crackpot name is that?" Rex scoffed to his cohorts.

"The name of a creature you shouldn't *fuck* with?" I blurted out.

Grandma gave me "the look" so I whispered an apology. I could be a hundred years old and still get checked for cursing in front of elders.

Rex's hand went up and everyone's attention darted from me to him. It must've been hard for him to submit to me.

"We need scouts to go check this out." He glanced around the room, and naturally he didn't look my way. "I'll take five men."

"No," Karey said firmly to Rex. "You'll be hunting in circles for days. The fairy path is enchanted. You can't see it or smell it."

"Then give me a location and we'll do a perimeter search," he said.

I knew what I had to do, but I faltered to step forward.

"It's not that simple." My voice started out as a rasp, but grew stronger. "If I'm understanding my fairy kin correctly, they can't give you a location other than somewhere to the north."

Karey nodded while Mevelyn shook her head at Rex. It hadn't taken her long to see he was full of shit.

"What do you want to do?" Erica asked. She gave me the same hard look as when we embarked after the trunk for the first time.

"The nymphs and I will head out tonight to find the fairy path's location. From there, we'll see if we can uncover any threats," I explained.

"What if whoever left those trunks is out there, too?" Erica warned.

I sighed, briefly catching Oliver's smug expression. "This is a scouting mission like Rex said. We go in, learn what we need to know so we can face our enemies on an even terrain, and then we get the hell out of there. We've seen the basilisks, and I'm the only one who's managed to kill not one but three of them. Trust me."

Everyone nodded. A decision had been made, but a knot in my stomach refused to untwist. On the far side of the room, my mom appeared with Sveta. The child sucked her thumb and rested her head against my mom's shoulder.

Seeing my niece and the faces of my pack strengthened my resolve. No one would harm my family. Not on my watch.

～

As much as I dreaded the phone call, I had to tell Thorn to return to South Toms River pronto.

I waited for us to drive north up Highway 571 before I pulled out my phone. Karey took over driving my Nissan Altima so I wouldn't be distracted.

The phone rang twice before he picked up. "Hey, you."

His casual greeting melted me but also made it harder for me to form a reply.

"Hey, Thorn." I caught the sounds of the wind whistling and nocturnal birds I didn't recognize tweeted in the distance. Was he outside relaxing for the night?

"Is something up?" he asked. "You're usually back home by now and I can hear others nearby."

I sucked in a deep breath. "We got trouble."

I didn't have to see him to recognize the change as his instincts raised. "How bad? Are you all right?"

I told him everything, from the trunk showing up at The Bends to the attack at Archie's and two basilisks attempting to track me down at the old house. The whole time he was silent until a car honked on the opposite side of the highway.

"And where are you going now?" he asked firmly.

The sound of the outdoors—city traffic and night animals—had grown louder on the phone. I closed my eyes. In the time I'd explained everything, he'd packed his bag. He was probably checking out of his hotel and heading to the airport.

"The nymphs and I are trying to learn more about what

we're facing—that's it," I replied. "No fighting. No confrontation."

"Nat, I know you." He was in a car now, too. I heard some dings as the engine revved to life. "You can handle whatever this is, but what if what you're looking for doesn't want to be found?"

"If you know me, then you know I'd never let the pack come to harm. Pups could've been hurt today."

"And I don't want you to be harmed either." A car door slammed. Was he at the airport already? Jeez, he probably could've walked there.

Less than a minute later, he spoke again. "There aren't any more flights to Newark tonight. Can you wait twenty-four hours?"

I glanced at the nymphs and asked, "How close are we?"

"Do you feel anything?" Mevelyn asked.

Was I supposed to feel something?

"Nat, I'm asking you, not them," Thorn said softly.

"I feel the pull, but I need help." From the backseat, Mevelyn closed her eyes and pressed her hand to the window. The metal bracelets on her wrist jingled.

"When I return home, I'll call you back," I said to Thorn. "Can you text me your flight information?"

Thorn couldn't magically show up out of nowhere like he used to do. It was a thirty-five-hour drive from Montana to Jersey. He was better off taking the first flight in the morning.

"Fine, but our conversation isn't over." Thorn hung up and my heart fell. Did I expect this conversation to go well?

Not really. I wanted him home. He wanted to be home. But I had to do this on my own.

"Natalya?" Karey asked.

I sighed, holding the still-warm phone. "I don't even know what you expect me to do."

"Feel for the magic," Mevelyn said simply.

I couldn't help but remember the first time I learned werewolves could perform magic. It seemed impossible to fathom until I learned magic required belief and a cost.

"Exposure to magic isn't a door you swing open and close on demand," Mevelyn explained. "Once you've tapped into the power you have within, there's no going back."

"What cost will I pay to *sense* this magic?" I said softly.

"Our Sister Wolf is wise." Mevelyn placed her hand on my shoulder and comfort coursed into me. "She knows about the fundamental power exchange."

"What's that?" Dione asked.

"Spellcasters, like witches, warlocks, and wizards, have the ability to draw power from a source like a wand or staff. They manipulate this power to cast spells."

"I see," Dione whispered.

Mevelyn continued. "Old Magic practitioners like our Sister Wolf here don't need wands—they are the source. They manipulate magic from within, but at a great cost to their bodies. Casting spells can be fatal if done too much. Rest easy, at least for tonight, Natalya. Reaching out to find light in the darkness costs nothing. Her light is bright enough, believe me."

Reluctantly, I rolled down the window, letting out the air conditioning. A warm breeze fluttered through the car and the forest's current drove into me. I drew in another deep breath. Beyond the scents and sounds of the nocturnal wildlife—the repeated calls of the whip-poor-will birds to the distant caterwauling of barred owls—something peculiar hummed and churned. This presence gave off a vibration I'd never encountered before. I leaned toward the door and stuck out my arm.

"What's that?" I whispered with awe.

"That's the fairy path."

"But I've driven down this road a couple of months ago —how come I never felt this before?"

"The fairy path has never been here."

I nodded. "It's growing stronger as we veer northwest."

"Yes, it is." Mevelyn's hand drifted away from the window.

An hour later, the humming grew so loud I couldn't turn off the sound no matter how hard I tried to focus elsewhere. Then another strange feeling came: A chill nipped at the tips of my fingers as we reached the outskirts of Sourland Mountain Preserve.

"It must be around here." I glanced at my hands. "Do you feel it? The cold?"

"I don't know." Mevelyn's voice didn't sound as confident. Even Karey had slowed down and Grace clutched Dione's hand. A prevalent scent of fear hovered over the nymphs.

But what were they afraid of? Were we close to the source of the attacks…or something far worse?

As we drove northward along Highway 601, my hands turned to ice. I rubbed them to generate heat. We had to be close. When we turned right to stay on Highway 601 instead of turning right down East Mountain Road, the chill began to dissipate. I tapped the dashboard. "Turn around, we were close, but we're not anymore."

Karey turned around and we followed the trail again— this time, deeper into the woods toward Sourland Mountain.

Right outside the park's closed entrance, we pulled over. Once Karey turned off the car's headlights, only the streetlights illuminated the road. Nothing stirred outside the car—and yet I sensed something was out there. The minute I opened the door, something tugged at me. A tickle itched along my scalp. With every step deeper into the preserve, a snowstorm gathered in my gut. Ice coursed up my arms. I'd never felt this kind of cold before.

"Hey, Nat! Wait for us!" Karey's voice trailed after me as my steps grew bolder. Stronger.

Slow down, Nat. For every single step I took forward, my grandmother's voice tried to push me back two steps.

Go back. The voice wasn't truly hers, but it was the human within trying to resist what the wolf couldn't. I hurried through the woods. Walking and running at a pace the nymphs couldn't match until the chill disappeared— only to be replaced with an unnatural heat from everywhere.

Soon enough, Karey's footsteps echoed behind me. All I could hear was the nymphs and the resonating hum. It came from everywhere: the sky, the ground, the trees.

But something was wrong. Through the treetops, the sky had gone black. The stars disappeared. I looked forward but saw nothing through the trees.

This isn't something my eyes will see, I thought. *I can feel her.*

When I glanced over my shoulder, the nymphs had fallen to their knees, their heads bowed in holy admiration. The heaviest weight I'd ever endured pressed against my shoulders to drench me in anxiety and pain. I joined them on my knees and curled into myself, seeking darkness. A reprieve from this seemingly never-ending feeling. My jaw clenched. My fingernails bit into my fists. My eyes were forced shut.

But the wolf within me soared. Circled and howled as if

the essence of She Who Always Walks the Path called to me.

Come shed your skin, a paper-thin voice whispered in my head. *The summer breeze is your blanket. The ever-moon your cloak. Feel me. Come to me.*

The strange voice continued to summon me as I crawled forward. My hands twitched. I unfastened the first button on my blouse.

Taste my power; run in reverence, the voice intoned.

And did I feel the power.

Suddenly, hands grasped my face. Warm fingers tilted my chin upward.

"Nat!" a woman's voice yelled. "Wake up!"

I opened my eyes to see Karey calling my name. She pinched my arm as she tugged me out of the forest. The effects lessened as we hurried farther south. The crickets chirped again and the night owls called out. The weight on my shoulders lifted but fear still pulsed within me.

Never had I faced such a mighty adversary. Every enemy I had faced *paled* in comparison.

Once we reached my Nissan Altima, we piled inside, but Karey didn't start the engine. We sat there in silence until Mevelyn spoke.

"We were lucky tonight, my sisters," she whispered, her voice weakened. "All creatures beneath her glorious presence must bow before her. Our pacification rituals saved us tonight."

She swallowed before she continued. "I don't know what we're going to tell the others."

"We shouldn't instill a panic," Dione said, her face ashen.

"No, but when her path draws closer to mortals, other creatures follow her," Mevelyn said.

"The leeches," I supplied.

Mevelyn drew in a shallow breath. "They'll come in droves. What I fear are the predators. This fairy path used to stretch from Europe to Canada. Now it's approaching us. Whatever is leaving those trunks seems to be attacking werewolves."

"But why us?"

Karey's aunt shrugged. "I'm not sure yet, but we'll deal with the *trunk* collector first, then we'll determine how we'll survive when She Who Always Walks the Path passes near."

"How do we survive?" Karey whispered.

"We may not," was all Mevelyn said.

I wanted to speak, but I refused to say what the wolf had heard not too long ago. Some words had power and speaking them brought them to life.

For I knew the true name of She Who Always Walks the Path.

And she'd eventually reach South Toms River and harm everyone I held dear.

CHAPTER 8

Just like last time, Karey wanted the house searched before I headed inside. With her younger sisters in tow, they inspected my home. Mevelyn and I waited outside the door. I was tempted to tell them not a single creature peeped within, but the determined look on their faces convinced me otherwise.

Months ago, back when little Sveta had been born, the nymphs ignored me. I was the sister-in-law from the crazy wolf side of the family. Hopefully, they liked me now.

I turned to Mevelyn as her hand clenched my arm. Sweat beaded her forehead.

The mysterious being the nymphs cautioned against was far away. At the rate she was approaching, we'd have plenty of time to form a plan—whether that meant making a final stand or fleeing.

And yet the nymphs were afraid.

Which meant I also should be fearful.

Karey and her sisters returned to us.

"Anything?" Mevelyn asked.

"The house is clear." Karey's right eyebrow lowered.

"There's a clurichaun in the cellar, but it's been sleeping for a long, long time."

"Excuse me, a *what?*" I blurted.

"A fairy from the Old World. You see, the original framing for this house is over two hundred years old." Karey brushed her fingers against a weathered wall in the foyer. "The house told me a pub owner and his family brought the clurichaun with them."

Wow, what a nifty trick. "Is this fairy dangerous?" I asked.

"Not really. More of a troublemaker and a drunk," Karey said. "You don't keep any liquor in the cellar so the clurichaun doesn't have a reason to wake up."

"Got it. No wine cellar in my future. Good to know." I bid the nymphs goodbye and locked up the house. As I walked through the living room, I shook my head. My senses always helped me, but magic seemed to hide everywhere. *Ignorance is bliss, I tell ya.*

I ambled to the kitchen, considering what else I should tell Thorn in the morning. I didn't want to alarm him, but he should know about She Who Always Walks the Path. And our many other problems. I sighed. I wanted so badly for Thorn to waltz through that front door and admit I'd taken care of everything.

He always made me feel like I could conquer the world. Why couldn't I show him through my actions?

I considered returning to my car to drive around again to hunt for anything suspicious, but what good would that do? Only a fool would hunt alone, and I didn't know what I was up against. I needed to rally the pack together and find whoever was leaving the trunks as bait before someone really got hurt.

Once I reached the doorway to the kitchen, I paused.

The back door was open and a warm breeze tickled my face.

Someone sat at the kitchen table. Their scent—one of dirty clothes and sweat—enveloped me. I didn't think the nymphs would've overlooked this, and my guest must've come in after the nymphs' security check. My muscles tensed until I recognized the blond-haired fellow. Thorn's younger brother Will sat at the kitchen table and looked up with a grin as I walked in. What was he doing here? He'd been gone for months searching for Aggie.

"Where have you been?" My smile faded as I took in the worry lining his forehead.

He jerked his head to the other side of the room. "Look who I found."

I hurried into the room. On the other side of the kitchen, a redhead beamed at me.

"Aggie," I breathed.

"Good to see you, too," my best friend said.

~

I couldn't believe Agatha McClure stood before me. While we sat at the table, Will pulled out the teakettle and three cups. It wasn't until after Will placed the kettle with water on the stove, and chose a seat beside Aggie, that we finally addressed where the hell she had been all this time.

"How did you find her?" I asked.

His Adam's apple bobbed twice. "It's a really long story."

I laughed. "I've got time."

Aggie got up to rummage through the fridge.

"Two days after you left town, I had to spend time with my dad out at the cabin," Will began. "There was a bunch of brush I had to clear."

I nodded to offer encouragement.

"Aggie was cool about it. She even offered to help clear out brush, but I didn't want her to have to deal with Dad. I spent a full day working, and when I returned to your cottage, she was gone." His jaw twitched. "At first, I thought she went to work, but there were four other scents in the house from werewolves I didn't recognize."

Aggie snorted, giving up on the fridge's contents to search through the pantry. Her overeating habit hadn't changed a bit. "My kidnappers snuck up on me while I asleep. I managed to bite one of them, but they knocked me out before I could escape."

Will continued. "Blood was splattered on the wall, and one of them tried to clean it up, even arranging her bedroom back to the state they'd found it, but you and I have done too much tracking in the woods not to uncover a bit of blood under bleach."

I was holding my breath and finally exhaled. "Have far were you able to track them?"

"Not sure how I did it, but I followed them all the way to Newark. On the way, I checked with every gas station in town. One of them serviced a fancy Cadillac Escalade with twenty-one-inch tires and tinted windows."

The tea kettle whistled and I gathered packets of calming chamomile tea. Carefully, I filled the three cups and allowed the tea to steep. Aggie joined us with a bag of barbecue potato chips in hand.

Will continued. "From there, I searched north and south along the Expressway. The pack north of us had spotted them. As a favor, they tracked them for me until they reached Newark. I'm surprised I didn't get any speeding tickets, Nat. I missed her by five minutes." He sighed. "One of the werewolves who works at the hangar revealed the occupants of the Escalade took a private plane to Chicago."

"Chicago?" Wow, they wanted her far away from home. I got up and gave everyone their cup of tea.

"I drove to Chicago and that's where the trail went cold," Will said. "Most of the packs there aren't too friendly to strangers. I searched the city for months and found nothing. I had no choice but to return home." He gulped his whole cup of tea in one swallow. "I sat in that cottage for a couple of days. I was so angry I couldn't think straight —until your answering machine went off. It was *full* of messages."

I leaned toward him, sensing where the winds were blowing.

"I checked the messages and her father had left five of them." The muscles in Will's face tightened. "In the oldest messages, he said some bullshit about Aggie running away from her obligations. The bastard sounded calm...and rich. But that wasn't what worried me. Some piece of shit asshole left nine messages before the machine filled up. You wouldn't believe what he said. He told her he'd *found* her and when he got a hold of her, she'd regret leaving him. I didn't know his name at the time, but I traced his number to Manhattan."

"Victor," Aggie paused in the middle of munching and said the word as if she tasted something foul.

"So her ex-husband was calling the house?" I asked.

Will sat up all the way. "I searched Manhattan for him, I never found him until I started watching her dad's place."

My gaze flicked to Aggie, but she didn't reveal her thoughts as she continued to eat. We never talked about her relationship with the Midtown Pack alpha or what went down as she grew up, but I suspected things weren't too good if she ran away in the first place.

"Low and behold, Victor Pershing finally showed up," Will sneered. "He probably thought nobody cared about her."

"Which was good for you," I added. I forced myself to get up and warm up some leftover soup. Aggie was hungry or agitated, given the way she rummaged my fridge. Had her husband held her all this time?

He nodded. "I followed his car all the way to Long Island. He has some fancy-shmancy mansion there, but little security."

I dumped the soup in a pan and turned on the stove. The outside seemed so tranquil compared to the rising tension in the room. Will's shoulders tightened and he clenched his fists. What had he faced in that house?

"I found her tied up in a back room like she was nothing but an animal," he spat. "So I freed her..." He swallowed deeply and didn't speak.

Then I saw their hands. They'd washed off the blood and other ghastly bits, but the scent was faint. All I had to do was suck in a breath and it was there.

And their eyes. Before I'd turned on the kitchen lights, I'd failed to see the feral glint in them.

"What happened tonight?" I whispered.

"Will set me free," was all Aggie said as if it was a done deal.

Alarm touched my voice. "If Victor tried to take her once, won't he return again?"

Aggie's calm demeanor darkened. "Not after what Will and I *did* to him. I dare him to show his face near me."

On Monday morning, I woke up in a cold sweat. My dreams were still vivid in my mind: Aggie and I faced an invading pack—the Long Island werewolves. They hunted down everyone who opposed them, most especially me. I'd never forget the night they'd attacked Aggie and me. We were cornered until Thorn came to the rescue.

Now my pack faced another foe and I didn't have my husband with me this time. At least Aggie was here now.

A familiar ache formed in my chest. Instead of allowing a panic attack to creep in, I got up and checked my phone.

Thorn sent me a text: *Got the midday flight to Newark. I'll be home by three.*

While I prepared breakfast for Aggie, he sent one more message: *Stay out of trouble, Nat.*

I snorted.

Eh, what do I do if trouble keeps finding me? I thought.

I made some bowls of oatmeal with blueberries and brown sugar on top. With gusto, I ate a serving and focused on what I had to do next. Pushing my concerns into a lockbox wouldn't work forever, but for now, the trick worked.

For me, following routines resembled a warm glass of milk with a couple of fresh-from-the-oven peanut butter cookies. Monday mornings especially. A new week meant a new opportunity to do everything—just like last week.

Growing up with a loud and rambunctious Russian family meant living in the moment. We experienced joy and sorrow together. Now that I didn't live with my parents, I forged my own path, but those golden moments still made me smile: Nothing beats receiving a hug from your *babushka*. And Grandma Lasovskaya wouldn't have it any other way.

After working the weekend shift, I had the next two days off. Most folks would sleep in after what I faced, but I refused to waste the day. I had a whole day to hunt down the culprit behind the trunks, but I was far too twitchy to start quite yet. Normally, I'd wait until tomorrow to attend group therapy, but the tension stretching across my scalp warned me I needed to tackle this problem before my anxiety worsened.

Time to see Dr. Frank.

The past year had been hard on me. I had no shame in admitting I was in therapy for not only my OCD, but my tumultuous past with my pack as well.

Once I finished a quick shower, I donned my usual wardrobe and headed into New York City. Showing up on Dr. Frank's doorstep without an appointment wasn't advised, but if I had to wait all day in Manhattan for an opening, I didn't mind *accidentally* browsing a shop or two.

Naturally, I arrived at Dr. Frank's office on the Upper West Side and his secretary gave me the bad news.

"Sorry, but he's out of the office until your group therapy meets tomorrow," she said.

Disappointment flicked at me, but I was the one who showed up to the party too early. With no way to see to my therapist, my compulsions tugged me deeper into Manhattan. The shop windows, with their beautiful, carefree wares, enchanted me. Two department stores already had Christmas in July pre-sale signs. Anything to grab a buck from compulsive shoppers like me.

Thirty minutes later, armed with two bags, the Great Northern Fairy Path was an afterthought. All I had to do to lessen my pain was browse, fall in love with a find, and then pull out my bank card. In the back of my mind, I knew this binge would end, and with it, I'd feel a tsunami of guilt every time I spotted the bags—but for now, I gave in and searched for my next fix.

I took the subway from Washington Square Park to Brooklyn. Once there I stopped briefly at a bookstore. The sign in front caught my interest: "Need leadership skills for your start-up?"

Why yes, I do.

The display included titles such as *Grow Your Business From the Ground Up* to gems like *Leader You. Build You.* Not sure what that one offered, but I liked what I read on the back of the book and I found the text to be well-edited. If I had to lead, I might as well learn a thing or two from something that wouldn't talk back: a damn book.

With a few self-help purchases in another bag, I left the bookstore and came to a stop in front a familiar pawn shop I hadn't seen for a long time.

Earl's Fine Antiques.

Visiting every corner of New York would take me a few lifetimes, but somehow today I ended up here. Memories flooded through me.

Dr. Frank had said, *"You guys need to head over to a pawn shop in Brooklyn this week or the next. Nick needs to face the prospect of returning an item, and, Nat, you need to resist your urge to acquire new things. I think this will be a low-stress exercise since you wouldn't be asked to remove anything from your home."*

Dr. Frank had sent another therapy group participant, a white wizard named Nick and I out on "missions" to confront our compulsions. We were supposed to browse and not buy. As one could see from my current jaunt, I was still working on that problem.

The store hadn't changed in the last couple of months. I passed two large, junk-filled bins in front of the window. Just like The Bends, Earl's used attractive baubles to draw in the curious. The protective barrier around the bins, heavy with the scent of cinnamon and magic to ward off thieves, hummed as I entered the store.

The exhilaration I'd experienced last time I entered the store increased ten-fold. Earl's wasn't The Bends—not with the superb merchandise on these shelves. The clerks here meticulously lined up glass goblets with clear potions along the far wall. Signs on each row indicated the contents. Each section of the store catered toward a particular clientele, and their stock had rotated since I'd last visited.

One section beckoned me closer. Antique Victorian Christmas collectibles sat in the center of a display. An unnatural light from above practically made me purr with delight.

"You look familiar," a voice behind me said softly.

I startled but forced myself to smile. Spellcasters like the wizard behind me had an uncanny ability to mask their scent and sounds.

I turned around. "I haven't been here for a very long time."

He nodded. "Oh yeah, you were here with Nick a

couple of months ago. Good to see you back. See anything you like?"

Don't look at the super shiny wares, I reminded myself. I knew the tricks of the trade. The clerk knew damn well I caught the scent of prey.

I glanced around the store and took a step away from the display. "Just browsing. Seems quiet around here."

"We had a quiet period this spring, but sales are picking up again."

I nodded. The Bends experienced a similar slow down, too.

The clerk wiped off an imaginary piece of dust off a figurine. I didn't take the bait to look. "Have you seen, Nick?" he asked.

"Not for a long time. Last I heard, he's in medical school overseas."

"That's a shame. He always came by every Tuesday to see my new stock. Maybe he'll come by tomorrow."

A beautiful vintage Christmas cake mold murmured sweet nothings to me so I edged toward the door. A half hour ago, I would've snatched up the dish, but now that the old exercise from Dr. Frank—and more importantly, Nick —crossed my mind, I knew it was time for me to return home.

"Maybe," I said wistfully.

At the doorway, I thanked the clerk and waved good-bye. As I made my way back to the subway exit, I'd hope Nick would be proud of the Herculean feat I'd accomplished.

∾

Thorn Grantham beat me back to the cottage. Little did I know, his flight took off earlier than expected and the traffic from Newark defied the laws of physics and whisked him away to our tiny town in a blink.

I pulled up to see Thorn leaning against one of the old oak trees lining the property. My throat dried and I lost all my thoughts of how to uncover the culprit behind the trunks. *Figures.*

By the time I turned off the car and grabbed the door handle, Thorn had crossed the yard and opened the door for me.

"A trip to the city?" He chuckled.

All my shopping bags were stowed away in the trunk, but I couldn't mask Manhattan's telltale scents: the pollution, a hint of the wizard's aftershave from the pawn shop, as well as the bookstore's scones. I knew from experience his nose was that damn good.

"I had a lot on my mind, so I tried to see Dr. Frank. He wasn't in," I explained. "Aggie's back too."

He drew me into his arms and my troubles blew away with a gust of humid heat. The sun warmed the top of my head and Thorn warmed my heart.

"You're not mad at me?" I whispered.

"Being mad at you is futile."

I edged to shut the door, but he quirked a grin and stopped me. "Pop the trunk, Nat."

I married the perfect partner, didn't I?

Bags in hand, we headed inside while I updated Thorn on everything that went down from the first trunk's appearance through how Will showed up with Aggie.

"Where are they?" he asked.

"I don't know. When I woke up, Will was gone, but

Aggie was asleep. I don't even know if Will stayed the night here."

He nodded. "I'll check to see if he's at the cabin with my dad."

After that, he didn't speak for a couple of minutes while I prepared a snack of pastrami sandwiches and homemade potato chips. I set the plates on the table, but he still didn't eat, staring out the kitchen window to the forest beyond.

"What are you thinking?" I asked.

"That we got a big problem. Has anyone reported seeing any other trunks?"

"I told Jake and the other elders in the pack to text me if they spotted anything suspicious. So far so good. There's only one place where I know there are trunks."

Thorn's eyebrows lowered. "Are they secured?"

"Oh, those suckers got chained up the moment they showed up at The Bends. It's the folks who don't know about the trunks I'm worried about. Especially the human population."

Thorn stood and my stomach grumbled at the sight of another abandoned meal. "I want to see them."

I hurried and took a massive bite of my sandwich. Oh, how wonderful it tasted. "How about you eat first?" I managed to say between chewing.

"I won't be able to eat until I get an idea of what I'm up against."

The pastrami and whole-grain mustard in my mouth turned to ash.

Way to go, Nat, stuffing your face while the world falls apart.

I wiped my mouth with a napkin. "Let's go."

"Stay and eat. Your stomach sounds like a grizzly bear. I can circle the property to investigate."

The sandwich, so perfectly arranged with the chips snuggling it, waved to me. Time to do the right thing.

"I can let you into The Bends."

Ten minutes later, I pulled into my work's parking lot. The most interesting sight was the faint lights through the window to the new building across the Parkway.

"That's new." Thorn peered at the windows, but the new occupants covered them with cardboard. Hope they didn't plan to open any time soon. Bill would complain up a storm if we had competition.

I led Thorn from the car to the back entrance. This late in the afternoon, I expected more traffic along the Parkway, but only a few cars whizzed past. The harsh June sunlight illuminated Thorn's back as he took point and approached the door first.

"What's that horrible smell?" he whispered.

I almost laughed. "Yeah, once the trunks open, no amount of air fresheners or bleach can get rid of the rotten-eggs-corpse stench."

I unlocked the door. The lights in the back office were off.

"Dead bodies don't smell this bad," Thorn muttered.

"Tell that to Quinton."

I headed to the light switch, but Thorn's hand rose to stop me. Then I spotted it. A set of wet footprints five feet from the door plodded across the floor.

"That's not water." The fluid had a peculiar odor—a bit sulfurous with saccharine undertones.

Thorn clenched his fists. "No, it isn't."

The footprints ended in the corner. Worse yet, the trunks were gone. Only the chains remained.

CHAPTER 10

After hunting through town and the surrounding boroughs all night with Thorn, I settled into a coma-like sleep until dawn. Knowing that the town was quiet should've given me peace as I woke up and dressed in a shirt and jeans, but my senses were piqued. A little too alert. At any moment, I expected to open a door and see a trunk waiting to be opened.

Just in case the dog shit hit the lawn the wrong way, I kept the goblin blade on me. Usually the weapon took on the form of a letter opener, which made it easy to stash in a purse or back pocket. By mid-morning, I thought it wiser to keep it strapped to my ankle in a switchblade carrier. If the thing transformed, at least I'd be able to grab the weapon before it chopped my leg off.

Thorn awakened long before me and left me a note: *Checking on my dad. Stay out of trouble until I return.*

He kept thinking I'd find trouble. He should stop saying that. My luck these days didn't fare so well.

Since today was Tuesday, I should be getting ready to attend therapy group, but I had guests this morning. To my surprise, Will had slept in the four-season room on the wicker couch while Aggie slept in the spare bedroom. Before I left town, they'd gotten cozy. Had something happened between them?

The urge to nudge him awake poked at me, but I grabbed a blanket and covered him instead. Whatever went down would reveal itself in conversation sooner or later.

Might as well head to the kitchen and fix some chow. While I was preparing a breakfast of sunny-side-up eggs along with gravy and biscuits—one of Aggie's favorites—Thorn returned and wanted to chat about our hunt last night.

"I don't get it. There's not a single trunk anywhere," he said. "We followed that sulfuric scent from The Bends to the lumber mill, but the trail disappeared north of here."

"It is weird." I scooped the cooked eggs onto a plate. The oven would ding any minute to let me know the biscuits were done and the gravy bubbled in the pot. Now was a perfect time for us to consider our options.

"Guess that means we keep up with the nightly patrols?" I suggested.

Using a fork, Thorn stole an egg off the plate and gobbled it up before I could protest. "I want one done every six hours. Since Will is back and doesn't have a job, he can do it."

As if on cue, Will sauntered into the kitchen from the four-season room. "I'm back and you're already bossing me around." He also tried to take an egg, but I slid the plate out of the way. One Grantham brother already tricked me today.

Will chuckled and helped his older brother with preparing buttered toast. They spoke in low tones about their dad.

"How about you let Aggie get some food before you guys eat everything in sight?" Then I caught her footsteps coming from down the hall.

When she entered the room, Will gave her a long look, but Aggie ignored him and approached me. She was wearing a familiar black T-shirt, but I couldn't place where I'd bought it. The shirt read: *I'm getting nothing for Christmas...So I stole this shirt.*

Had she raided the shopping bag full of Christmas shirts I wanted to hide back at my old place? Asking her where she got the clothes would only incriminate me, so I forced a smile.

"Need any help with cooking?" she asked.

"Nah, I'm good," I replied.

Thorn patted his brother's shoulder in support and directed Will to set the table. Did Thorn know what was going on between them?

The tension between Aggie and Will eased as they sat on opposite sides of the four-seater table. Thorn sat between them at the head while I added the biscuits from the oven and the bowl of hot gravy. Steam rose from the biscuits and filled the room with the mouth-watering smell of fresh bread. The moment the eggs hit the table, the Grantham men helped themselves.

"Do you mind?" I laughed. "Can we please let Aggie get some first?"

They froze. Will with one bite in his mouth and Thorn with his fork stabbing an egg.

"It's all right." Aggie snatched some biscuits. "Victor's cronies fed me well—even after they tied me up. They only slipped up once."

"I'm sorry we didn't help you sooner," I said.

Will ate with his eyes on his plate.

"I held my own. They untied me one time so I could use

the ladies' room." The side of her mouth slid up with a sinister feline grin. "They were smart enough to not do it again."

I shuddered, wanting to ask how she managed to use the bathroom, but I didn't want to know.

I said softly, "I had no idea you were missing."

Aggie took my hand briefly and squeezed it. "Last night, Will and I talked. He caught me up on everything. I can't believe you went all the way to Russia by yourself to learn Old Magic."

"I did what I had to do," I said as I gave Thorn a quick glance. "Some prices are worth paying."

Thorn gave me a small smile.

Five years ago, Thorn disappeared from my life, but he hadn't done it on purpose. A warlock had imprisoned him and Thorn earned his escape the hard way: my mate used one of the warlock's dark spells against him. In the process, Thorn cursed himself.

"Believe me," Thorn said. "I wasn't too thrilled she ran away to learn Old Magic to remove the curse I had, but then again, that's Nat for you."

He made the curse seem simple, but less than six months ago, my mate was close to dying. No one knew how to help him, even Nick, and I was forced to take the matter into my own hands and learn how dark magic like curses worked.

When I really thought about it, even now, I knew I needed to stop acting like the town pariah and play nicely with others.

"Did she really lift the curse?" Aggie asked. "Wow."

Thorn nodded. "Yep, I'm good as new, but I don't know if Nat is the same anymore. A lot happened in Russia."

Aggie quirked a grin. "She's different all right. She's a badass now."

I shook my head. "I did what I had to do, and now it's time for me to forget what I learned and move on with my life."

Aggie snorted. "You never forgot when I left food out on the counter; there's no way you'll forget Old Magic."

I scoffed as if all those words I'd seared into my mind could be blown away like dandelion seeds. "I've already forgotten *a lot.*"

Thorn rolled his eyes, smelling through my lie's stench.

I shoved a generous bite of biscuits and gravy in my mouth and tried to recall the spell Tamara taught me to conjure fire. The words bubbled from my subconscious with ease.

Damn it.

I tried to think of mundane things—like what inventory hadn't been sorted back at The Bends or what trash the necromancer janitor hadn't cleaned up. None of those tasks wiped away the words. Maybe if I believed I couldn't do magic anymore, then I'd be okay. Nick had told me, *"Magic isn't a simple formula. It comes from your heart. When you have the right tool, the right words, and you believe without a doubt, magic can happen."*

Operation Believe-in-Shit-I-Could-Do-Myself started today. I had a bunch of self-help books from my trip to the city the day before. Time to put those to use.

Thorn's phone beeped, pulling me from my reverie. He glanced at the screen and frowned.

"What's wrong?" I asked.

"Rex was patrolling all night...and he wants me to join him today."

I rolled my eyes so hard I heard the marbles in my head clicking. "Bullshit. How come we never smelled him while you and I were out there?"

"Exactly." Thorn's voice lowered. "Over the last couple

of months, Rex has gotten antsier than I'd prefer. He's pushing boundaries. Be careful around him."

"I know. I know."

"He was never like this when we were younger. He was competitive, sure, but he changed after college."

I picked up my plate and put it in the sink. "Did something happen there? Where did he go to school again?"

"He stayed in town and went to Ocean County College. Not sure what went down while you and I were at Pitt."

I smiled, recalling how two South Toms River kids found each other at the University of Pittsburg. There and I had good times there.

Thorn continued. "He never finished though—I know what much. Guess I need to dig deeper over a couple of beers and get back to you on this."

Like a friendly chat for old time's sake would really reveal what the hell was going on with Rex.

I slowly nodded. "I wish he'd just get it over with you and try to challenge you instead of pissing in everyone's yards."

Thorn snorted. "He's been doing that, too."

"He's marking?" Aggie said with distaste.

"Every couple of weeks he'll go outside of the pack's boundaries to leave a mark here and there," Thorn said. "I called him on his actions, and he said he was trying to *help*."

"Help, my hairy ass," I said stiffly.

"Pack members who crave power are more dangerous to their pack than an external foe," Thorn said. "Remember that, Nat."

He kissed my forehead and left the house. As I watched him leave, I wondered if I should fear Rex's maneuverings more than I had. Who else smelled my weaknesses and would sweep in to hurt those I loved?

For the rest of our breakfast, I listened to Will and

Aggie make small talk. They didn't talk about their relationship, but I snooped until I realized I was pressed for time. With my books in hand, I hurried to the door. Aggie volunteered to remain behind to tidy up. Will offered to help and she didn't refuse. Maybe they could talk it out. Without my prying ears.

As I left though, they had other things to say.

"Does she really want us to clean?" Will asked as I grabbed my keys in the foyer. "She...wants things done a certain way."

Aggie laughed. "Watch and learn, young grasshopper. We're gonna be killing off some microscopic sentient beings with the stuff she's got."

Maybe things weren't so bad between them—even if they made a joke about my cleaning standards. Cleanliness meant their food wasn't contaminated and wouldn't make them sick. A win-win in my opinion. Who knew when the next pandemic would hit? I had enough antiseptic wipes to protect the whole town.

~

Tuesday passed swiftly without any trouble, but I jolted awake again around three in the morning and couldn't go back to sleep. Thorn snored away, not a care in the world. Nothing stirred outside of the house, yet I slipped out of bed and curled up on my couch to read. Interestingly, the pile of self-help books had a new book on top. The paperback's edges were slightly worn, but the title was still easy to read on the front and side: *Bill's Introduction to Management and Leadership.*

I nearly choked on my spit trying not to laugh. How did Bill manage to slip this into the pile? I'd only left them in the car briefly.

I had to see this disaster, especially considering how that goblin could scarcely manage The Bends. The book's spine gave a quiet pop as I opened the cover. The dedication in the front read,

Leadership is derived from actions. The action to inspire. The action to complete what can't be completed.

That wasn't too bad, but the chapter headings didn't promise a great read. There were gems like *Recreate Your Success Post-Dark Ages*. And even: *You Too Can Con Your Way to Your First Buck.*

I tossed the book onto the heap and grabbed one from a more *reputable* author.

I didn't always try to use a self-help manual to fix my problems. Back in college at the University of Pittsburg, I was often selected as group leader for assignments. Why? 'Cause I *never* turned in incomplete work. Sickness, a part-time job, and even the full moon wouldn't stop me from fulfilling my obligations. Becoming the de-facto group leader should've given me respect and friends, but I was constantly reminded of my faults.

One sociology assignment came to mind. The incident was like a carpet burn seared into my memories. At the time the teacher issued the homework, groups were formed then my teammates met up with me. They smiled and made small talk. One guy even ordered pizza. But their body language revealed a mountain of bullshit. Even my werewolf hearing caught their true thoughts.

After one work session I thought I'd done well, one gal left the study room and ran her mouth. Not more than ten steps away from the room she blurted out, "Did you see the inside of Natalya's backpack? Weirdo alert. I've never seen so much random junk."

Another group member replied, "I don't give a shit. I need an A and I can pretend to like her if necessary."

And those were the nicest comments.

Keeping the wolf within me from lashing out was diffi-cult—and believe me I wanted to go wild—but that wouldn't have helped. My dad used to say you couldn't teach kindness to stupid people. You either had home training or you didn't.

Afterward, I steeled myself against their words and I led. I picked up the slack for good-for-nothing students too busy gaming to contribute. I even smiled at the back-stabbing bitches who talked about me when they thought I couldn't hear them…because I wanted to be accepted. Even if I behaved differently.

Now that I was older, yet not necessarily wiser, I was back at square one. A student opening a book expecting the knowledge of the world to change me, perhaps ply me like Play-Doh into an acceptable form.

What I feared the most was that I'd always be this way and nothing would change for the better.

~

A few hours later, I woke up feeling refreshed.

"I love that sound," I murmured, stretching my arms out.

Beside me, my mate yawned, and he rubbed my back. "The silence?"

"You're home and everything is *sort of* right with the world again."

He chuckled and wiped the sleep from his eyes. The faint shadow of a beard darkened his jaw. "Don't worry. Just when we think everything's fine, somebody will show up with chainsaws, a clogging dance crew, and *mimes*."

"Not the mimes." I said. "They're the worst for noise."

I'd lost my two days off, but I refused to let that slow

me down. I almost grabbed my usual garb but snatched a brand new T-shirt I won during a summer music festival in Beachwood instead. The orange shirt didn't give me the same honeyed feeling as my business clothes, but wearing the top and jeans reminded me that every day was a new chance to see a new Natalya.

Thorn nodded with approval and added, "You're not completely abandoning the skirts, are you?"

"Oh no, I'm just trying this out for personal growth." I made air quotes around *personal growth*. "If I want to be a better alpha female, I should act and look like everyone else instead of standing out all the time."

His face grew serious. "You don't have to try to be like other people to lead."

"Doesn't it help though?" I gave him a small smile.

"Wonder Woman doesn't need tight clothes to kick ass."

"True, but she looks awesome in them. I wish my pencil skirt didn't make it so hard to kick ass." I kissed his lips then he left the house for his shift at the mill.

The drive to The Bends should've taken me a couple of minutes—until I noticed the new thrift store across the street was open. The sign in front read *Huldrefolk Collectibles*. Instead of pulling into my work parking lot, I decided to scope out Bill's competition. Might as well see what they had since I was twenty minutes early for my shift. It wasn't like I wanted to shop or anything.

I'm doing research.

Like any savvy business, this flea market had balloons stretched along a banner proudly stating, "Open Now!" The enticing scent of popcorn and hot dogs drew me out of the car toward the building.

Many familiar faces smiled my way.

"Morning, Nat!" said one woman, a wind witch who often visited The Bends every couple of days.

"Mrs. Weisz, dare I ask what you're doing here?" I was being playful. A little bit.

I quickly caught up with her. Might as well do some reconnaissance shopping using a cover like the elderly witch. Mrs. Weisz, who had a fog of vanilla perfume and the patience of a saint, shuffled down the sidewalk toward the entrance.

"Have you already been inside?" I asked her.

"This is my first time." She giggled, revealing a bit of red lipstick on her pearly white dentures. "I hear they've got some pretties." She leaned toward me. "Don't tell the folks across the street I came here."

I paused then shrugged. Looks like my disguise was working overtime.

Beyond the entrance, I had to do a doubletake. Along the front of the building's rock-filled garden, if I could call it that, someone had planted crooked rows of red and green tulips. Those were the same tulips the Sisters of Divine Grace had placed in front of their church. Oh, dear, I hope the SDG wouldn't soon make an appearance.

I hurried to catch up with Mrs. Weisz. She smiled up at me. "Can't wait to see what's inside!"

The double doors, about ten feet tall and made of aged oak, were wide open. Once inside, I checked the showroom from the booth-filled space to the skylight windows above. To my left, a short line formed near the doors for the free hot dogs and popcorn. A rotund man, with a glamour covering his true form, welcomed costumers and placed shriveled up hot dogs and a wrinkled bag of popcorn on a paper plate. Two eager customers snatched them up, apparently not seeing what I saw.

I passed the food and checked out the booths. This store used a format like most other flea markets. Individual vendors probably rented their booths, placed their goods inside, and the owner facilitated the sales and took a margin off the top.

A woman walked past Mrs. Weisz and me. She bit into her wrinkly hot dog. "So good," she remarked.

I cringed. She wasn't gonna digest that well.

"See anything good?" I asked the elderly witch.

"Over there." Mrs Weisz pointed toward the nearest booth with a selection of wands.

I walked after her. There were glamours all over the place. They covered the dirty floors under a veneer of worn oak planks that the humans saw. Another spell made the windows shine for the humans whereas I couldn't help but notice mud splattered all over the place. I shook my head in disgust. Bill had given me a window to a world nothing like The Bends.

This particular booth had nothing I wanted: one side had a shelf with withered wind wands while another side had a rickety stand overflowing with bubbling mason jars full of squirmy things inside. Not sure if those were squid or crawfish or…I dared to take a sniff and caught the faint odor of dead things. *Ugh, that's a hard pass.* What did witches do with this stuff?

I said to Mrs. Weisz, "While you look, I'm going to check out another booth."

She waved her hand to shoo me off like she always did. Every individual wand would get her attention. I wouldn't have to worry about her anytime soon.

Each stall appeared to have different goods from other supernatural creatures. Cheap centaur saddles were offered in one while another booth sold subpar trinkets from a mermaid family. At the end of the row, I spied wares lining the walls: dragon heads, phoenix tails (still on fire), and mounted medieval weapons. Before I could ponder if any of those swords were used to capture the dragon head, something shiny glinted from a booth in the next row. As if tugged by the magnetic pull of the sun on other stars, I was compelled to walk toward a stall with a singular object on a pedestal: a set of Christmas reindeer bells. Bright red ribbon, without a single blemish I might add, was perfectly tied around a ring holding three bells. I could practically see my reflection in the shiny metal. I dared to get closer to see if a glamour played with my senses. There were no illusions I could detect. Just the faint musk of deer and a hint of a snowstorm—as if snowfall would soon be approaching. I reached for it and my ears popped. Was that a good or bad thing? I grasped the bells and the jingle made me giggle with delight. The three digits on the price tag didn't even deter my imagination. I could imagine running with my younger brother through the living room as kids during Christmas. Mom would be heading out the door to fetch a whole cow or pig for dinner while Dad would be snoring on the couch next to Grandma and Aunt Olga. The TV would be blasting away, but we were all together. Safe and happy.

The holidays always represented the best time in my life.

Footsteps behind me made me turn sharply. A black woman dressed in business slacks and a dark blue polo shirt approached me. Her skin appeared youthful and luminescent even though her shoulder-length hair was gray peppered with white.

"My boss told me you don't belong here," she said.

I swung my find behind my back. The bells jingled. Shit. "Pardon?"

"You need to leave. My boss doesn't like goblins," she said.

"I'm not a goblin."

"Well, apparently, you smell like one. He said and I

quote, 'No stinkin' goblin folks welcome here.'" She shrugged and smiled as if she wanted to be nice but had no control over the situation.

"So I can't be a paying customer because I work across the street?"

"Pretty much."

I sighed.

She held her hand out—not to shake mine but to take my prize. "Can I have that please?"

"If you think I can't afford it, I assure you—"

"—sorry but this isn't about money. Believe me, Kramkar would swindle a satyr out of his last dime, but Bill and his employees aren't welcome here."

Reluctantly, I surrendered my find. After the bells waved goodbye to me from her hand, my heart broke to see a stained, torn ribbon wrapped haphazardly around a single broken bell. Damn, that was a top-rate glamour.

"Was that cursed?" I asked.

"If you were a selkie, I'd be worried," the woman replied, "but lucky for you, you're a werewolf so you should be okay."

We made our way back toward the entrance. The woman didn't complain when I lingered here and there to take a peek.

"Are you a human?" I asked. She didn't smell supernatural. "What's your name?"

"I'm Jocelyn the human. Yeah—it's a long story."

"If you've worked for Kramkar as long as I've worked for Bill, I'm sure we could gab for days—by the way, what's up with all the rocks in the front? They weren't there yesterday."

"They're from his homeland. Wherever he goes, a part of his mountain comes with him."

When we reached the entrance I said, "Thanks for letting me take a look around."

"Sure thing."

Before I crossed the threshold, she added, "If Kramkar wasn't here, I would've sold this to you. My customers don't buy holiday stuff as much anymore."

I quirked a grin. "There's always a home for holiday cheer at my house. Especially the hopeless junk."

Empty-handed and pensive, I went to work. According to my watch, I made it just in time to see Bill staring at one of the computers in the back office.

There was one trunk in the corner, but someone had secured it.

"Nice to see you graced us with your presence." I stored my purse in my desk drawer and walked over to him. "When did this little gift show up?"

"Middle of the parking lot around six A.M."

"Damn it." I snapped a photo with my cell and sent it to Thorn. "Has it made a peep?"

"Nope. And the nut job who left it on my property needs to up his game."

I took a step closer to him. For once, Bill's glamour wavered briefly. His wire frame glasses thickened and thinned as his skin took on a tinge of moss-green. More hints to his true form, particularly his iron-rich scent, were revealed as the fabric of his spell unraveled.

"Bill? You feeling okay?" I asked.

"Damn trolls across the street are screwing around with my magic," he grumbled. "Back in the day if another man pitched a tent in your glen, you could raid his camp."

After a curse or two, he mumbled a few words and the magical spell over him strengthened.

"So Kramkar is the problem?"

Bill's blond eyebrow lowered. "You know his name?"

"I went across the street to take a peek and I got a warm reception. The place is probably a dump under all that magic they're tossing around."

"It's more than a dump. If you could see what I see, you'd wipe your feet off after you left the property."

Troll shit? *Oh, now that's nasty.*

I glanced at the bottom of my sneakers to find them troll shit-free.

My phone dinged with a message from Thorn: *Rex and I are on the way. Don't touch it.*

Yeah, right. Like I'd make that mistake again.

"Do you mind if Thorn takes a peek?" I asked.

"No problem. The wolves are facing as much trouble as I will be."

"Do you know who is behind all of this?"

"I have an idea, but I'm not sure. Kramkar could be the one dumping this shit everywhere to make me look bad. Those trunks didn't show up until his wrinkly ass barreled into town."

I rolled my eyes at the idea. One of the basilisks attacked a tourist. Why leave those things around to gnaw on your customers? Someone else was behind the trunks.

Ten minutes later, Thorn and Jake arrived.

"Where's Rex?" I asked.

Thorn shrugged. "He said he had other things to do."

After his little speech about offering a helping hand, this guy couldn't even show up? How noble of him.

Jake circled the trunk. "So we need to search for anymore trunks and that rotten smell, right?"

"Yep," Thorn said.

"Why don't you and I see if we can track anything weird?" Jake suggested. "Do a five-mile search around the market?"

"Agreed." Thorn kissed my forehead and left.

I added, "Be careful," but he already hurried out the door.

The morning crowds at The Bends were far thinner thanks to the new business opening across the street. The fire witch bit at her short nails while Erica re-sorted the magical capes by color. I couldn't stop thinking about the cursed bells either. They were ugly as hell, but the memories they'd drawn from me were so vivid I craved seeing them again. To distract myself, I got to work.

It was business as usual until a familiar face walked through the door. At first, I thought he was an illusion, but the customer's all-black attire made his identity unmistakable. Nick, the white wizard, had arrived, but his assertive steps toward me meant I wouldn't like what he had to say.

CHAPTER 11

"Nick?" I whispered.

My friend gave me a familiar smile and all the old memories we'd experienced: hanging out together in Brooklyn, browsing antique marts for items to hoard, all those adventures—the good and the bad, came to mind.

If I didn't have Thorn in my life, I would've opened my heart to Nick's affections.

"You were supposed to be at group therapy yesterday." He strode into the room. Nothing about him had changed since I'd seen him right after the New Year began. He wore the same 1940s-style gangster's uniform: a black trench coat, black slacks and shoes. Back when we'd first met, he joked that, due to his OCD, he didn't like colorful clothes since black hid most stains.

"Is that really why you're here?" I hissed. "No, hey, how are you doing? It's been a while?"

"It's Wednesday," was all he said.

"Believe me, I know the date. And it's good to see you, Nick."

He finally nodded. "Good to see you, too."

My brow wrinkled. "Aren't you supposed to be at medical school right now?"

The unnatural brightness in his dark eyes dimmed a bit. "You could say that. Things didn't go as planned."

I opened my mouth to ask more but shut it quickly. We had plenty of time to catch up. Since we last spoke, so many things happened, certainly to me and probably to him as well. Far too much for a quick chit-chat.

"How did you know I'd be here?" I asked.

"Dr. Frank." He gave me a knowing look and I had a feeling that sneaky therapist dished on my whereabouts so Nick could check up on me. "Group therapy starts in *ten* minutes."

I gestured around to show the store. "And The Bends has been open since eight. Your point?"

"You didn't show up on Tuesday so you should see Dr. Frank today." He gave me that firm wizard-knows-best expression: A growing frown and tilt to his head.

"I can't leave. Today isn't my day off."

Nick glanced around. "I don't think they'll miss you. There are three people in here."

"Three?" I only spotted two. A water witch checked out the staffs while a tiny brownie sniffed around the enchanted goods on the lower shelves.

"One is wearing a heavy glamour," Nick explained, "but the Hippoi Monokerata is just browsing and will likely leave soon."

My mouth opened and closed. I'd ask later what the hell a Hippoi Monokerata actually was. "I'll go next week like a good girl. I promise, Nick. But I can't take time off."

"What about lunch? We can do a simple exercise, catch up, and I'll have you back here before your break ends. As much as you'd like to pretend you don't need help, you do."

I sighed. That damn wizard was too *helpful* for his own good. "Fine, but where can we go with only an hour?"

Nick pulled a medallion out of one of the many magical pockets in his long, black coat. "Courtesy of Dr. Frank. We'll head to NY and return in less than hour."

Erica sauntered over to us. "We'll be fine, Nat. I can take care of everything."

Out of all the times to have a co-worker show up. I was grateful for Erica's offer, but my cheeks grew warm at the prospect of having my former rival see me leave to attend therapy. With a white wizard, no less.

As her face didn't reveal her inner opinions, I simply thanked her.

Of course, none of this stopped me from worrying about what might happen if I left: What if one of the trunks turned up and people were hurt? I crammed the fears into my mental deal-with-it-later box and nodded to Nick. He activated the medallion with a click, and soon we materialized right in front of Dr. Frank's office. We hurried out and headed outside.

The quiet of the office changed into the roar of the City that Never Sleeps. All around us, pedestrians walked about, heading to lunch or personal business. Cars zipped past us and honked. Deliverymen on bikes veered around fast-moving traffic. I used to work here a couple of years ago, but now that I lived in a small town, I loved getting a dose of big city energy every now and then.

"What now?" I asked. "Did you want to do an exercise?" In the past, Nick always stuck to his wizard's guns about adhering to Dr. Frank's orders.

His face grew pensive but he asked, "Care to eat instead?"

Eating in New York rather than of experiencing the joy

of my sad sack lunch sounded divine. "Yes, please. How about we grab some food from Mike's Magic Cart?"

I loved the grub on Mike's Magical Cart, but as an enchanted food seller, Mike never appeared in the same place. He jumped from neighborhood to neighborhood, eluding the most clever wolf's nose. Spellcasters like Nick, though, had a trick in one of his many wizard pockets to figure out Mike's location.

With a grin, Nick said, "He's in Washington Park today. Let's go."

Nick teleported us to a business office right off 5th Avenue. The place didn't have air conditioning and I about passed out from baking in the fourth floor hallway. In order to teleport, Nick had to have visited the location before. By the time we got outside, I was drenched in sweat and Nick barely had a trickle.

"Does your coat have air conditioning?" I gasped.

He chuckled. "Not really. Just a spell or two to keep out the heat."

Damn wizards and their magical perks.

As we passed pedestrians on our way to the square, many stared at him in his coat, but he didn't mind so I didn't either. My nose told me we'd found Mike's Cart before I'd spotted it. The decadent aroma of werewolf meat skewers, sweet shapeshifter candy, and fluffy fairy puffs wafted past my nose.

On the way, I asked the question that had crossed my mind the minute he'd showed up at The Bends. "Got any plans to let me know why you're not at medical school anymore?"

A muscle in his cheek flexed. That was the only indication my question touched a nerve.

"I've had time to think about what I'd say to my friends,

but now isn't the time. Just know I'll be ready sooner rather than later."

Questions lingered in the silence between us as we entered Washington Park and found Mike's Magical Cart parked off the street. I still wanted to know if something horrible had happened to Nick. Did he flunk out his first semester? Or maybe he accidentally brought one of the cadavers back to life during his anatomy class. Hell, I didn't know how medical school worked when the student was a wizard, but he wouldn't have returned unless something big went down.

Nick was a good friend and I didn't want to see him fail.

I'd failed enough times for both of us.

Mike's Magical Cart couldn't be missed. The plum-purple food truck leaned slightly to the right, but that didn't stop customers from approaching on the opposite side of the street. Baskets with fairy puffs hung off the sides. A four-foot window revealed a tiny kitchen with a short wizard and witch working inside. Mike and his co-worker had to be no more than five-feet tall. The witch never stopped moving as she deftly flipped over skewers and burgers on a wood-fire grill. Then she scurried to the drink station to fill two plastic cups with what appeared to be ale. Well, my nose caught a whiff of malt and hops.

Not more than ten feet away from the cart, a peculiar tingle danced along my back.

"So the cart has a glamour," I marveled.

"Yep, he'd never be able to operate in a public place," Nick replied.

We stood in the line behind a set of centaurs in business suits and a warlock stood in front of them.

"What do humans see?" I asked.

"The one thing New Yorkers avoid—"

"Overpriced tourist baubles," I finished.

"Exactly. Humans know a bargain when they see it."

I laughed. "True, but what about the desperate folks who are on the way to the airport and will buy anything? Even if it's the ugliest thing they'd ever seen?"

"The wards kick in and they go elsewhere."

My mouth watered the closer we got to the front of the line. I could practically taste the blend of salt, spices, and grilled meat on my tongue. My fantasy ended when Nick spoke.

"I know what you're facing in South Toms River. How long did your pack believe they could stand their ground against the Basilisk King?"

At the sound of the unfamiliar name, I slowly turned to him. "That question came out of nowhere."

"Since you've put me on the spot, you should expect the same. Dr. Frank told me you've had some trouble in town and I checked things out."

"So we're up against a creature called the Basilisk King." I'd never heard of that creature before. "Have you met one?"

Nick crossed his arms, and we stepped forward. "There's only one Basilisk King, and the minute I returned to North America, I felt him. The whole magical community senses the fairy path shift, but back in northern Jersey, I couldn't shake another feeling. It was like watching a storm far away from the shore. The darkness floated up from the ground with the morning mist." He slowly shook his head. "This effect will increase as the fairy path draws closer."

I nodded. She Who Always Walks the Path was behind of all these changes.

"What do you know about him?" I asked.

He took a step closer to me, his dark eyes flashing.

"Even a wizard like myself knows the Basilisk King isn't a creature to be trifled with. Long ago, when gods walked among men, the Basilisk King was a demigod with followers in ancient Greece and Mesopotamia. He was what you'd call a dictator these days. You either worshipped him or his followers made you fall to your feet."

None of this news was good.

"And the basilisks?" I asked.

"They're abominations he can conjure at will from another realm similar to hell."

"Do you have any idea why he's in South Toms River? Why does he follow…" I almost said her true name and stopped myself. "…her around?"

"She Who Always Walks the Path's a source of true power. By following the fairy path from the beginning to the end for all eternity, she'll always offer vitality to those who trail after her. The Basilisk King siphons off her strength. No one has had to deal with him since her path used to thread through northern Europe to the Canadian wilderness."

"And now she's coming here."

"Precisely."

We reached the end of the line, and gleeful for the distraction, I ordered not one, not two, but six skewers. Might as well get as many as possible to take home. Mike, the cart's owner, chuckled as he handed me my change.

"Been a long time, Ms. Stravinsky," he said with a bright smile and a heavy Brooklyn accent. "You should visit my cart more often."

I stole a quick bite. "If I could find this place, I would've setup a tent."

His head cocked to the side and the tufts of his dark

brown hair flopped over. "You don't know how, hmm? Seems like an excuse to me…"

What excuse did I have?

He looked over my head and greeted the next customer.

I shuffled to the side, wanting to ask Mike what he meant, but Nick was already leaving, munching away on a bag full of fairy puffs. Briefly, I glanced over my shoulder and considered the cart owner's words. Did Mike mean that I could use Old Magic to find the cart? As tempting as the idea was, I couldn't use magic to find food—no matter how perfectly seasoned I found the snacks.

I switched to a more important topic as Nick directed us to the nearest alley: the Basilisk King.

"Can we kill the big BK or do we have to play whack-a-basilisk until we can drive him away?" I asked.

"I'm still researching with some associates in the Wizards Guild. Once I learn more, we can act. For now, we need to be on the defensive until a solution is found."

"Lovely. Whack-a-basilisk it is then."

"You're not alone. As long as your pack stays out of his way, you should be fine until we can strike."

"What if I'd love to leave his dangerous ass alone, but he's targeting me?" I reminded him about how the basilisks ran to my old house.

"Then while we're waiting for answers from the Wizard's Guild, we need to figure out why he's targeting you."

A shiver danced down my spine. The creature prowling my territory had a name, but I'd yet to face him. "What do you mean by *we*?"

"I mean the pack won't have to face him alone. You'll need the magical community—whether you want it or not."

We reached an alley between buildings and Nick opened the portal back to The Bends.

The back office was empty and the sounds from a crowd shopping leaked through the double doors. Hopefully, Erica and the others didn't have to deal with too many customers.

"I need to gather the necessary supplies," he said firmly. "If you see one of those trunks, contact me. Day or night. Otherwise, you'll see me soon."

I walked through the gate into the store.

As the portal closed, I knew what Nick meant by soon. Time to prepare the pack for spellcasters in the area.

CHAPTER 12

Thursday morning arrived, and I woke up not long after the sun rose. Thorn held me close. I rested my head on his left arm while his right arm circled my waist. His steady breaths and relaxed features should've left me at ease, but every time I closed my eyes, they shot open again.

My heartbeat quickened. Unease tightened the muscles along my jaw. Something was wrong. I listened for sounds beyond the house. The early morning robins tweeted and crickets sang. A breeze pushed the rocking chair on the porch. Nothing else stirred.

Then I caught it.

The very faint sound of a latch clicking.

The groan of a trunk cracking open.

Get up, Nat.

My head shot up. Thorn jerked awake. I hurried to the window, pulled the curtain aside, and glanced outside. Thorn followed.

"What's wrong?" he murmured.

My mouth dropped open. What blew me away was the

line of beige trunks from the woods leading up to the house. I counted at least fifteen of them. One gray stone sat in the middle of the yard.

"No way…" I breathed.

Thorn left the room wearing the jeans he wore to bed while I threw on a T-shirt and jean shorts.

With my goblin blade in hand, I thundered down the steps to find Aggie and Will conversing with Thorn.

"Have any of them opened yet?" Will asked Thorn.

My mate peeked out the peephole on the front door.

"One of the trunks is open, but it's empty," he reported.

If you see one of them, contact me, Nick had said.

Ugh. I didn't want Nick and Thorn butting heads, but with that many trunks outside, we were about to slam our faces into a doggie-door.

I shot the wizard a text message: *There are trunks outside of my house leading into the woods.*

A reply came a few seconds later: *It's a trap.*

No shit, Admiral Ackbar! I thought.

Another message came from Nick: *Stay inside. I'm on my way.*

Good grief, now the Storm Troopers were coming.

Thorn clutched the doorknob. "We got movement to the right along the trees. We can't stay here. Everyone's leaving."

"We can't leave," I said. "The guy behind all this *wants* us to go outside. Did anybody else see the Hansel and Gretel-style trail of breadcrumbs out there?"

"What are we gonna do if all those trunks open?" Will asked. "We'd be cornered."

Aggie paced the hallway. I noticed she had a baseball bat ready to go. "Are reinforcements coming?"

"Yeah," I said quietly. "Nick is back in town."

"Not the wizard again…" Thorn grunted with a shake of his head. He still didn't like spellcasters.

As if on cue, someone knocked on the back door. At least Nick hadn't used the front entrance. I hurried to let him in and Aggie joined me.

"What's up, Nick?" Aggie said. "You're a sight for sore eyes."

"I wish we were seeing each other under better circumstances," he replied.

Nick wasn't alone this time. A dark-haired girl with alluring androgynous features followed him. The early morning sun's rays hit the top of her head as she entered the house and the reddish sheen to her ruffled chin-length brown hair caught my eye.

What really got my attention was the wrinkled, lime-green shirt she wore over a pair of jeans. What an interesting shirt. With an amused snort, I realized that was the same shirt I'd given Nick for Christmas. I almost laughed. Did that mean Nick and this new friend were shacking up together? If I survived this madness, I would definitely tease him.

"Who's this?" Aggie asked.

"And what a cute shirt," I added.

Nick flashed me a quick look—a not-now-please expression.

Why wait until the end of the day when I could tease him right this second?

"Yeah, you gonna introduce me to everyone?" the woman next to Nick asked with a hint of a Southern accent. A dimple formed on her right cheek as she smiled.

"Oh, sorry about that. Everyone, this is Brenna Bourbon. She's one of the instructors at my school."

Brenna waved at everyone. With a brief inhale, I caught the faint telltale scent of a spellcaster. As to what type, I'd learn sooner or later. Witches showed their true nature in time.

Thorn and Will joined us in the kitchen and more introductions were passed around.

"Were there any trunks in the backyard?" Thorn asked, all business now.

"I teleported to your backyard. We didn't spot any on the way in," Nick replied.

Will stepped forward. He was ready to kick some butt with a hockey stick. "Which means we can escape from the backyard if we want."

Nick strode through the house until he reached the front door. Holding a staff in his left hand, he opened the front door with his right. He crept outside with Brenna bringing up the rear.

"Didn't you tell me to stay inside?" I hissed.

"Yes," he said as he walked up to the first open trunk. "I'm not sure what we're up against, so I'd rather take the brunt of the attack."

Thorn stepped out onto the porch and blocked the view from the doorway. I wanted him to move so I could see, but I knew he did that for our protection. I refused to miss out on the action and crept over to the living room to peek out the window. Aggie and Will followed.

"What's Wizard Boy doing?" Aggie asked.

I scooted over to give them a better view. Nick used the edge of his staff to close the first trunk.

"These are all empty." He walked to the stone and picked it up, then he strolled to the next trunk and kicked it. The trunk jostled but didn't open.

"Did you just kick that? Seriously?" Thorn barked. "Even if they're empty, aren't they still dangerous?"

Brenna placed her hands on her hips. "They must be. When he passed the trunk, Nick sealed it."

"These vessels are peculiar," Nick murmured as he palmed the rock. "Are they doorways?"

Unable to resist, I left the house and the others joined me. By now, Nick was on the edge of the front yard.

"Are there more?" I asked.

"The next one is a hundred yards south," Nick replied. "I can feel another even farther away."

"What's that in your hand?" Thorn asked.

"It's some kind of beacon and there's very old writing on it, but I can't read it." He turned away from us and headed toward the woods. "I need to see where the trunks go."

Thorn hurried after Nick.

"What do we do?" Will asked us.

"We bury them." Using an oak wand drew from a jean pocket, she opened a hole in the ground and the first trunk disappeared inside.

So she was an earth witch. Interesting.

Curiously, I watched the earth swallow the trunk. Something caught my eye.

"These trunks are slightly different compared to the ones that showed up at The Bends," I said. "The markings on the sides are different."

"What does that mean?" Aggie asked.

"I don't know since I can't read them, but I don't want to find out." The goblin blade in my hand hadn't changed form yet. It didn't detect a threat. Did that mean all these trunks were a decoy to lead us into the woods as Nick claimed?

Time to find out.

Our path of trunks headed south. Nick, Aggie, and Thorn took point and made sure the trunks were locked or empty before Brenna and I took turns burying them—or should I say Brenna did all the hard work. Gradually, we ventured farther and farther south through the woods until we left South Toms River and entered Jakes Branch County Park.

As we traveled deeper into the forest, I burned to know what happened to Nick. Didn't Nick say she was an instructor at his school? I wanted to pry, but I kept my mouth shut. Asking Brenna to dish on what went down would bother the hell out of Nick, too.

Finally, the woods led to a gravel road next to a vacant lot. Something was familiar about this place. I'd been here before. The lot had a small building and toolshed for storing snowplows. We were quite off the beaten path now. At least five miles from South Toms River.

"Where are we?" Brenna asked.

"We're inside Jake County Branch Park." Nothing had changed since my last visit. "And we're close to *something else.*"

"Something else?"

We kept following the trunks. The path ended at another toolshed of sorts, surround by haphazard piles of scrap metal, televisions, and other bits of decade-old junk. Of all the places they could have led, why the hell did the trunks end here?

My friends and I had found the *zmee.* The same Russian dragon that had stolen a package from me a year ago.

CHAPTER 13

The *zmee* still hadn't cleaned up this dump. Not a single piece of trash was cleared since I'd ventured here. A year ago, after winning an online auction, I learned my glorious prize had arrived in the mail, and I raced home to retrieve the package. Only to discover my precious parcel was missing.

The culprit behind the kidnapped package lived in this rubble. He'd sent me on a mission into Philadelphia to get my belongings back. A year ago, the trip here triggered my OCD badly, but today I had other things on my mind—the trees and dirt be damned. I'd deal with shit on my shoes later in the privacy of my bathroom with a bottle of bleach.

Thorn, Will, and Nick stood at the edge of the clearing and waited for Brenna and me.

"Any more trunks?" I asked.

"I don't detect any, but this clearing is enchanted," Nick whispered.

"There's no need to whisper," I said. "I know what lives here and he can hear us. Well, *they* can hear us."

"They?" Aggie asked.

While the others waited, I marched right up to the familiar shed. The unsteady shelter was composed of rusty bits and pieces of scrap metal and crumbled bricks. Over the past year, the elements had corroded more of the metal, but the oak tree jutting out of the back held true and provided ample shade over the house and shed.

As I rounded the house toward the front, I caught sight of a new structure. No more than ten feet from the door was a rocky pile. As I got closer, I realized it wasn't only made from those peculiar pebbles I'd seen next to the trunks, but rocks and skulls.

Both human and basilisk skulls.

Had the *zmee* done this? Was the dragon the true Basilisk King? No way.

"*Zmee*, are you in there, you dirty thieves?" I belted out in Russian.

From inside, I caught the sounds of movement in the house as the dragon shifted.

"I can hear you in there," I said in English. "You might as well come out before I come in there and set your shack on fire."

The dented metal door shuddered. "You wouldn't dare!" a gravelly voice screeched.

The opening swung inward with a yawn. A scaly hand with a four-fingered claw appeared as the others joined me in front. The *zmee* crawled their way out. When I mean crawled, I meant slow enough for Nick and Brenna to have a *full* conversation and count the number of basilisk skulls on the mound and discuss the markings carved on the stone.

It was as close as one would get to a History Channel show.

"Do you know the language?" she asked him casually.

"One of the ancient Mesopotamian tongues."

"Sumerian or Akkadian?"

A grunt from the house caught everyone's attention again as a dragon with tiny arms and legs pulled its body out section by section. Inch by inch. Three heads popped out of the hole and the one in front paused to take a breather.

Thorn's serious expression was quite the contrast to Aggie and Will's poor effort to keep a straight face.

"You done yet?" I asked the *zmee*.

There was a point where the dragon couldn't pull their rear end out. The last time I had to come here, I never saw their rear end either.

"What are you doing here, Wolf?" the first head snapped. "I told you last time I don't bother the South Toms River Pack and they should return the favor."

I pointed toward the stack of stones in front of the house. "You might not be bothering the pack, but you're sure as hell collecting humans on pack territory."

The second head rested on the ground, its eyes drooping. The third head poked it while the first spoke. "That pile is not our doing."

"We know it belongs to the Basilisk King," Nick said smoothly. "Why did he lead us to *your* house?"

The first head shrugged. "We can't leave so we don't know—only that we respect the Great Reptile King. He is the Master of Mysteries. The Great Purveyor of Blood who will make the puny the humans fall to their feet."

"All these skulls are the humans that…got in the way?" Aggie said with a grimace.

"Probably," the second head said. "The Great One's *helper* brought them here for us to create an altar. He wants those who can wield the ancient power to bow before him."

Nick and Brenna exchanged a brief look.

"Those with power?" Thorn said.

"The Great Reptile King only drinks from the well of pure power. The fairy path allows him to sip, but creatures that are true sources of power will allow him to truly quench his thirst. Like a can of Cherry Pepsi, but much more refreshing."

The second head was snoring now, but that didn't stop Nick from approaching the *zmee*. "This is a fascinating arrangement. When did this 'helper' create this beautiful altar?"

"They came—" the first head nipped the third, stopping it from speaking.

"Do you want the Great One to strike us down?" The first head bit into the third one's ear again. "Shut up!" It turned to Nick. "You're a tricky one, Wizard. I should bite off your head!"

Nick blinked back at the *zmee* with a lack of interest. Even as the first head drew in a deep breath, the scales along their neck blossoming from dark brown to a brilliant red. Alarm circled my chest until the dragon coughed and spat out thick smoke.

Yep, the *zmee* hadn't changed a bit.

That poor creature needed to work out and chase down some villagers or they wouldn't be setting anything on fire.

"What a great feat of strength. Are you proud of yourself?" the wizard asked with a hint of amusement.

The third head sneered. "Why don't you come a little closer?"

"I could help you with that cough you got there," Nick offered, "but I doubt you'd be grateful for my help." He stayed where he was. The yard was pretty disgusting, but I knew he'd cross the muck to help anyone in need.

"Other than this stubborn cough," the first head said,

"I've been perfectly healthy—either way, the Great One will bestow shiny gifts if I stay in his good graces."

"And his minion?" I slid into the conversation. "Will the lowly minion who built this altar also bestow such gifts, too? I might have something you'd like."

The third head's brow furrowed, and it flashed its many teeth. "You wolves think you're smart, just like the Great Reptile King's wolf minion. I won't be tempted by your deception."

I could feel us inching toward more clues, but the first head glared at us with a gaze sharp enough to cut through any bullshit. If we could've directed the third head away from the rest, we might've had a shot at more info.

"I'm tired of this talking," Aggie snapped. "Why don't we drag them out of this shithole and kick their ass until they tell us where we can find the Basilisk King and his little punk ass helper."

Both Nick and I grimaced. Based on the putrid smell of the dragon's home, I didn't want to see what kind of trash the *zmee* hoarded inside.

"You're a brave one, Red. Let's see how brave you'll be after we bite into your backside," the first head spurted, managing to wake up the second with hard pokes to its neck. "I'll use your skull to replace the head of this good-for-nothing."

The second head snarled and bit down on the first head's snout.

We stood there and waited.

"Was this what happened last time?" Nick whispered.

"About the same. The first one's crankier now though," I replied. "At the time, I wished I had popcorn."

Nick shook his head in disgust while Thorn rubbed the side of his face.

Aggie leaned toward Will to say, "Ten bucks says the second head fucks up the first one."

"You're on," Will replied.

Thorn groaned. "This is getting us nowhere. Hey! Hey!" He waved his arms as the second head slammed into the first. The opening to the tiny house shook from the shifting dragon and the sounds of broken glass emerged from within.

The tussle advanced toward us. Aggie jumped out of the way. Nick vanished in a flash of white light just as the second head hit the ground and crashed into a mound of broken flat screens.

"How long did the fight go on last time?" Thorn yelled.

"Not long. Give them a second," I replied. As I predicted, the tussle got the three heads tired and soon enough they were panting. After all, they were all attached to one body.

"Let's be reasonable here," I began. "We both know the Basilisk King can offer you many things, but I doubt he's brought you what you *really* want. Something shiny. Something precious and holiday-oriented?"

The first head perked up while the second tried to catch its breath; the third smacked its lips as if the dinner bell had rung.

"The Great One doesn't have time to answer such frivolous prayers," the third head said.

"They're not frivolous to collectors like you and me, right?" I said. "Look, a year ago, I got you those photos for your research. I'm sure you're done and you need something new to examine. If you want, I'll be happy to supply more research materials." If I had to break into another museum and snap of bunch of photos that would be easy-peasy.

The first head darted forward to speak first, "Well, I'd enjoy close-up photos of this new exhibit in Berlin—"

"Shut up," the second head snapped. "We don't want your stupid shit."

"I agree. I want something shiny..." the third head hissed.

"Something precious and rare..." the second head added.

Damn, I should've rephrased my words. Had I gotten us into deeper trouble?

Nick reached into his coat and pulled out a rare green glass Christmas ornament. The piece had to be from the 1950s. "Is this tempting enough for you to tell us who is helping the Basilisk King?"

The second head was mesmerized, its eyes going from a topaz to molten gold. "Breathtaking—"

"—but not good enough, we have plenty of broken ones inside," the first head added. "I'm still mad you rolled over our property—our expensive property."

The third head whispered something in Russian to the second, but I didn't understand the grunts between the words "bring now." What were they doing?

"Yes..." The long tongue of the second head curled out. "There is a *new* store in town."

A knot formed in my stomach, knowing what was coming.

"Our nymph courier got some rather disgusting popcorn in there, but she spied the most beautiful treasure. A set of reindeer bells enchanted with magic from the *Huldrefolk*," the second head said.

Thorn glanced at me for clarification and I mouthed the words, "Trolls."

The second head continued. "We want those bells. The nymph couldn't find them after she saw them the first time. Some busybody human told her they were for sale, but only for those who truly desired them."

I crossed my arms. "Fine, we'll get you the bells, but you have to pay for them."

"It's a bunch of stupid bells. I'll pay for it," Will offered, but my hand shot up to stop him.

"No, if the dragon wants the bells, they will pay for them."

"Half," the first head said.

I tilted my head to the side. "I saw those bells not too long ago. They cost a hundred dollars."

Will shuffled back, his offer receded. I doubt any of us —other than me—would be willing to pay that much for some cursed junk.

The *zmee*'s heads conversed again.

"Do you take PayPal?" the third head asked me.

"Oh, for fuck's sake." Aggie groaned. "Are you serious?"

"They are." I gave the dragon my PayPal email address.

"Fine." The first head's eyes formed slits. "Then a bargain has been made. You, and only you, Natalya Stravinsky will bring us the *Huldrefolk* bells and we will reveal how to find the Basilisk King."

"What about the minion?" I asked.

"One item," the first head said. "One answer."

"Fine," I grumbled.

"We will know if someone else," the second head eyed Will and Thorn, "mishandles the merchandise."

"Fine, we'll bring you the bells, but we expect an answer," I said crisply.

"Agreed. We fulfilled our end of our bargain last time, didn't we?" Eagerness shined in the first and second head, but the third gave me a strange grin, revealing rows of sharp teeth.

CHAPTER 14

An hour later, we stood outside of The Bends. I had the cash in hand, but we had a new problem.

"I'm not allowed to be inside," I told the others. "They wouldn't sell me the bells either when I wanted to buy them."

"Why?" Brenna asked. "Most of the trolls I've met under bridges sold me whatever I wanted."

"Not these entrepreneurs." I motioned toward The Bends. "Apparently, I've got goblin cooties. Bill has covered me in goblin enchantments. The owner Kramkar can sniff me coming from miles away."

"That's a problem." Nick eyed Brenna. "Would a counter-spell help?"

"I could dose her in floral scents?" She shrugged as I backed away from them.

"I'll pass," I said. "The last thing I need is to smell like potpourri for the rest of my life."

Nick approached me and Thorn stiffened, but my mate kept quiet. "Even if we tried a counter-spell, I don't know whether it would work. Nat's different now."

"What do you mean she's different?" Aggie asked with concern.

"You mean that *signature* is natural for her?" Brenna asked.

My brow furrowed. What did she mean by signature?

"What did you learn back in Russia?" Nick asked. "Any curses or dark spells? Powerful ones?"

I laughed. "Tamara taught me the basics."

"Old Magic has changed you." He frowned a bit.

He must've caught my confused expression. He added, "Imagine if the sun gave off a different hue than the one you're always used to seeing."

I wasn't sure if that was good or bad, but I didn't want to use Old Magic again anyway.

"Why don't we try a counter-spell and see if we can blur her out?" Brenna suggested.

The two spellcasters surrounded me. Their spell fluttered over me like a hot summer breeze around my head to a brisk winter flurry along my toes. Then a sucker punch hit me in the stomach, and I dropped to the ground.

"What the hell was that?" I grunted. The goblin blade on my ankle flared to life and seared my skin.

Thorn stooped and scrambled to help me take off the blade's holster. The blade had burned me and left an imprint on my skin.

My mate bit out a curse.

Well, I guessed the goblin blade didn't like that.

"What does that mean?" Brenna grimaced and kneeled next to Thorn.

"Nothing good," Thorn said to her.

Nick placed his hand on my shoulder and the healing took over. "Your goblin employer must've placed protections on you to keep your enchantments intact."

I released a heavy sigh. "All in the name of business. I'm supposed to be able to see magical things and chip away low-level glamours. I had no idea the spell was that powerful."

"The goblin blade magnifies the spell's strength." Nick pinched his lips together. "Will and Aggie should try to sneak inside first. We might get lucky."

With our first plan squashed, I gave Aggie the wad of cash and she winked at me with a mischievous grin. "Mom, can I buy some candy if there is any money left?"

I rolled my eyes. "Sure, but I wouldn't eat anything out of that store if I were you. The rock candy might really be rocks."

We waited for them on the docks at The Bends. Quinton didn't pay us any mind, nonstop in his shuffle to haul goods from trucks into the back office. On such a sunny day, I expected him to have a tan of sorts, but his skin was still pale and the dark circles lining his midnight blue eyes had lightened.

As he continued to work, I realized I should greet him in the morning more often. He often kept to himself, but I learned last year that he'd moved here from Iowa to settle down closer to the sea. Quinton hoped to refine his craft before starting a family to continue his legacy. A legacy of stuffing zombies like Thanksgiving turkeys.

Movement to my left caught my eye.

With amusement, I watched Brenna kick a rock to a bush next to the building—only to see the bush rustle and the rock shot back out.

"Did the bush 'kick' that back?" I took a step toward the bush until I heard her reply.

She beamed like a cat cuddling a freshly caught canary. "Wouldn't you love to know."

Yeah, I wasn't gonna mess with sentient shrubbery.

Nick shook his head with a smile. "Behave, Brenna." Then he asked me, "Do you think they got a chance?"

"Aggie is persuasive," I said, "but the *zmee* said the bells are only visible to those who truly seek it."

"We all want to find the Basilisk King. Isn't that motivation enough?" Brenna asked.

Half an hour later, Aggie and Will returned, empty-handed and annoyed.

"We searched the place from top to bottom," Will reported. "I found some boxes of dusty Christmas paraphernalia, but nothing else."

Thorn sighed. "I expected as much. Nat, can you try to sneak in the old-fashioned way? Perhaps walk in with other customers?"

I shrugged and jump off my spot on the dock. "We don't have much of a choice but why not?"

Like any clever predator, I waited for the early afternoon rush. Tour buses driving north from Atlantic City came around this time. As the buses parked, I pulled in behind them and waited for the doors to open. Groups formed of middle-aged and senior shoppers wearing fanny packs and over-sized visors. Many of them gabbed of what they hoped to find. None of them mentioned visiting The Bends across the Parkway, but that didn't matter. As the line formed toward the front, I filed in, making sure to look around and admire the scenery like any tourist would.

One middle-aged lady in coveralls and a sunhat said to her friends, "I hope this one is good. The Port Republic shops left little to be desired. Not a single antique figurine."

"Who knows," I chimed in. "I bet the stuff across the street is better. Especially if you're looking for Victorian-era antiques."

They gave me a weird look for butting into their

conversation but kept flowing forward. I adjusted my tote on my shoulder. The entrance loomed ahead. My heart fell to see Jocelyn standing outside with her arms crossed. My gaze connected with hers. She slowly shook her head.

Shit.

I tried to ignore her and blend in with the crowd, but I didn't even reach the sidewalk to the entrance. Once I reached Jocelyn, a compulsion to turn around slapped the back of my neck. With every step I took, the urge to flee increased. The feeling was familiar—like the gathering of a storm in my chest before a panic attack hits. Sweat gathered on my brow. My breath quickened. I sucked in deep breaths, but nothing reduced the desire to knock over everyone and get the hell out of there.

"I warned you," a gentle voice whispered.

I turned to see Jocelyn next to me. Not standing; she stood above me. I'd collapsed to my knees. The other shoppers flowed around us, unaware of my condition.

The goblin blade twitched on my ankle, but the weapon's form hadn't changed. Was the movement a warning or a message?

"I just want to browse," I murmured. "A little."

She shook her head.

I scooted back and the panic retreated a little. "I won't tell him. I need something in there so I can find the Basilisk King and stop him from hurting people."

Her finely curved eyebrows lowered. Did she recognize the name?

"He's here?" she whispered. "Kramkar had a feeling we were followed from our last town."

"The Basilisk King followed you here?"

"No, no." She trailed after me as I finally managed to stand. "The fairy path is a lucrative circuit in terms of supernatural sales. Have you seen the Basilisk King in person?"

"Not yet. He's left trunks all over town. My friends and I have a lead to find him, but we need the reindeer bells from your store."

A flash of pity fell over Jocelyn's face. "When we're *open* during the day, he's around. Sorry."

I sighed. However, once I reached the parking lot, I briefly turned around. Why did she emphasize the word *open*?

By the time I returned to The Bends, I had an idea what she meant.

Jocelyn had given me a vital clue as to when I might seek my prize.

CHAPTER 15

The sun escaped and dipped beneath the horizon, bringing radiant streaks of burnt orange and lavender toward the sky. As the night deepened, I waited on the docks. I shooed the others away until only Thorn remained, and even he gave me space. This would be my mission to accomplish alone if necessary.

I couldn't see my mate, but I sensed him hovering nearby.

"You might not see me, but I'm always around," he always said to me.

Once the sun retreated and the waning crescent moon greeted me, I stood. Erica pulled into the parking lot as I prepared to leave.

"What are you doing here?" I asked.

"Late shipment from New York. Bill was complaining about it being left on the back door."

I motioned to the empty dock. "I've been here for hours. Nothing's arrived."

The Bends had closed already. Did she really come here for a shipment? I couldn't smell a lie in her words, but suspicion flicked at me. The *zmee* said he had a wolf minion. Could that helper be Erica?

"Maybe it hasn't shown then. I guess I'll eat dinner and return later." She turned to leave but glanced over her shoulder. "What are *you* doing here?"

I explained to her about the trunks and how I could find the Basilisk King if I retrieved an item from the troll thrift shop. Naturally, I didn't tell her about the minion.

"Why don't you coerce the *zmee* into giving you the information you need?" The way she stood there, placing her weight on one leg, her annoyance came off her like a fog.

"A thousand-pound Russian dragon can't be coerced—only bargained with. Even the witch and wizard with me didn't bother."

She sniffed. "I would've tried anything, but..." She left my lack of action in the air, so I marched away.

Footsteps echoed behind me. Was she following me?

"Where are you going?" I asked her.

"The Basilisk King is attacking my territory, too. If you know a way to find him, I should help you."

"I don't need your help."

She ignored me and followed me to the empty troll mart parking lot. A breeze passed over my nose, and I inhaled. Nothing stirred here recently. I caught the delicious scents from the nearby fairy bakery, the noxious fumes from cars along the Parkway, but not much else.

Erica scanned the outside of the building. "I don't see any security cameras."

"The troll guards his property during the day," I murmured, not really wanting to work with her tonight.

"And what guards the place at night?"

"I don't know—" My words ended when I checked the garden. The tulips stood tall, yet there were less rocks in the front now. Only indentations from where the rocks had been. Had someone pulled them up since my last visit?

With the cover of darkness, we circled the property, finding no one around.

"How did you plan on entering?" she asked.

That was a good question. The loading dock to the rear of the building had locks on the doors. As I drew near, I caught the scent of both humans and enchanted creatures. Had Jocelyn locked these doors or perhaps one of Kramkar's supernatural employees?

I crept toward the door. The dim light from the night sky shone on the dark metal. Electric shocks danced along my fingertips as I rubbed the surface.

"Is it enchanted?" she whispered.

"Yes, we'll need to find another way inside."

With a quick glance at my watch, I noted the time. "Let's keep this trip under ten minutes."

"Understood." Erica pointed upward. "I doubt they've locked the skylights."

Good observation.

I took point and jumped up to the second story windowsill. From there, I scaled the side of the building with Erica again on my tail. Clutching the wood wall, a warm breeze fluttered my hair into my face. To my left, Erica scampered past to the nearest skylight. Surprisingly, the window opened with ease and she slipped inside.

I took a final look around—I'd never surveyed The Bends from this high in the air. In the daylight, my workplace appeared like any other. Simple. Non-threatening. But now that night descended, shadows prevailed. Suddenly, The Bends' roof *shifted*.

A second later, the troll store fluttered in return. I felt the movement beneath me. So weird and disorienting. The walls on The Bends stretched and contracted as if the store drew in deep breaths like a living being.

I shuddered and hurried after Erica. She perched on one of the roof's support beams.

"What were you doing?" she whispered.

"Nothing." I leaped onto the beam and crept across to join her.

Below us, only moonlight bled through the skylights and revealed the showroom floor below.

"What are we looking for?" she asked.

"Reindeer bells. They were in booth 2B, but this store might be enchanted…"

"…meaning they could be elsewhere," she finished as she scratched her nose.

"Unfortunately."

During my excursion with Mrs. Weisz, I hadn't smelled any guard dogs or any other creatures that might be used for protection like a moody brownie. Bill didn't use a security alarm, but he did use wards. Did that mean a similar method was used here?

"Reaching out to find light in the darkness costs nothing," Mevelyn had said.

I closed my eyes and drew in a deep breath. Held it. I cradled everything that represented the *outside* within me. Even with my eyes closed, Erica's essence flared beside me like a bright beacon in the dark. Beyond her, the entire troll thrift store glowed. Briefly, my stomach quivered from the beauty of strange, firefly-like sparks flittering around vases in one booth to hanging urns vibrating in another. Swirls, as beautiful as the vermillion streaks in a hunter's moon, undulated from packages of fairy dust in one stall to a rack selling void-black clothing.

This whole place was alive with supernatural activity.

I searched further.

There. The magic emanating from the reindeer bells was dark-blue, similar to the shifting shadows along the deepest points in the ocean. When I examined it the first time, I'd glimpsed what it wanted me to see, not its true nature.

My awe died a grisly death as, suddenly, a crack formed in the corner of the store and a hunched-over creature ambled out. Compared to the dancing lights, this being pulsed with dark gray shadows.

I opened my eyes. Erica stooped beside me still scratching her nose. How much time had passed? It felt like close to fifteen minutes already, but my watch confirmed we'd been here less than five. I jolted myself out of the time shift. We had a mission to accomplish and ominous company coming from one of the showroom corners.

"We got a problem," I whispered. "Something's crawling out of the wall."

"Where?" she asked. "I don't smell anything."

"In front of us to the far left. See those double windows? Near that corner."

She squinted. "Is that a rat?"

"Rats aren't that big." Erica's description appeared to be accurate. Whatever it was, it had an elongated tail and a thick torso and legs. A faint *swish-scratch* reached the rafters every time its tail and nails brushed the floor.

Swish, swish, scratch. Swish, swish, scratch. The sound grew louder.

The reindeer bells were on the other side of the store. If I made a run for it, I could grab the bells and then we could get the hell out of here.

"Got a plan?" Erica asked.

"Can you attract its attention while I grab the reindeer bells?"

She nodded and jumped to the nearest rafter. From there, she reached the top of one of the booths' shelves and climbed down. The guardian twitched and shuffled her way. Meanwhile, I made my way down the opposite wall. This high up, I didn't expect to find so much dust and cobwebs. The Jersey spiders had made themselves at home, and I dodged their housing developments to head down. Once I was close enough to the ground, I jumped and hid behind a booth wall.

A crash erupted—the clang of a metal bin hitting the floor—and my heart jumped to my throat. More sounds, a table turning over and metal objects banging about. I turned the corner to peek.

At the far end of the aisle, Erica ran toward me with the guardian hard on her heels. It huffed and puffed, but that tiny body picked up speed. Any second now it would catch up with her. The goblin blade on my ankle hummed and I withdrew it. The weapon's hilt twitched in my hand and stretched out to form an axe. Nice and heavy, too.

Erica glanced over her shoulder and missed noticing a table in her path.

"Hey!" I called out to her, but she crashed into the table and a whole display fell over. So much for sneaking in and out without leaving a trace.

The creature advanced and its tiny mouth opened, revealing rows of gleaming white fangs.

I braced myself to jump out and help her, but the most peculiar thing happened. Instead of pouncing on its prey, the guardian picked up the nearest product in its mouth, a wicker basket with gaudy stick figure dolls, and placed it back on a shelf. Then it stepped closer to Erica, saw another item and arranged that, too.

Erica looked back at me, and I shrugged. She got to her feet. The rat-dog snarled and advanced again. With the tip of her pink-painted fingernail, Erica pushed over a small bin. Only cats knocked over things with such finesse, but the guardian stopped to clean up the mess. The process repeated over and over again.

Damn, Bill would love to have an employee follow people around and tidy up behind them. Where could we get one? Probably not from the local Animal Control.

Erica whistled sharply and shot me a wake-up-and-get-what-we-came-here-for expression. I sprang into action and raced down aisle two, trying to remember the arrangement of the booths from above. Two stalls later, I recognized my target. The pedestal sat in the middle of the stall with the glorious reindeer bells on top. I picked up my prize and about booked it out of there but realized I was stealing.

Good look there, Ms. Stravinsky.

I retrieved the envelope of money from my pocket and left it on top of the pedestal. I didn't need to leave my name or identifying information. The troll would only know I'd bought it at the price on the tag. Surely, that'd make up for breaking into his shop.

With my prize in hand, I said a prayer that this stealthy purchase wouldn't be the beginning of an all-out troll-goblin war, then I got the hell out of there with Erica not far behind.

CHAPTER 16

Thorn and I refused to venture through the woods at night to visit the *zmee* so we set out to do the handoff first thing in the morning. Will planned to start his new job at the mill today, and Aggie joined us as backup.

Personally, I didn't fear the *zmee*. That three-headed dragon wouldn't be gobbling any hikers in Jake County Park, but I did fear the Basilisk King. Why did he build the altar for the *zmee* and who were these sources of power they were blathering about? Did we need to find these people before the Basilisk King attacked them, too?

The three of us trudged through the woods with the rising sun peeking through the oak and pine trees. This early in the morning, the cooler weather gave us a pleasant breeze filled with the scents of wildflowers, honeysuckle, and mushrooms. The nocturnal birds had fallen silent and now goldfinches and woodpeckers freely flitted from tree to tree.

Eventually, we reached the *zmee*'s ramshackle home. Smoke rose from its chimney and the scent of meat—not sure of what kind of meat and I didn't want to know—wafted from inside.

We didn't have to wait long for them to appear.

"You brought it!" the second head slipped out before the other two.

The third head attempted to shove the second one out of the way. Their tiny fingers eagerly reached out to me.

No way was I giving up the goods until it answered the agreed upon question. "Where's the Basilisk King?"

Each head frowned in unison.

"The Great One doesn't sit still," the third head screeched. "He is drawn to power therefore, his location changes from one day to another."

"You said yesterday he seeks power sources," I said. "What *are* power sources? Shapeshifters?"

In the past, warlocks had used shapeshifters for their spells. It was cruel and torturous.

The third head gave me a sinister grin that skittered up my spine. "True sources of power. Those who can draw power from within and manipulate it."

My veins filled with ice, but I held myself steady. Now wasn't the time to breakdown. The *zmee* referred to Old Magic practitioners.

Like Grandma and me.

I whipped out my phone and dialed my parents' house. No one picked up.

This early in the morning, my dad should still be there as he usually worked the afternoon shift as a machinist at a local factory. I tried his cell phone and that went straight to voicemail.

"Dad, pick up the phone!" I hissed.

My dad slept like a bear head-deep in hibernation. Mom got creative years ago and hooked the television to a timer to wake him up.

I need to go home. Now.

"Nat, where are you going?" Aggie called out.

"I'll explain on the way. Let's go!" I replied.

The forest blended around me as I sprinted back to the car. The others weren't far behind, barely panting by the time we reached the car. Thorn jumped into the driver's seat.

"Grandma, right?" he asked.

He'd read the situation quickly. I nodded then shot a text to Nick: *BK wants old magic spellcasters. Heading to Grandma.*

Barely adhering to the speed limits, Thorn leaned on the accelerator and got us to my parents' house a few minutes later. I scanned the street. Honestly, I expected to see a row of trunks heading down the road, but with only a woman walking her schnauzer, the scene was one of quiet calm.

I had a feeling a hurricane was coming though.

Nick arrived at my parents' home before us. He sat on the front step like a sentinel.

"Any signs of trouble?" Thorn asked him.

Nick sighed. "He's been here, but he hasn't entered the property."

"How do you know?" Aggie had circled the house and appeared around the corner.

"The residue you spoke of is all over the backyard," Nick replied. "Water evaporates, but the basilisks are enchanted from an alternate realm full of caverns with sulfurous pools."

"Eww." Aggie made a face.

"Is Grandma inside?" I asked, already at the door.

"Yes," Nick replied. "She's watching television while your father is sleeping. I'll wait here while you check on them."

"I'll keep you company," Thorn said to Nick.

I had only a half-second to wonder what the hell Thorn and Nick could talk about before Aggie and I hurried into the house. The way we barged in, you'd think there was a major emergency, but Grandma Lasovskaya merely watched a recorded Russian gameshow from the 1990s called *Hundred to One*. She giggled away as the host asked families a series of questions *Family Feud-style*.

Grandma's features softened. "Natalya, what are you doing here? What is wrong?"

I knelt in front of her and brought her wrinkled hands to my cheeks. "I'm so glad you're safe."

Aggie searched through the house, checking all the rooms downstairs. The moment she opened my parents' door, a heavy snore bled out, only to cease when she shut the door again. She hurried up the stairs two at the time to the next floor.

"Of course, I'm safe." Grandma Lasovskaya smiled. "Why wouldn't I be?"

I drew in a deep breath. "The creature behind all of those trunks is called the Basilisk King."

While I explained everything that happened so far up until what we'd learned from the *zmee*, she nodded at the appropriate moments.

"I was worried you were in danger," I added.

She stroked the side of my face. "He was here last night, but he didn't bother me."

"Why didn't you tell me? Or even Mom and Dad?"

"I didn't want to see you like you are right now. You're worried about things you can't control."

"I can't stop the Basilisk King from leaving his little care packages around, but I can at least protect you."

She gave a *tsk-tsk*. "All of you believe the elderly should be cared for, but many of us still have some tricks up our sleeves."

I immediately recalled the day she used Old Magic to protect me, but at a great cost.

"Some prices shouldn't be paid unless absolutely necessary," I said.

"True, but he hasn't gotten desperate yet. The time may come for me to face him, but I'm not afraid."

Grandma might not be scared, but the tightening in my stomach signaled how deeply I feared for her. Just one basilisk was a handful for Erica and me. How would Grandma fare against double or triple that number?

Aggie came down the steps and joined us. "All clear. I made sure the windows were locked."

Grandma patted the seat next to her, and Aggie gladly took the spot.

"Want one?" Grandma offered Aggie a piece of candy from a tiny pocket in her blue shift dress. Agatha thanked her and unwrapped the shiny, crimson wrapper. I smiled, recalling the familiar feeling. My grandma always knew how to make us feel better.

"I'll wake up my dad and tell the others what's up," I told them.

After rousing the eldest Stravinsky and explaining the situation, I joined Thorn and Nick outside. The two kept a respective distance from each other and chatted.

Maybe this was a sign my mate trusted Nick.

"I've learned a spell or two of Old Magic," Thorn said while leaning across his SUV. "Why hasn't the Basilisk King sought me out?"

"Good question." Nick crossed his arms from where he stood next to the house. "For some reason, you're not a potential meal."

Thorn grumbled, "He should come for me if he wants a

real fight." He paused as if in thought. "Tracking an enemy that doesn't leave a trail is very difficult."

"The *zmee* said he *does* leave a trail," Nick said. "Therefore, we need a plan to trap him."

"How do we trap someone who's constantly moving though?" I asked.

"It's hard as hell," Thorn said. "Hey, how come the magical community hasn't intervened?"

Nick slowly shook his head in frustration. "The Wizard's Guild prefers to sweep the matter under the rug unless there's a possibility that the humans might see the supernatural world."

"Guess a bunch of dead tourists in front of the *zmee*'s shack wasn't enough," I said.

"No, it's not unfortunately, but you don't have to face this alone. Brenna and I are willing to help however we can."

"As much as I distrust spellcasters, I appreciate your help," Thorn said.

I hid a grin. My mate could be congenial when necessary.

"So, we can't track him and he's constantly moving. Do you know if he can be trapped or killed?" Thorn added.

"He's a demigod capable of opening doors to another realm and he subsists on power from other magical beings —which means we should be able to weaken him and force him back on the fairy path."

"Can he be *killed*?" Thorn asked again slowly.

Nick pinched the bridge of his nose. "He's lived through multiple world wars into the modern age. I wouldn't want to try to kill him, but I'm assuming yes."

This wasn't the time to *assume* anything, and we all knew what was said about people who assume things.

I tried to swallow, but my throat was far too dry. We

had yet to see what powers the Basilisk King had beyond controlling his minions and summoning their gateways.

"I say we wait for him to come to us," Thorn suggested, "then we drive him back north to the fairy path. If he refuses, we *kill* him."

Nick's nod seemed reluctant and the confidence I'd felt facing the *zmee* withered. Instead of hunting the Basilisk King, we had to wait for him to come to us. We were sitting ducks.

I wanted to fall deeper into my thoughts, but my phone rang. The name on the Caller ID elicited a groan.

"Who is it?" asked Thorn.

"Bill." I rubbed my forehead. "And I have a feeling he's not happy. I might've started a neighborhood flea market war."

CHAPTER 17

Thorn and Aggie offered to stand guard with my dad. At first, Dad declined their offer, but I doubt anybody could pry Aggie from the goodies at the Stravinsky household.

"I need your family to adopt me," she gushed as I left.

When I was younger, Grandma loved to spoil my cousins and me. She'd wait for our parents to look away and then she'd dart into her pocket to retrieve snacks and sweets.

"We need to keep your belly full and your claws sharp for the next hunt, Little Ones," she'd say.

Can't hunt on an empty stomach.

I smiled at the memory, but the glow from those pleasant memories dulled as I pulled into The Bends parking lot. The first sign that I'd messed up was the torn-up front lawn. It was as if a gigantic hand clawed through the grass, leaving clumps tossed about here and there. Also, the dumpster beside the building had been turned over and the rancid contents funked up the parking lot.

Lovely.

Would it be honest to admit I took my time to go inside? Yep. Somebody needed to pick up the minuscule pieces of trash in my backseat. While I was tidying up though, I was surprised to see Rex pull into the parking lot. He never came here unless absolutely necessary. Alarm circled my chest—was something wrong with Grandma? No, someone would've texted me in an emergency. So why was he here?

Not long after he picked a spot near the building, Erica came out and walked up to his car. Rex rolled down his window and waved to her. Interesting. The particulars of their chat didn't jump over the four cars to mine, but I wondered what those two would talk about. From my perspective to the far left of them, I couldn't see Erica's face. I only caught Rex's smug grin and the way he gestured out the window as if they had a casual conversation.

Suddenly, my phone rang. It was Bill again. Time to go inside. I bought ten minutes before my doom. Today, I didn't have to clock in for my afternoon shift until lunchtime, but Bill's first phone call tugged me in by the scruff of my neck.

During the call, all he'd said was, "I know what you took from Kramkar. I want to see you. Now." *Click.*

Bill rarely called me, and if he hung up early, a bomb had dropped in the back office. Soon I'd be mopping up the victims from the aisles.

I hurried inside to face the goblin. My boss sat at his desk with an expression you could either call furious or absolutely enraged. If he frowned any deeper, the wrinkles along his forehead would've filled his face.

And, even worse, his glasses were on the desk.

Bill never took off his glasses.

"Hey." I edged toward him. "I can explain everything."

His right eyebrow rose. "You're looking for the Basilisk King and you made a stupid bargain with the *zmee* for information."

"How did you know?"

"The fairy folk talk. Now they're running their damn mouths about how you *broke* into Kramkar's business and stole his property."

"I didn't steal it. I left the payment."

He scoffed. "Does it matter? Can you break into McDonald's, steal a couple shakes, and then *kindly* leave some cash on the counter?"

I didn't reply to avoid digging myself a deeper hole.

Bill wasn't done griping. "Why don't we march on down to Archie's after hours, fire up the grill, and make a late-night snack? Sounds great, huh? As long as we *pay*."

I lowered my head.

"Kramkar was at my doorstep the minute you broke his wards," Bill said, his voice low and deadly. "He wants compensation."

"How much—"

"Don't say a word." Breathtaking magic with the scent of red pepper flared from the goblin and I fought the urge to cower. "I'm speaking right now."

I bit my upper lip.

"Back in the Dark Ages, a troublemaker like you would've had their hands chopped off, but since for your sake that's *illegal* now, you'll have to pay up through other means."

Fear crept into my backbone. How deep did I jump into a shit pit this time? "I don't have much, but if Kramkar is reasonable, I'll do what I can."

Long ago, I learned to never tell the fairy folk I'd do *anything*. Idiots with big mouths ended up on a brownie chain gang working in mines.

Bill said, "Kramkar doesn't want *monetary* compensation. He wants you to work for him for a week." He picked up his glasses and wiped off the lenses with a tiny silk cloth. "With no pay."

Fuck. My face fell.

Damn, I wanted to ask for time off to protect Grandma. Now I had to work—for free, no less—at the troll thrift mart. Today catapulted from horrible to catastrophic.

I turned to leave, but Bill had additional words for me.

"Not sure if you don't know this already, but you should be careful out there. The fairy folk also told me one of the shapeshifter delivery men at the Bashful Brownies Bakery Company was killed last night."

"How? A basilisk attack?"

"Nope. No claw marks or other signs of an attack." Bill's expression darkened again. "The Basilisk King killed him. The shapeshifter's life-force was drained and all the fairies found was a dried-out husk."

CHAPTER 18

With orders to report to work at Huldrefolk Collectibles on Saturday morning, I returned home. Why bother working at The Bends today when I had to endure a week at a new job? On the way home, I clutched the steering wheel hard enough to dent it. My breath hitched and mind raced. I'd visited that troll's shop twice and that was more than enough. The show room floor had dust and cobwebs everywhere. They stole the flowers from the local nunnery. Kramkar probably thought excellent customer service was excellent for including subpar cursed merchandise and offering customers overcooked food covered in shiny glamours. Who knew what other problems they had?

I spent the rest of the day cleaning the cottage. Scrubbing the floors and organizing my fridge twice didn't help. The Stravinsky clan planned to meet again at my parents' house to make arrangements to protect Grandma and I dreaded facing my family.

For past few days, I didn't feel like a powerful alpha female. Matter of fact, I had yet to find the Basilisk King and now I had to work for Kramkar. How much lowlier could an alpha female get?

To cheer me up, and perhaps fill me with even more dread, Aggie asked about baking a cake for tonight.

"You know I never miss a meal with the Stravinsky clan," she said softly.

I slumped on a kitchen chair. "Is now really the time to bake our problems away?"

"Now is always a good time to stuff our faces. Food is the universal language of caring. You give a frozen lasagna to families after they pop out a kid. During birthdays, you cook barbecue and serve cake to everyone. I really believe food makes people happy."

I smiled. Aggie did have a way with words.

To waste perfectly valuable time, I watched Aggie gather the ingredients on the counter.

"What the hell are you making that needs canned rhubarb and fresh raspberries?"

Her grin lit up her whole face. "I'm making a raspberry and rhubarb drizzle custard Bundt cake."

Uh, did I even have a Bundt pan? "Seriously? Where did you learn the recipe?"

Aggie didn't have a great history of cooking well.

She hummed. "I've been watching *The Great British Bake Off*... Food porn at its *best*. I get off every time somebody says *biscuit* in an English accent." She drew out the S in biscuit.

"Lovely." I grabbed one of my leadership books, not Bill's hot mess title, and read while she worked. Might as well witness her grand baking skills and throw support in her direction. Her last masterpiece, a pineapple upside-down cake, had a lovely presentation. No one got a chance to eat though after the cake fell off the table at my parents' place. It turned into a pineapple-oh-hell-no cake.

Perhaps this cake had a better shot at greatness.

Aggie searched through the cabinets, pausing here and there as if deep in thought. For a moment, I felt like it was old times back at my previous home. The Long Island Pack had lurked nearby, but we'd gabbed and pretended the outside world didn't want to hurt us.

"What did Bill have to say?" she asked as she gathered sugar and pistachios. She added butter, eggs, milk, and cream to the counter, too. She surveyed the ingredients with a warm smile as if they were her children.

I told her what went down with the goblin.

"Ugh, one week with Kramkar, huh?" She flashed me a thumbs-up. "You got this! You'll be fine."

"I'll be fine," I repeated sourly.

I'd be fine or I'd leap out the window and see how far I could run down the Parkway screaming.

"You've been through a lot," she added, "and you're stronger now."

I opened my mouth to voice all the things that run through my head at the most inconvenient moments. The things my OCD made me fixate on from the moment I woke up until I slept, but Dr. Frank had taught me many coping mechanisms. It was time to put them into play. Change was good for the soul. Too bad my soul was perfectly content with my life as it was.

Aggie set the oven to preheat. With her back turned to me, I couldn't spy on her, but her soft humming relaxed me.

"How you holding up?" I asked.

"This dish is coming along nicely."

"I don't mean the food, Aggie."

She paused. "Yeah, I know. And thanks for waiting a while before you asked me that," she whispered as she combined the cake's ingredients into a bowl.

I nodded. She couldn't see the gesture, but the intention mattered. I waited, always patient when she usually wasn't.

"I'm doing the best I can," she finally said. "Like I always do. Will's trying to help me adjust, even if I don't want his help right now."

"I'm sure he is."

She glanced at me over her shoulder. "I'm not interested in a relationship right now and Will respects that."

"I was wondering what happened between you two."

She sighed. "He's not happy about my decision, but he understands I need time after what happened with my dad and Victor."

"Has your dad reached out to you yet?" I asked softly.

"He's not that dumb," she said flatly. "Desmond McClure's time is coming. We will be having a little *talk* about what he did to me."

I wanted to tell her to let him go. To forget about him. But I was talking to Agatha McClure here. Alpha females like Aggie didn't forget. They remembered, and if the opportunity arose, they settled the score.

"If you need a backup quarterback to throw the pass, I'll be there for you," I said instead.

"You can't throw a ball worth shit," she said with a snort.

"Yeah, how about a backup goalie?"

"When we were kids at that camp, you sucked at sports, Nat."

I stuck out my tongue at her.

"Saw that." She put down her mixing spoon. "I miss camping. We had a good time at Camp Harold, didn't we?"

"I didn't have a good time, at first, but after I met you, it was so much more fun."

"Same."

Back when we were kids—troubled youth was the

polite way of putting it—our parents sent us off to a were-wolf camp. I was awkward and weird while Aggie's rich parents were hoping sunshine and the backwoods would keep their kid from overeating. Little did they know that Aggie needed more than therapy. She needed friends. She needed someone to appreciate her instead of throwing too many obligations her way. And I just needed someone who understood. We made the perfect pair.

Aggie put something in the oven, but she blocked my view the whole time. What did she put in there?

I peered around her shoulder. "What are you doing?"

"Baking pure happiness." She quickly shut the oven door and pushed me to sit. "Get back to reading and get a *real* leadership book that would apply to werewolves. Like *Wildlife Behavior 101* or something. Those self-help books don't apply to packs, by the way."

"Packs are like corporations. Kind of."

She gave a short laugh. "Before I came here, I used to work at a corp. You don't challenge the CEO to a fight to lead the company."

She had a valid point there.

"Not every leader has the same style." She tapped the table with her finger for emphasis. "I've seen asshole bosses who make billions of dollars to nice guys who get run over. No matter your personality you must find what motivates your people. You adapt and learn to run at the speed of your pack."

I caught myself wanting to rub my face to ease the growing tension. "I have doubts."

"We all do. It's how you deal with doubt that matters." She scratched her head and accidentally streaked batter in her curls. I opened my mouth to say something, but she spoke again. "I need to get off my ass and see if Barney's has any openings."

"Craving their sizable pickles or the sandwiches?" I flashed her a grin.

"Oh, stop it. I actually liked working there. The owner believed in me and my employment was based on my merits, not my background."

When Aggie arrived on my doorstep last year, I had no idea what she'd experienced with her dad, only that she'd planned to eventually move on. Like a stubborn flea, she attached to me and settled into life in South Toms River, and her job at Barney's allowed her to thrive.

Which meant she could thrive again.

"Need me to write you a letter of recommendation?" I asked.

"No need. I already sent my old boss a text to check up on him and let him know I'm in the area. Apparently, he needs help training the new high school and college students he's hired."

The rich scents of Aggie's cake filled the kitchen with a divine, fruity fragrance. That was a good sign she wouldn't kill us.

Forty minutes later, the oven timer dinged and I glanced up from my book. Aggie had left the room, but I offered a hand and fetched my Santa's Little Helper oven mitt.

After I opened the oven, my mouth dropped open. "That's not a Bundt cake."

Aggie had used a Christmas C-shaped pan, and unfortunately, the pan was far too small to hold the expanding cake. Sticky sweet batter spilled over the bottom of the oven, and the fruit bubbled under a layer of char.

That was gonna be fun to clean up.

The resourceful baker hurried into the kitchen and gushed over my shoulder. "Isn't she pretty? You didn't have a Bundt pan so I got creative."

With the shake of my head and a chuckle, I removed the cake from the oven and left it on the stove to cool.

"Don't worry about the oven. I know how to clean them out," she added then sat next to me at the kitchen table. "In a couple of hours, I shall wow you with my festive Raspberry and Rhubarb Drizzle Custard Christmas Cake."

I laughed. Her bright smile made a bad day much brighter.

Once evening approached, we headed to the Stravinsky family meeting. Thorn had stayed with them all day, so we met him there.

"Any problems?" I asked him.

He shook his head and drew me into a long hug. Relief flooded me and I rested my head against his chest, not caring if my family was close. Once this was all over, I was going to book that fly fishing trip sooner rather than later. Maybe some sunshine and time for us to snuggle in a hammock would make this madness go away.

"No problems," he said against the top of my head. "From the Basilisk King, that is."

The boisterous noise from my uncles watching a freestyle diving competition from Norway filled the room and I let go of Thorn. What the heck was so exciting to them about dudes in Speedos hitting the water? I read the text at the bottom of the television screen. *The World Championship of Death Diving*, huh? Yeah, participating in that kind of foolishness would be a hard pass from me.

Their laughter after each painful-looking dive made it difficult to hear conversations. If Grandma wasn't hard of hearing at times, they would've lowered the volume, but she was engrossed, taking in every detail.

"Those humans do this for fun?" she asked Uncle Boris in Russian.

"I'd do it for money." He shrugged.

Aggie left our side to head to the kitchen with her masterpiece. She had to weave around my younger cousins as they played tag in what little space was available.

"Precious cargo," she announced. "Coming through!"

I caught Mom's squeal of appreciation in the kitchen. Having Aggie around again for chow was welcomed.

I turned to Thorn. "Is Dad at work?"

"He left this afternoon, but he promised that he'd try to get off earlier."

On the television, a well-built young man catapulted himself off a high platform and sailed toward the water. His trajectory was off and he belly-flopped on the surface.

A resounding "Ouch" filled the room.

"He might not be able to reproduce after that," Uncle Boris said in Russian.

"My balls shriveled up just seeing that," another uncle replied.

"As much as I'd like to watch until the meeting starts, I'm heading into the kitchen." I left his side, briefly checking on Grandma, and entered the kitchen to find my mom, Aunt Olga, and Aggie gabbing away.

I checked out the back window but found everything quiet. My parents took good care of their backyard and I spotted signs of my mom's perfectly straight rows of summer vegetables. The hydrangeas in the back swayed with the evening breeze.

The scene should've fed me a large dose of tranquility, but I knew from the past that relaxing meant I wouldn't be ready if a surprise came out of nowhere.

I left the window to find Aggie sampling Mom's pot roast while Mom and Aunt Olga discussed Aggie's relationship prospects now that she was back in town.

"Are you sure you're not serious about Will?" Aunt Olga asked. "Your best friend could be your sister-in-law!"

Aggie shoveled another portion into her mouth. "We've been dating for a while now, but I need to be alone."

"Why do you want to be alone?" Aunt Olga asked softly. With well-manicured fingers, she drew Aggie's hair out of her face. "You're young, strong, and pretty. You should date more."

"I got married, divorced, and then my ex *kidnapped* me. The next guy who hits on me might have his arm ripped off."

My aunt pursed her lips and nodded in agreement. I wouldn't have a comeback for that reply either.

Less than an hour later, my father trudged into the house from work. Of course, Rex was right behind him. Lovely. Everyone greeted my dad and our family meeting began.

Thorn and I stood in the living room in front of the television. Rex leaned against the back wall and surveyed the room like the place was his kingdom.

"As many of you heard," Thorn said, "our territory is under attack." He explained in easy to understand terms what we knew about the Basilisk King and the trunks.

The Stravinskys nodded at the right moments. Even the children paid attention.

He continued. "At first, we thought he might be targeting anyone, but we discovered he has individuals in mind."

I told everyone the news I heard from Bill about the slain shapeshifter.

"Does that mean all shapeshifters are targets? Like us?" Aunt Olga asked.

"No, he was just the first course before he gets to the real meals," I murmured. "Those who practice Old Magic."

Everyone exchanged worried expressions.

My mom, on the other side of the room standing next to my father, glanced at Grandma in horror. No matter how much my mom adhered to the Code, Grandma was still her mother.

"When will he attack?" Mom asked.

"He's already been here," Grandma said simply.

All eyes turned to the small woman.

"Are you serious, Mama?" Aunt Olga approached Grandma.

"He won't enter the house," Grandma explained. "Lowlives like him want their prey to come to them."

"And what will drive him to go to you, Mrs. Lasovskaya? Hunger will bring him to you," Thorn said.

That drew a moment of silence.

Thorn added, "He attacked the shapeshifter right outside of the bakery. I believe like any predator, if the trap isn't sprung, the wolf hunts for the rabbits in their den."

His words laid a solemn blanket over the room.

I stepped forward. "I want Grandma protected twenty-four-seven. Do we have any volunteers?"

"I will take time off from work and protect my mother-in-law," Dad said firmly.

Four hands went up. One of the volunteers was twelve. That kid was a sweetheart, but a harsh breeze could've pushed that pup over. Others murmured to show support, but we wouldn't have enough people to cover spaced-out shifts. And now I had to work for Kramkar for a week, too.

Rex's voice rose above the whispers. His smile was a slippery as he was. "Everyone in South Toms River should do their part. Whenever I'm not at work, I'm willing to help."

I sighed. My family consisted of the working class. I

had to be understanding, but seeing my grandma sitting there, so tiny and vulnerable, set me on edge.

I sharply said, "I plan to do my part and sleep here from now on." The flames in my stomach rose higher as pack members glanced away. Many were afraid, but I sensed indifference, too. "I don't want to *force* people to help their own, but I will make—" A large hand gripped my shoulder from behind. The tension in my shoulders eased as Thorn's serenity slipped into me.

Across the room, even Aggie frowned at me.

Thorn took over. "The Basilisk King is hunting Old Magic practitioners, but we all must be vigilant. Children should stay close to home. And if you see any old-fashioned trunks outside call Natalya or myself."

"If they don't answer, you can call me," Rex chimed in. "I'll always be available to help."

I sealed my mouth shut and counted to ten. Would I mind that much if he wound up as Basilisk breakfast?

The meeting ended and those who couldn't wait to leave hurried out the door. Rex continued to stand there, even accepting a plate of food from Mom. He murmured thanks, but Mom merely nodded in reply.

Rex took his plate and had a seat on the couch—right where I could see him all relaxed and content.

"Natalya?" Many voices filled the room, but I recognized Grandma's immediately.

I hurried over to her.

"Do you need anything?" I asked.

She swallowed and stared at me a little as if she collected her thoughts.

"I don't want our pack ordered around like this. I'm old," she finally said firmly. "I can take care of myself, and I don't want you or anyone protecting me."

"*Babushka...*"

"No, I don't want to hear it." Her soft brown eyes hardened. "I know your heart is pure, but up here," she touched my forehead, "you are steel. Unmoving. You're not willing to bend."

"I'll never be willing to bend when it comes to you."

"That's not your choice, *devushka*. I'd never give your life for mine, girl." She leaned back, adding space between us. My heart clenched painfully.

"Grandma, we're still going to leave guards outside."

She cringed and shook her head.

"Grandma?"

Her chin trembled. Damn, I'd made my grandma upset. I'd never done that before.

Without a second thought, I left the house. I couldn't stand staying there another minute.

"Where are you going?" Thorn asked.

"Home." I made it to the Nissan and headed to the driver's side, only to have Aggie block the door.

"Leave me alone," I growled.

"No."

Aggie motioned for Thorn to head back inside. Reluctantly, he nodded.

I reached for the door and opened it, but she closed that, too. The frustration coiling inside unfurled.

"Stop it." I tried to push her. With ease, she sidestepped my attack and left me sprawled on the concrete.

I came at her again, claws out, but she blocked me again, grabbed my blouse collar, and shook hard. Damn, nimble wolf. I snarled, and her grip switched from my collar to my neck. She shoved me until my back hit the car hard.

"Stand down, Nat." Aggie bared her teeth and her blue eyes flashed purple. "Or I will end you."

She drew a deep breath while my anger grew and the rising tension in my stomach threatened to overwhelm me.

"You almost lost control back there," she said. "Those people are your family. Your blood. You need to be more flexible."

"Grandma needs protection and people are dying—"

"Yes, they are dying, but ordering your family around won't solve the problem."

Aggie's steel-like grip tightened as I fought against her hand. No matter how hard I scratched or hit her, she refused to yield. How I wished I had her strength—her raw power.

"Fine!" she barked. "Get it out of your system then. When you're done wetting your pants like a pup, I'll let you go."

Soon, my fast-beating heart stilled and the rage writhing under my skin eased. As quickly as my anger surfaced, the feeling subsided.

"Done?" she asked with a straight face.

I grunted. "Yes."

I shook my head. "You should be the pack leader," I added with a whisper.

"Don't want it." She crossed her arms.

"Why not?"

Aggie stared at the overcast sky. A cascade of emotion danced across her features. "We all have our place in this world. Years ago, I'd bet my left ass cheek I'd end up as the Midtown alpha female. I'd be carting my kids to some Upper East Side private school." She shook her head. "That isn't my destiny. Thanks to my ex-husband, I really know that isn't for me."

She rested her hand against the same shoulder Thorn had touched and offering me a reassuring squeeze. "Now I choose what I want. My mate. Where I live. What job I have."

I managed a nod.

"South Toms River is my home now," she said, "but this is your proving ground. Take care of it. Take care of your pack or you're gonna wind up a rogue, and you don't want that again."

She opened the driver's side door and got in. My bold best friend even snatched my purse to retrieve the keys.

"Where are you going?" And how come she was taking *my* car?

"To get a sandwich at Barney's. Want one?"

Relief fluttered over me. Even though I'd tried to fight her, she'd forgiven me just as quickly.

"Uh, sure?" I got in on the passenger side. "Are you sure you want to be driving around with the Basilisk King out there?"

She smirked. "Good luck to the bastard who gets in the way of my next meal."

I was too ashamed to face my grandma and camped out in the car with Aggie that night. Thorn didn't return home either. He pulled up behind us in his SUV and fell asleep. Aggie did the same from the backseat, but slumber never found me. The shadows kept shifting from the fast-moving clouds. A summer storm passed through around two AM, rattling the trees and leaving me restless.

By the time the harsh weather passed around six AM, I was bleary-eyed, but a couple cups of coffee would get me back on track. Aggie still snored in her resting place, and I tried to shut the door softly as to not wake her. She didn't stir one bit. Damn, I wished I could do that.

I got out of the car to circle the house. From one end of the street to the other, all was quiet. The rain left a bit of debris, some branches and leaves on the street, but anyone would say this was great weather to water their backyard gardens.

I checked around the house and everything was quiet and clear. Just like Grandma predicted. I stuffed my hands into my pockets. Maybe I was worried for nothing, but the fear settling into my bones remained.

The sweet scents of breakfast wafted from my parents' chimney. If I closed my eyes, I could taste a fried egg between two pieces of buttered toast. Grandma would be sitting at the kitchen table with coffee.

Instead of heading inside to shake off sleep with my family, I trudged to my car and started it up. I'd be back to apologize later.

"We're leaving?" Aggie said, her voice thick with sleep.

"Yeah, you hungry? I gotta report to Kramkar's at eight."

Through the backseat mirror, I caught Aggie's grin. "Donuts with sprinkles are my best friends. Hot cake and sausages are my friends with benefits."

Of course, sausage was where it was at for Aggie.

Aggie climbed into the passenger seat from the back. "I want a permanent relationship meal this morning," she purred.

I laughed her way. Aggie's hair was tangled and her morning breath questionable, but I relaxed a bit as she rolled down the window and rested her head outside the window.

"What would I find in a permanent relationship meal?" I asked.

"A gigantic cinnamon roll...covered in not only pecans and powdered sugar, but also with strawberries, pineapple, and blueberries." The happiness in her voice made me roll my eyes.

Off to find a permanent relationship meal, I decided and pulled away from my parents' house. Thorn remained behind. A quick text showed he caught my departure: *Stay safe.*

As we reached the drive-through at Dunkin' Donuts, I

was ready for some of that cinnamon and sugar Aggie was talking about. "I can practically smell the steam rising from fresh donuts."

At the order window, I bought a sizable breakfast feast: a dozen donuts, two pancake platters, and four cups of coffee.

A few minutes later, breakfast was in my car, and Aggie bit into a sausage with gusto, talking as she chewed. "Breakfast beats boys every time."

Time to pay the piper, his booking agent, and everyone else I owed a debt.

I dropped off Aggie at the cottage and drove to the troll thrift store at eight AM. I wasn't the only wolf here. My brother Alex reclined in his Ford Taurus on the far end of the lot. He nodded my way.

Guess I had protection today, too.

From the backseat, I fetched my sack lunch and tote bag. Today, I wore a dark-blue pencil skirt and crisp, white blouse. The clothes comforted me, but in terms of weaponry, they weren't as friendly for hiding stuff. Therefore, the tote bag held my goblin blade.

There was no way I was leaving that sucker in the car.

Jocelyn didn't wait outside for me, and with the front doors locked, I had to use the rear entry at the dock—without breaking in this time. My hands grew clammy with each step. I forced my back to straighten. This shouldn't be hard. Hadn't I figured out everything at The Bends?

That took five years and a million panic attacks, my internal worrywart reminded me.

I said a prayer to not go full werewolf and maul my employers.

Here we go.

There were no locks on the doors, and I walked into my new job then almost waltzed right back out. The back room in The Bends wasn't perfect by any means—but at least Quinton stacked The Bends's new stock in a designated corner. Here, cardboard boxes blocked the door, and I sucked in my stomach to squeeze through the gap.

And sky above have mercy, what a sight I found.

Heavy dust coated everything. A canvas tarp was left in one spot while wrapping paper filled another. It was as if they'd moved here, dumped out their goods, then they didn't bother to dispose of the packing materials.

Lucky me to win the golden prize of working here.

I danced around the piles, searching for a place to stow my belongings. Finding not a single hook, locker, or drawer, I gave up and left my bags against the cleanest spot along the back wall, after I kicked away more paper and Styrofoam peanuts.

A fine sheen of sweat formed on my brow. Soon enough, I'd be stress sweating out of my clothes. I pasted a smile on my face and did what I knew best: organize the hell out of this shit. I slid on a pair of plastic gloves and started sorting the boxes. Ten minutes later, which may well have been longer since I was working in purgatory, Jocelyn showed up carrying sacks of groceries. Fresh hot dogs and popcorn, my nose told me.

"Got any more bags?" I asked her. "Need some help?"

"No, this is it." She surveyed my work and sighed. "Sorry you had to be brought into this mess."

"You and me both."

I'd cleared some space on a worktable hidden under boxes, which allowed Jocelyn to leave her groceries on top.

"You work fast," she observed. "Have you ventured out to the main showroom yet?"

"Do I want to?"

She chuckled. "I should've warned you that Kramkar trashes our stock and storage space every evening. Tomorrow, it's going to be a mess in here all over again."

I shrugged. "Across the street is just as bad. Have you got a fridge for my lunch?"

She fished out a cooler from under some boxes. It had to be from the Eighties based on the outdated design. "It's clean and enchanted to stay cold. A football fan died while on the way to a tailgate. Guess his spirit is keeping it cold until his team goes to the Super Bowl."

I shuddered. Maybe an upset stomach from spoiled tuna fish wouldn't be so bad compared to working here.

Reluctantly, I left my lunch inside the cooler and followed Jocelyn out to the main store floor. The troll thrift mart didn't have a back office. Just a closed-off area with curtains and large merchandise blocking customers from easily getting in.

Not much in the showroom changed since I snagged the bells. Any evidence that Erica and I visited was long gone. All the stalls were arranged as before.

"Let me give you the tour," Jocelyn said. We started down the main aisle near the entrance. "There are twenty booths in the store. All with stock from enchanted sellers from around the world. Even from an otherworldly dimension or two."

I opened my mouth to ask from where but decided ignorance would be bliss during my stay.

She continued our tour, showing me the set of four cash registers. All of the point-of-sale registers were from the late Nineties. I could spot an IBM SurePOS 790 from twenty paces away. Those things were notoriously buggy if they weren't setup correctly.

I held in a long sigh. No computerized system here. At least they had credit card scanners and I wouldn't be stuck with an ancient manual credit card imprinter like the one Bill once tried to get me to use. The stains from the carbon paper gave me hours of grief.

"We have four temporary register clerks," Jocelyn explained. "I trained them to use our registers."

"Do you want me to work with them today?" I cringed at the thought of banging away at those dusty registers, but I came to work.

Jocelyn folded her arms and her soft features reflected deep thought. "Kramkar wanted you to scrub the floors and clean the rafters since you showed off how much you liked swinging from them, but you're an experienced flea market manager." She leaned in close to whisper, "This place could use a harsh hand to put us back on track. I need to do better, too."

"So that's why you bought the hot dogs and popcorn," I said.

She smiled a little. "The Bends is a really nice flea market—I guess I'm embarrassed I let Kramkar run the place into the ground to make a buck."

I nodded in sympathy. "If you've met a greedy goblin, then you've met a greedy troll."

"I'd say make yourself at home, but this isn't home base for you so walk around and familiarize yourself with the stock. Oh, and just one thing."

"Yes."

She looked at me very seriously. "Don't disturb the rocks in the front."

How strange. Did she think I planned to do some gardening? The thought had come to mind to give the

Sisters of Divine Grace their flowers back, but I hadn't considered lugging any rocks around. After working in another magical market, I knew better than to trust anything based on appearance alone.

"Got it," I said. "I'm going to wrap up my work in the back room and then I'll come up front once the store opens."

The quiet back room helped me to collect my thoughts, but the area wasn't quiet forever. Not long into sorting the piles of moving materials—and I made a sizable dent in the mess within twenty minutes—the temporary workers ambled inside. Two young men, a middle-aged woman and an older man who wandered past while whistling "Firebird" by Stravinsky (no relation, sadly). The staccato melody was unmistakable.

All four workers were trolls covered in blankets of glamours. Also, they didn't smell local. The mountain pines trailed after them with hints of iron and copper ore mixed in. I squinted harder to see if I could chip away at the glamour, but the spell covering them flared and nipped at me.

"Do you mind not staring?" a squeaky, young voice asked.

I turned around to see a teenager—maybe sixteen or so based on how my cousins looked—frowning at me. He wore a bright orange Fortnite T-shirt and skater-style khaki shorts. A fisherman's cap covered his shaggy white-blond hair.

"Sorry about that." I jerked back. "Are you one of the temp workers?"

The boy frowned. "I'm Kramkar."

My mouth formed an O. *Whoa.* This guy had a next-level glamour. To my senses, he was nothing more than your average human. Hell, he even smelled like he'd pulled an all-night video game marathon while chowing down on pineapple and ham pizza in his messy bedroom.

I offered my hand—might as well show that I had good manners. "Hello, I'm Natalya."

He didn't take my hand. "I know who you are and what your problem is."

"Excuse me?" My hand fell to my side.

"You're too inquisitive and analytical, a dangerous combination back where I come from."

My response dripped with syrupy sarcasm. "Last I heard, inquisitive and analytical people survive more natural disasters because they're alert to danger."

"Depends on the danger," he replied dryly.

Remembering that he wasn't actually a teenager was all that stopped me from shooing him back to his *Minecraft* world.

Kramkar surveyed my progress. "Not bad, Wolf. Just do your job and keep your nose clean. I'm sure you'd like to return safe and sound to Bill's Slop Shop, eh? By the way," he looked me up and down, "are you cleaning up or fixing a toxic dump site?"

Both?

I donned an apron from my tote as well as extra long plastic gloves and a mask. I shrugged and got back to work. The reply I had in mind wouldn't have scored any points to getting me the New Employee of the Month badge.

An hour later, the back room sparkled. I could even see my reflection on the polished concrete floor. The over-powering, lemony scent of Clean-It-Rite filled the air. With one job out of ten thousand completed, I removed my apron, gloves, and mask. Time to see what was happening in the showroom.

I squared my shoulders and headed out. Many customers browsed the aisles, far more than The Bends on a Saturday to my dismay, but then again, Kramkar's market was a shiny new destination. Soon enough, the antique hoarders like myself would pluck the place clean and move back to their regular haunts.

Instead of heading right to the registers, I swept through the aisles to check for any problems. As to be expected, the human visitors shifted the goods in a few booths, and I gave in to the urge to line up everything. I always got tingles whenever I rearranged clothes by color. Wasn't the natural order of things how the world's meant to flow?

In the middle of setting up a display of haunted shells in the mermaids' stall, I caught a familiar screech from the registers.

"I want to see your manager," a woman's voice yelled. "I bought this antique washbasin and it's damaged."

I sighed and hustled up to the registers. A frequent customer from The Bends stood in front of the second register with her hands on her hips. This morning, Mrs. Kite wore a dark red tunic covered in garish plastic stones over capri pants with bright pink Croc sandals.

Mrs. Kite was no a human, but rather a harpy, a ghastly creature with a human head on a bird's body. She was also a serial complainer at The Bends, and now she'd showed up here with ruffled feathers. The harpy leaned against the counter while kicking an antique washbasin at her feet.

Like any good manager, Jocelyn stood across from Mrs. Kite and calmly offered her assistance. I kept my distance but stayed close just in case she needed backup.

If she lets that harpy get one over on her this time, she'll never see the end of her complaints.

Mrs. Kite turned to Jocelyn, her bedazzled tunic catching the sunlight through the skylights. I was about blinded.

"I bought this rare 1910 washbasin. I used it to wash my grandbabies, and look at it now—" She tilted the basin to show some rust near the rim. "It's ruined."

From my perspective, Mrs. Kite might've had a good argument, although I'd never use a beautiful antique for personal use. I focused on the basin. The metal was indeed rusted, but very tiny scratches marred the inside. Looks like the grandbabies did more than use it for a birdbath.

"I'm sorry that happened," Jocelyn said with a tight face, "but once you've used your merchandise, you can't return it for a refund."

"It's a wash basin," Mrs. Kite snapped. "You're supposed to be able to put water in there without ruining it."

I couldn't resist stepping forward. "Are those scratches inside?"

The harpy's head slowly turned my way and her frown deepened into a sneer. "I was talking to her—someone who can help me—honey." She added *honey* like a kick to my face.

Jocelyn jumped on my remark. "When you bought it, that wash basin was pristine. Where did those scratches come from?"

The harpy huffed and the bitter smell of black pepper wafted off her. "Where is Kramkar? I want to see him now."

"Kramkar isn't available at the moment," Jocelyn said firmly. "I have the authority to issue refunds—if the customer's claim is valid."

"Valid?" the word came out with a barely concealed squawk. The harpy quaked, kicked over the washbasin with a clang, then left in a huff. Other customers murmured at the disruption, but the checkout lines kept moving. One loud customer would never get in the way of the hunt for treasures.

"Thanks." Jocelyn picked up the basin. "You know her?"

"Yeah, she's a problem child at The Bends."

I tried to pay attention to Jocelyn. I really did. But like a hound dog catching a scent, my gaze drifted to the free food near the door. The enticing scent of grilled hot dogs reached my nose. Even the popcorn in the popper smelled fresh and buttery with a hint of salt. So much better than it had looked during my first trip to the troll's thrift store.

"Want a hot dog?" Jocelyn asked. "You're looking at the grilling machine like it's whispering sweet nothings to you."

"Smells good, but no thanks." As appetizing as the food looked, it could be another glamour, and frankly, I planned to decontaminate the grill machine tomorrow. A nuclear blast or two should do the job.

"You can eat lunch whenever you want..." She trailed off and looked behind me.

"What's wrong?" I turned to see two customers admiring an eighteenth-century Norwegian chest. I hadn't seen it before or I would've stopped to examine the weathered iron handles and the hand-painted rosemåling of gold and black swirls on top.

The trunk twitched, and a little pebble fell off the top.

"Is that what I think it is?" she whispered.

Jocelyn scrambled around me, but I was far faster. I reached for the lid seconds after the customers, a couple in their fifties, opened the trunk.

CHAPTER 20

The spindly legs of the basilisk snaked out and swiped at the man. He sprang backward with a yell. "What in the heavens is that?"

His wife just stood there screaming.

"Shit!" Jocelyn grabbed the nearest weapon, a sad-looking broom.

I was empty-handed since I'd left the goblin blade in the tote bag. Damn it. I should have worn pants and the ankle scabbard.

The basilisk emerged from the Norwegian trunk screeching and squawking. The serpentine body slipped out with a soggy plop, leaving a foul trail of bubbling fluid dripping down the once-gorgeous trunk. While the rooster head snapped at Jocelyn, I searched for a weapon. The nearest booth had jars. Great. I spied the wash basin. *Batter up!*. I snatched the basin and walloped the Labrador-sized beast like I was swinging for the bleachers.

We had to get the basilisk under control before it grew any bigger.

Around us, human customers scrambled to the door in

a chaotic eruption. They tumbled over each other and banged into antique furniture. To their horror, an unseen force slammed the doors shut.

I swung the basin again as the basilisk swiped at me. "Kramkar, open the doors!"

Jocelyn arced the broom at the beast, but its beak snagged the wood handle and bit clean through it.

"Son-of-a-bitch, I paid for that broom myself!" she roared.

The basilisk leaped at her. Not thinking of the consequences, I jumped in the way. The basilisk hit my stomach hard, and we tumbled into a clothing display. Colorful robes fell over us, but that didn't prevent the beast from scratching and biting at my arms and shoulders. Each strike burned with an unnatural fire that spread deep beneath my flesh.

Suddenly, the lights went black. Not even the windows or skylights let in any sunshine. Every muscle in my body froze, and though I couldn't see the basilisk above me, I felt its weight hold still and got a face full of its breath as it hissed.

Without warning, a gray spotlight shone down and flared in strength before focusing on the pile of clothes where I lay with the basilisk.

I tried to twitch—anything to draw myself away from the growing agony in my body. Only my eyes gave way, but I couldn't turn my head. The ground shook as something large and ominous approached. My heart hammered beneath my ribs and an involuntary tear slid down my cheek. Was the Basilisk King coming? Would I finally see his true form?

I looked up to see a giant shadow. No, this couldn't be the Basilisk King. This creature reeked of the underground, and an earthy, musty scent like the back of a cavern that had never seen moonlight filled my nostrils and bathed my face in damp and cold.

Was that Kramkar?

With awe, I stared at his true *Huldrefolk* form. If he weren't a giant, I might've mistaken him for a middle-aged man. Wisps of white-blond hair hung from his shoulders and he wore nothing more than a simple pair of black cloth trousers and a tunic. He bent forward, the miner's cap on his head twitching, and he reached for the basilisk. The creature resembled a statue in the giant's hand.

To my right, a set of double doors sprang open, allowing in beams of light from the outside world. It took all my strength to strain to see what happened around me. At the giant's feet, human-sized trolls also wearing miner hats ignored the dust falling from their clothes as they hurried about to reposition the awestruck humans.

My breath caught.

Great magic flared and rocketed through me. How I wished I could turn my head to see.

"The Basilisk King will pay for encroaching my territory," the great giant intoned. He peered down at me and his eyes formed slits. "My new employee endangered our business. You must leave this place now, Wolf."

The gray spotlight on his hat went out, and daylight returned. All around me customers browsed as if nothing was out of the ordinary. Was I an extra in an episode of *The Twilight Zone*? I lay, curled up in pain, on top of the robes. The trunk was gone, thank goodness, and the couple who set off this whole debacle left the store in laughter.

You gotta be kidding me.

I tried to stand, but my torso and shoulders screamed in pain. I glanced down to see growing blood stains on my blouse.

"Nat, you okay?" Jocelyn knelt in front of me to make sure the customers didn't see me.

"Is she all right?" one concerned woman asked.

Jocelyn placed a musty-smelling robe over my shoulders, and I didn't shrink away. Pain had a great way of overriding other instincts.

"She's got bad cramps," Jocelyn explained.

That got a snort out of me. "I'll be fine," I managed to say with a wince.

"You poor thing." She fished some Midol out of her gigantic purse. "Take the max dose, sweetie." She winked and walked away.

If only Midol could fix this.

Jocelyn helped me to my feet, and I limped with her help to the back room. Once we were safely behind the curtain, I said, "What the hell just happened?"

"I don't know. I tried to help you when everything went dark," she explained.

Wow, even Jocelyn had no idea.

"I see." I hobbled to the workbench and slumped against the side. My body was expelling the basilisk's toxin, but based on how long it took Erica to recover, I could expect my healing to take some time. "You didn't see the miners rearranging everyone like we're a bunch of Elves on the Shelves?"

"You saw the *Huldrefolk*?" she said in wonder as she fetched me a bottle of water.

I gratefully sipped the cool liquid. "You've never seen Kramkar in his natural form?"

She shook her head. "A long time ago, I promised to work in his shop for what he did for my family. It was a bargain and worth the price. Even then, he wore a glamour. I've never seen the real Kramkar." She stared at me closer. "Can all werewolves see trolls?"

"No." Now wasn't the time to discuss the gifts Bill gave me. I gave her a gentle shove. "I need to rest. Check the floor and make sure everyone is okay."

"Are you sure? You don't look so good."

I probably looked like a fresh pile of goblin shit. I smiled to reassure her despite my pain. She placed her hand on my forehead then gently stroked my cheek like my mom did. The gesture had the same soothing effect that helped me to relax.

Her eyes softened. "Don't move, Nat."

As she headed back through the curtains, I wondered what bargain she'd made with the *Huldrefolk*. And why.

~

Not sure how long I sat propped up by the wall. I dozed off at some point only to startle awake from my own drool. Eww. At least I felt somewhat better, less like roadkill. Time to get that awful robe off me. I'd tolerated the musty thing for long enough. Raising my arms made me yip with pain so I rolled the garment off my shoulders and stepped out of it. The whole process took twenty minutes of groaning and shifting.

I checked out my clothes. My top was ruined—that was a guarantee. As I ambled into standing, I noticed more tears and blood stains. Like one of Quinton's zombies, I shuffled across the room and reached for my tote. And damn it all to hell, the goblin blade must've transformed into the lance and pierced through the sides of a perfectly good bag.

To my surprise, Jocelyn had left a note on the bag and another bottle of water: *Go home and rest. You were sleeping so soundly I didn't want to wake you. Call if you need any help.*

She even left her cell number. Nice lady, that one.

With some duct tape since there was plenty in the back office, I patched the holes in the tote bag. The fix job was a backcountry hot mess, but for all I knew, somebody in New York would've called this Duct Tape Chic.

You're such a trendsetter, Natalya. Always on the cutting edge.

Ouch. It hurt to laugh at myself.

The mid-afternoon sun shone far too bright once I ventured outside. With each step to my car, my breath turned shallower and the pain amplified. At least I held my keys and wouldn't have to fish them out of the tote bag.

The temptation to call Thorn strengthened, but he wouldn't take my current condition well and might storm into the goblin mart to confront Kramkar. A few more hours of healing and I'd be fine. Really.

A hand tapped my shoulder.

I winced as I pivoted to face Erica.

Shit.

She glanced at me as her mouth dropped wider and wider. "Nat, what happened?"

"Aren't you supposed to be working?" I whispered.

I know, not the best reply after you got your ass kicked and someone showed concern.

"I'm taking a late lunch," she explained. "I saw you across the Parkway walking really slow and was worried something was wrong."

"You know, you could've told me how much basilisk poison sucks ass. One attacked the troll shop," I said, clenching my teeth against the pain.

With care I didn't expect, Erica drew her arm around me and guided me toward my car. She shouldered my weight with ease and my head bent forward as hurt flashed through my arms. I tried to straighten my back and tilt my chin higher and failed. Everything hurt so damn bad.

"Breathe through it," she whispered. "We're almost there."

Did she really drop her head so it was lower than mine? Or was I so jacked up I hallucinated?

We finally reached my car and I unlocked it. Erica opened the passenger-side door. Alarmed filled me when I spied stains on her shirt. My wounds were oozing *something* and I'd stained her luxury linen top.

"I'm so sorry," I said. "That's an expensive shirt..."

She scoffed. "It's a knock-off. A good one, but still a fake. I can't afford that kind of stuff anymore."

It was hot and stuffy inside the Altima, but I didn't care. Erica walked around to the other side of the car and got in behind the steering wheel.

"Oh, my God, it's so hot in here. Sorry Nat." She put out her hand for the keys and I handed them over.

The whole sequence of events felt strange—out-of-body. What happened to the woman who'd bad-mouthed me in hope of gaining Thorn's love?

The car started, and soon all the windows were open to fill the interior with the breeze, hot and humid. Despite the heavy pollen from the nearby oak trees coursing through the car, I sucked in the fresh air.

How I wished the air conditioner was enchanted. A blast of cold would've been welcomed with open paws.

"Do you want to go home?" she asked as we pulled onto the Parkway.

I shook my head. Aggie shouldn't see me like this either, but I needed fresh clothes.

"Your parents' place?" she suggested.

Then I'd have to face my family.

"Dollar Mart?" I whispered. "These clothes are dirty."

"Um, okay." Erica activated the air-conditioning, but with the town being so small, by the time we reached the

Dollar Mart, the air blasted by the car's vents would be anything but chilled.

We passed the low-cost store and continued into South Toms River. I forced myself to sit up from slouching.

"Where are we going?" I asked, sliding back down my seat.

"You're not walking into the Dollar Mart looking like you got mugged. I'm taking you to my apartment."

"You don't have to do that." The ache in my arms should've eased, but the pain only worsened.

"Yes, I do. Believe it or not, I know what you're about to face with those scratches and bites."

"What do you mean?"

"After the first basilisk used me as a basketball, I got home and tried to sleep to let my body get rid of the toxin, but that wasn't enough. If your cuts are deep, you won't heal, at least not as quickly as you usually would. What your body is expelling can re-enter through the deep cuts. You need a shower."

This was getting better and better. At least Jocelyn hadn't gotten hurt.

"I don't want to inconvenience you—don't you need to go back to work?" I wondered.

"Fuck Bill. He'll be fine."

My head whipped to the left, and I flinched.

I caught the hint of her smile. "He complained about you all morning."

"Great. Now Kramkar *and* Bill can trade war stories of employing me."

We took a left on 5th Ave and drove around a series of apartment complexes. The buildings were white with carnation flowerbeds in front and brick posts along the driveways. We pulled into a parking spot under a carport.

"I've never been here before," I remarked.

"Yeah, it's on the edge of town and relatively new. Most of my neighbors are commuters."

Erica pulled into the parking lot. Naturally, at that moment, my phone buzzed with a call from Thorn. I used the annoying Bugle Wake Up ringtone for his number.

"Do you need me to answer the phone for you?" she asked.

"No, I can call them back."

She stopped in the middle of the parking lot. "Stop being so stubborn."

Before I could say anything, she fished the phone out of my purse. When she spied the phone number, she paused.

"Yeah, you can answer it." She activated the phone and placed it by my ear.

"Hey, you." I feigned strength in my voice and held the phone as Erica parked the car.

"Hey, you," he replied. "You want a sandwich from Barney's? Rex is about to take over my shift at your parents' place."

Erica climbed out of the driver's side then maneuvered around to my door and helped me stand. I held in a groan as she helped me up a step.

"Nah. I'll eat lunch at..." Another step. "Erica's place. She felt sorry for me...Kramkar's store is a mess."

That got a moment of silence. There was *no* way Thorn would come here. Hanging out an ex's place had to be on the no-go list in any dude's head.

Erica kept a straight face the whole time.

"Okay..." he began to say. Then he added, "Are you all right? You sound out of breath."

I chuckled as Erica buzzed us into the building and cool air drenched us. "I've been running around like mad."

"Right." He didn't sound convinced. Shit.

Erica, thank God, had a first level unit down the hall

from the outside entrance. Once inside, she said in a too loud voice, "You want some leftover barbecue ribs?"

"Sounds great." Ugh, the enthusiasm in my voice was as fluffy as cotton candy.

"I'll check on you later then," Thorn said.

I closed my eyes, knowing very well that was Thorn-speak for, *I know something is up and you're going to tell me exactly what is going on when I see you next.*

I ended the call. How long did I have until he showed up? It seemed an evasive wife trumped avoidance of an ex's place, and if I was lucky, I'd be able to wash up and redress before Thorn arrived.

"Have a seat," Erica offered.

From my left, an orange pet darted down the hallway and into a bedroom. My nose told me that had to be a cat. Werewolves rarely kept pets. Having them around when we went into heat or around the full moon wasn't wise. Not to say we'd eat our pets, but if we spent a couple of days during the full moon out hunting, Hannibal the Hamster would have to fend for itself.

I looked around the picturesque room you'd expect to find in a spread for Martha Stewart's magazine. And damn, was it pink. Accent pillows covered in pink tartan were arranged on a chic, peach-colored loveseat and couch. Two more tufted chairs in soft brown broke up the pastel over-load nicely. Here and there, I spied silver framed photos of Erica with her best friends and many others with her dad.

"You have nice furniture," I remarked. "How about I sit in the bathroom? Less likely to get basilisk goo on something."

She rolled her eyes and fished out an old blanket from a closet. "You can sit on this." She placed the blanket over the loveseat.

I eased onto the couch. "Don't you care about the blanket?"

"It's from an ex-boyfriend from Connecticut. Back in college, he cheated on me with some chick who slept with him after waving hi. Now I loathe Pottery Barn bedding with the passion of a thousand fleas, which is a shame 'cause Pottery Barn's nice stuff."

The blanket looked perfectly fine to me, but I had to admit I'd probably burn the blanket if I was mad enough.

On the way to the bathroom, she hit play on her answering machine. The machine blurted out that she had two messages. One was from her college alumni association asking for a donation and another message was from her dad. I tried not to listen, but I was right next to the darn thing.

In between the sounds of the shower starting, I caught Oliver Holden saying, "Hey, sweetheart, it's Dad. Did you get my phone call yesterday? I know I've been quiet lately, but we need to sit down and talk about the changes I have in mind for the pack. Call me back soon!"

What was that all about? *Changes in mind?*

My thoughts about Oliver's message trickled away as I heard Erica moving around in the bathroom. I still had to take a shower. Damn, this day wasn't ending well. Could I keep my clothes on and maintain my dignity?

Not with OCD, sister, my heart reminded me.

I was too weak to rip off my clothes and I had nothing to replace them. Thus, I sat there and ignored the stains. Dr. Frank would be proud of my progress.

Steam wafted from the bathroom down the hall. Erica returned and stepped up to me. "Time to get you clean."

When she reached for me, I flinched. She glanced away, sensing my discomfort.

"I know you're not thrilled about this." She folded her arms. "But it is what it is."

She looked me directly in the eyes, only for her gaze to dart away again as if she recalled her place. "Let me help you, and then we can forget this ever happened."

As Erica helped me stand, I knew there was no way I'd ever forget this.

Eventually, we reached her bathroom, a beautifully updated space with chocolate brown and pastel pink accents. She even had a small vase of pink poppies. A pop of playfulness. This bathroom was everything I'd expected from Erica Holden.

Right outside of the shower, I said, "I can manage it from here."

She stood there briefly, and I waited. After she drew a deep breath, she pointed to a pile of fresh linens. "Here's a towel and washcloth. I'll leave you some sweats outside the door. There's also a fresh loofa in the shower..." She let her words hang in the air. Maybe my former rival realized how our relationship had evolved, too.

I tried to stand as long as I could before I slumped against the nearest wall. It took me ten minutes to get out of my clothes and step into the shower. The lukewarm water slipped over me and I settled into sitting on the bottom. My head rested against a support bar, and I slipped into a painless oblivion.

CHAPTER 21

The shower water pelted me, a gentle drizzle lulling me in and out of sleep. Memories fluttered in and out of my head. Most of them fleeting, but one stuck and the scene unfolded like a fractured fairy tale.

Two women were alone in front of my old house in the woods. It was a chilly evening in December.

The blonde woman stood over one with dark hair.

That brunette woman was *me*.

Less than twenty-four hours before that scene occurred, Thorn and I had made love. I'd defied Erica's order as alpha female to stay away from him.

Now she wanted me to pay the ultimate price. Seeing everything unfold from a distance felt out-of-body.

In the evening light, Erica's eyes resembled the midnight sky. Dark and foreboding. She drew her arm back and struck me with a crowbar repetitively on my leg.

I cringed from the metal bashing tender flesh. My leg blossomed with blood and bone. Seeing myself choking out cries nearly drove me deeper into despair.

Erica leaned into say, "When burned, a lesson learned."

Then she reached into her jacket pocket and pulled out a box of matches.

Please, no.

Erica lit a match and pressed the hot end to my hand. I shrieked and cowered. But Erica's lesson wasn't done. She stepped back and circled me before tossing her crowbar in the snow. With a smile and a steel-toed boot, she kicked my side.

While I gasped for breath, she leaned down and grabbed my hair to force me to look up at her. "I told you over and over again to stay away from him. I guess you're too stupid to figure it out."

Just as quickly as the scene appeared, the memory vanished in smoke, leaving me hollow and scraped down to nothing.

The world would never know what happened that day, but pretending it never existed allowed a wound to fester between Erica and me.

The time would come—sooner than later, I feared—for us to rehash that night and come to terms with how it changed us. For I had learned: forgive but never forget the people who harmed you.

~

No one interrupted my shower or witnessed the tears I shed in my sleep.

When I propped myself up, the water wasn't as warm, but my wounds seeped less and strength returned to my limbs.

Time to kick some ass in the living-here-and-now world.

I stood, much more easily than before, and considered

washing myself—until I spied her soap and hair products. Erica might've been on a budget, but she splurged on expensive-looking bottles of hand soap, shampoo, and conditioner. Two bottles had labels in italicized languages I couldn't read. To my misfortune, the floral-scented shampoo and conditioner smelled like her. Yeah, not a good idea, considering I wanted my husband thinking of me, not her.

I used the hand soap. Not the best choice compared to a sudsy bar of soap, but the cleanser was antibacterial and soothing with hints of eucalyptus and mint that both cleaned my wounds and dulled the pain in my muscles. The water turned downright frigid by the time I finished in the shower. My teeth chattered, and I shook like a dog coming in from the cold, but a quick glance in the mirror revealed pink scars. No longer oozing and infected, yet there is no way Thorn wouldn't notice them.

After drying off, I peeked outside of the door. As Erica had promised, a set of clothes lay in a neat pile. A pink pile of clothes. The closest I came to wearing pink was downing a bottle of Pepto-Bismol after eating too much at my mom's house. And a good wolf didn't traipse out into the woods wearing clothes that screamed here-I-am!

With a sigh, I considered the possibility Erica did this on purpose.

I took the clothes anyway. Erica had left me a body suit. Huh? People still wore those? What did she do? Raid the bin of clothes she intended to donate? I climbed into the garment, then slipped on pink velour Juicy jogging pants and matching jacket.

And God help me, the word *Juicy* was scrawled in white cursive across my ass.

Everything fit too snuggly—which suggested Erica had

a smaller figure. At least I wasn't naked. A win-win, my uncle Boris would probably tell me.

After I was fully dressed and tamed my hair to not look like a knotted-up Tibetan terrier's tail, I refused to look in the mirror. Nope, didn't need this memory of my attire seared into my gray matter.

I ventured out of the bathroom to the inviting scent of baked barbecue ribs.

And Thorn waiting for me in the living room.

With a straight face, I joined them. Erica sat on the couch—while on the opposite side of the room, Thorn leaned against the wall near the door. Even in my exhausted state, I could smell a new aroma in the air: awkwardness.

"You look better, Nat," Erica said.

"Thanks." I forced myself to not touch my waist where the pants dug into my skin.

"You hungry?" she asked.

"Starving. Are the ribs, ready?" I remained at the edge of the living room.

"I left it in the oven on low heat. Let me get you a portion with some sweet tea." Erica got up and went to the kitchenette to the left.

Thorn's gaze was fixed on me as she passed him.

"Did you plan to leave me a message?" he finally said.

"You were protecting Grandma. I didn't want to alarm you until I got home." Then I added, "I'm stronger than I look, you know."

He crossed the room in rapid strides. "Where are you hurt?"

"The basilisk made my arms and chest Swiss cheese, but I'll be fine." On the other side of the room, I caught Erica opening the oven and placing the platter of ribs on the stove.

Then the sounds stopped. Not even a breath from her. Why did she hold it?

A familiar feeling tugged at me. Was she feeling the jealousy and pain I'd experienced? Half a year ago, I was forced to watch Thorn stand next to Erica. She fawned over him, even though he didn't want to be with her. I longed for him to the point of physical pain in my heart.

"I'll be fine," I said gently and pulled myself out of his embrace. I stroked his cheek, and he leaned in to kiss the top of my head. Everything was right with the world again as we shared a breath.

With a sigh, I went into the kitchen. "I'm starving. Need any help?"

Erica faced her wall of cabinets. There was no window there, though, and she gripped the counter hard enough for me to feel guilty. She had put three plates on the counter along with utensils and stopped right there.

She turned around with a false smile. "Sure, can you get some glasses from the cabinet next to the fridge? You can pour the iced tea for us."

I did as she asked while she arranged the plates on the four-seater table between the kitchen and living room. How did she expect us to eat?

"You're not hungry, are you?" I asked Thorn. Maybe he'd take the bait and give Erica some space.

"After sitting in the truck all day, I'm hungry," he admitted, glancing briefly at the steam rising from the beef ribs.

Damn, he didn't take the bait.

I couldn't let this go on. "Erica, this looks fantastic and smells delicious, but do you have any Tupperware containers?"

A wave of confusion flashed over her face. "Sure, I grabbed some from the store before I moved in."

She pointed to the second to last cupboard and I got

what I needed. As quickly as possible, I placed Thorn's and my portion into the containers.

"What are you doing?" Erica asked lightly. "Are you going somewhere?"

"I've inconvenienced you long enough. I realized you probably had to call Bill and ask for the afternoon off. Right?"

She nodded. "It's no big thing. The pack helps one another."

Helping shouldn't equate to hurting.

"Bill can be an asshole if you ask for too much time off." I sealed the containers shut and returned Erica's false smile. "Since I'm stuck at the troll mart, he's gonna need your help to keep the fire witch from burning the place down."

Erica nodded, her face unreadable, but the tension in her features and shoulders eased.

I edged toward the doorway and Thorn followed. "Thanks again, Erica. I really appreciated your help."

"Not a problem," she replied, her voice not as bubbly as her face.

"See you around," Thorn added.

"Sure."

I closed the door and hurried out of there as fast as possible.

In the parking lot, Thorn said, "What happened back there?"

I kept going, trying to add distance between myself and Erica. Thorn grabbed my elbow. "Hey, slow down."

"Couldn't you see?" I hissed, trying to tug him toward my Nissan.

"See what?"

"Why did you come here? I know you wanted to make sure I was well, but I was hoping this time—out of all the times you magically showed up—that this was the one place you wouldn't appear."

Thorn's hazel eyes bore into me, then realization flashed in his eyes. He lowered his head.

"She's still hurting," I said softly. "And I couldn't let you fawn over me in front of her."

"This might sound cruel, but she needs to get used to you and I being together."

That was the alpha in him talking.

I rested my hand over his heart while I held the food with the other. He cupped his hand over mine.

I said, "Getting used to seeing the one you love with someone else doesn't mean the *longing* goes away. I know this from experience."

He drew in a deep breath.

I tugged his hand. "Take me home before I eat the ribs *and* the Tupperware."

CHAPTER 22

The minute I got home, I wanted to take off these awful clothes and slide into a fresh pencil skirt and blouse. My wardrobe was probably reaching for me from miles away. Just as luck would have it, Aggie had finished her interview at Barney's and arrived at the house at the same time.

"What are you wearing?" she blurted. "You're one step away from a *Jersey Shore* reunion."

I flipped her off and left my keys on the kitchen table. "How did you get here?"

She sighed. "Will gave me a ride."

"How's he doing?" I shrugged off the pink jacket from hell.

Aggie's nose twitched, and she eyed the containers of ribs on the table. "Where did you get that? It smells delish."

Way to change the subject, Aggie McClure.

As I left the kitchen, I tossed words over my shoulder, "You can have half of mine. Half!"

While Aggie and Thorn scampered to grab their plates and scarf down their chow, I was forced to do gymnastics to tumble out of my borrowed bodysuit. A disturbing, wiggle-like dance wrenched off the too-tight Juicy jogger pants, and soon enough, the offensive pink pile lay on my dresser. When I had the time, I'd get the clothes washed and delivered to the owner.

My plate of food and a glass of ice water waited for me in the kitchen. I sat down to stuff my face. Of course, Aggie and Thorn cleared their plates quickly, but Aggie stared at my serving. I dug in to claim my kill.

My mate gazed out the kitchen window to the forest beyond the cottage. Did he sense any danger?

"Thorn said you were attacked at Huldrefolk Collectibles," Aggie said. "How bad was it?"

Between bites of beef from the ribs, which actually was pretty tasty, I explained what happened up to the point where Erica offered me a ride to her house.

"Jeez," she said. "That basilisk bastard doesn't quit, does he?"

"He's definitely persistent," I admitted. "And he's getting bolder, too. Usually, he leaves his shit outside for folks to discover, but this time, he planted one inside of the troll mart."

"Which means someone told him you were working there," Aggie said with a snort.

"But who knew I had to work at there?" I murmured.

"Every employee at The Bends," Aggie said. "You don't think the culprit could be one of your co-workers, do you?"

"Or someone's been following me around and waiting for the right opportunity to strike," I replied.

"The minion," Thorn and Aggie said at the same.

I nodded and stuffed another delicious bite into my mouth. Erica hadn't bought these ribs from Costco—the barbecue sauce was flavorful and the meat fell off the bone as if she'd slow-cooked the food all day. The others had licked their plates clean. Literally.

"We need to stop this *helper* and the Basilisk King," I said, not bothering to stop eating. "If one basilisk can poison a werewolf and knock us down on our asses, I can't imagine what they could do to humans."

Aggie said, "I don't like the idea of waiting until this Basilisk Butthead sets another trap for Nat or even Grandma. Why don't we gather the pack and hunt down his crazy ass?"

I frowned. "We'd be hunting in circles. We're better off setting a trap of our own."

She appeared thoughtful. "Back at your parents' place on Friday, I wondered if your grandma was doing that very thing."

Now that got my attention. I hadn't considered that possibility.

"What do you mean?" I wondered.

"When I brought her a plate of food, she mentioned how she needed all her strength for the struggles to come." Aggie's forehead scrunched. "At the time I laughed it off— you know—there'd always be someone around to keep an eye on her, but what if she planned to face him alone?"

I swallowed my food with a gulp of ice water. "Yeah, Grandma does have an independent streak. I'd like two guards on her instead of one from now on."

"I agree," Aggie grumbled. "Who's on guard duty right now? I can take over until the morning."

Thorn turned to us. "Rex took over my shift around lunchtime."

Hearing his name made the beef in my stomach feel like lead.

Aggie shook her head in disgust. "Once you're done eating, Nat, you and I will send him on his *merry* way."

I snorted. "If only there was a Pied Piper to draw out jerks like him from the pack."

Aggie laughed, and I welcomed the throaty sound. "They'd have to use a dog whistle."

~

The sunset barely clung to the horizon as Aggie and I pulled up to my parents' home.

The new moon hid behind the cloud cover, which obscured the brighter celestial bodies. Without the tug of the moon, I felt quite human tonight. The night creatures still sounded vibrant to my ear, but my senses were noticeably dulled. The night blooms were less fragrant and chirps from the crickets less intense.

I trudged up to the house. Time to focus on what needed to be done.

"Only Aunt Olga's car is out front," I snapped. "Where's Rex?"

"Maybe your aunt sent him home." Aggie paused right outside the door. "I don't hear anyone moving inside."

I sucked in a deep breath and listened. She was right. By now, I should hear someone moving around. Mom mentioned having to volunteer at church and Dad had to work, but someone should be here.

The goblin blade in my tote bag twitched and I retrieved it. To my dismay, it transformed into a lance.

Aggie didn't wait and tried to open the front door. "It's locked," she whispered.

I produced a key, and she used it to open the door.

"Is it a good or a bad sign you're holding a lance?" Aggie whispered.

"Bad. Very bad."

The foyer was dark. The only light illuminating the

space came from above: the light over the staircase leading to the next floor. Aggie peered into the living room to the right. No lights on there either. The TVs were off—usually someone left at least one on for the late-night TV watchers.

I peered to the left into the dining room. No signs of disturbance.

I opened my mouth to call for my family, but Aggie grabbed my hand and squeezed.

No sound, her gesture conveyed.

Suddenly, a thud from the kitchen drew our attention. It was the basement door.

"Something is propped against the door," Aggie whispered.

We hurried double time through the living room into the kitchen. The faint scent of ozone made my heartbeat thump in time with a rabbit's.

Someone had used Old Magic here.

Even in the murky darkness, I could tell the whole kitchen was trashed. A plate with cold food sat on the kitchen island while cutlery and glass were scattered across the floor. Two cabinet doors barely hung on their hinges while the light over the kitchen table was precariously close to falling onto the floor.

Something rustled on the other side of the island, but what alarmed us further was another frightening sight: the door to the backyard was open.

And a trunk sat right outside the door.

A moan drew our attention back to the kitchen. Aunt Olga lay on the floor on the opposite side of the island.

"Oh, my God!" I crouched in front of her.

Bloody cuts covered her whole body, and she shook as if a fever overtook her. It was the basilisk poison. She needed help right away.

The basement door shook again, and Aggie braced herself against the fridge holding the door shut. "Shit, that's a strong fucker."

Aunt Olga shivered and blinked before she focused on me. "Mama?" she murmured. "Where's Mama?"

From the other side of the room, Aggie propped her phone up with her shoulder while she held the door. "We got a problem here, Thorn. We got one of those things in the basement and Aunt Olga is hurt."

I caught his curse through the phone.

"We still need to find Grandma," Aggie added.

I stroked the side of my aunt's face. "I'll find her," I said softly in Russian. "We need to get you cleaned up before the poison hurts you further."

I turned to Aggie. "She needs to be bathed or the poison will slowly kill her."

"I'll guard her. You search the house," Aggie ordered. "Another one of those things might have Grandma. Help is coming."

I headed toward the living room again but paused. The odor of ozone led out of the house. Not in. I returned to the back door.

Yes, the scent was stronger here. I could imagine Grandma's soft footsteps as she reached this doorway and walked over to the open trunk. Her tiny footprints were clear in the soft grass.

The lance vibrated in my hand. At the other end of the yard, another trunk materialized. My breath got caught in my throat.

The path to the Basilisk King.

"Do you see her?" Aggie called to me.

"No, but I know how to find her."

Aggie groaned as the door shook harder. The beige

steamer trunk inched backward until it hit the wooden fence.

Come hither, wolf, it taunted.

I took a step back.

Wait for Thorn, Nat.

Wait for the cavalry.

The trunk dematerialized as if someone was in the process of changing the channel.

Every time Thorn told me that I leapt before I looked ran through my head. My time to make a decision was running out. Thoughts of Grandma crossed my mind, and rage built in my stomach. If that bastard hurt her, I'd unleash the power of a thousand full moons on his ass.

I marched up to the trunk, knowing it would be empty. With a running start, I darted over the fence into the next yard. Another trunk waited for me. Then many more spaced farther apart.

The Basilisk King drew me farther south into Double Trouble State Park.

~

Twilight turned the sky from dark purple to midnight-black. Through the thick trees, I could barely make out the sky. The goblin blade quivered in my hand, giving me strength for what was to come. Stomping through the woods in low heels and a pencil skirt didn't give me the best mobility, but the wolf within me yipped with eagerness at the prospect of a hunt. I had to find Grandma before the Basilisk King hurt her. I picked up my pace into a run.

The trail of trunks grew farther apart, but my nose tugged me where I needed to go. With each step the sulfurous scent raced through my nostrils and left a foul aftertaste in my mouth.

I briefly glanced back, but no one chased after me. I checked my watch. Fifteen minutes were gone already, long enough for Thorn to reach the house with other pack members to help Aggie take down the basilisk in the basement.

As I ventured further into Double Trouble, past the cranberry bogs and Cedar Creek, the trunks were harder to find, but the trail was there. He wanted me to find and confront him. Well, if he wanted to get a taste of me, his first sample would be from my fist down his throat.

Familiar landmarks popped up. The pack hunted here during the full moon, but with the waning moon barely perceptible in the sky, only the shadows illuminated any dangers.

Suddenly, the urge to hide fell over me.

Something was close.

My enemy was near.

The goblin blade shuddered and elongated. I backed up until my spine pressed against a tree, the sturdiness of its trunk giving me strength. I widened my stance as the blade curved into a form I'd only seen in books: an Egyptian scimitar. My fingers rubbed the hieroglyphs on the hilt as the blade radiated a harsh, scarlet glow.

I inhaled to prepare myself for what was to come. Hadn't I fought scarier foes with this weapon?

And hadn't I been hurt in the process?

I took a tentative step forward. The night sounds ceased. Maybe every bird, bat, and bug held their breath like me.

The glow on the blade deepened from scarlet to the color of blood. Fire danced at the tip, illuminating the forest before me. I walked along the creek, leaping onto rocks and fallen trees to avoid the mud.

One step at a time, Nat.

When I came to a fork where the creek separated to a lake, I spied someone sitting on another felled tree. Two heaps of marked stones sat between him. Altars of worship for a fool. A circle of five mud-brown steamer trunks surrounded him and Grandma lay on the ground before him. Her mouth was covered with duct tape and her hands tied behind her back. With relief, I saw her breathing but barely. Dark bruises marred the side of her face.

I crept closer, hoping I wasn't seen, but my olive-skinned adversary's head turned my way. There went sneaking up on him.

With a snarl, I advanced on him. Heat from the goblin blade warmed my face and drove me harder. The closer I got, the easier I could make out the sharp angles of his face. The deep set of his black eyes and the multi-colored robe he wore. My foe looked like he stepped off the set of an epic *Conan the Barbarian* movie.

The Basilisk King's hand lifted, and I froze while he spoke words I didn't recognize in a low voice. When I remained silent, he tried again in a tongue I understood, Old Russian.

"You are definitely worth the wait," he said smoothly with his hands planted on his knees. "The old woman is a morsel, but you're a banquet worthy of a god."

I hoped he'd choked on me. "Any chance you want to turn around and go about your business? Maybe eat at Burger King like regular people?"

Confusion then anger flashed on his face. "What nonsense do you speak? Shut your mouth and kneel before me!"

Superman didn't kneel before General Zod, and I

wasn't complying either. I took four more steps when every trunk latch clicked and the lids opened.

"Do you think I'd make it that easy, Old Magic Mage?" he sneered.

"Let her go, or I'll kill you," I growled.

"You'll kill me?" He laughed. "I've seen empires toppled and great leaders sacrifice their children to me."

"Why don't we test your mortality then?" I pointed the blade in his direction.

From the nearest trunk, a four-finger claw edged out. The creature squawked and its feathers rustled—as another basilisk from the other side of the circle emerged.

Shit. This wasn't good.

"I can summon them, and I can make them go away," he said evenly as if we were negotiating the price of a charmed waffle iron at The Bends. "You can suffer or accept your fate."

I smirked as the rage bubbling in my chest swelled. I let the fury feed me for what was to come. He wanted more than worship—he wanted to consume me before moving on to his next victim. I was nothing more than lunch to him. I refused to let anyone, even this son-of-a-bitch, make me feel like I was nothing ever again.

"My friends tell me I'm stubborn. Guess what? They're right." I raced hard at the first trunk and swung the blade through the middle. A thunderclap slapped my ears as the trunk and basilisk were cut in half. Sparks danced in the air, and the singed wood glowed bright.

With a flick of the Basilisk King's hands, the four other basilisks were unleashed. They converged on me at once, beaks opened wide, claws extended in my direction. They circled me like a pack on the hunt.

Run, the wolf in me warned. *Escape before you've sealed your doom.*

But there was no running this time.

Two basilisks surged forward, their wings flapping. I stabbed at one, but the other on my right latched onto my arm. Raw pain raced up to my shoulder, and I howled. The discomfort from my last fight was too recent, but I couldn't let it deter me.

Using the fiery blade, I set the first attacker on fire and the basilisk retreated in flames, bounding in a smoky flurry until it hit the water. The second basilisk knocked me over and the others swept in for the kill.

Was this the end?

I scrambled in the throes of the mob, growling and swinging, trying to escape at any opportunity. Every bite and scratch held me down until I drowned in a bottomless well of pain. Blood wet my arms and legs, saturating my clothes. The fire to fight within me was dying. I had to act.

Aren't some prices worth paying?

I whispered five words. A sting hit my gut and blossomed into an all-encompassing agony I'd never experienced before, as if a piece of my body were sliced out in exchange for this moment of power. The basilisks around me burst into flames. They retreated and swooped into their trunks and the lids slammed shut.

Yet the spot where the Basilisk King had sat was empty.

God help me, had I defeated him? I struggled to stand and managed to crawl to Grandma.

"*Babushka?*" I whispered.

She didn't stir.

Meanwhile, the goblin sword's flames continued to flare then died as the trunks dematerialized around us. No, I hadn't beaten him, but I'd survived. One thing was painfully certain: I was horribly wounded, but I hadn't even managed to touch him.

What condition was Grandma in? I pressed my face against her cheek.

"Just keep breathing, *babushka*. I'm right here."

I struggled to stay awake. What would stop the Basilisk King from returning and taking us if I couldn't remain conscious and guard her? My eyelids drooped, and the strength that kept me motivated to survive wavered. I couldn't stop shaking and the pain on my arms and legs magnified with each passing minute, but I refused to close my eyes. I crept over to the Basilisk King's perch, knocking down his foul altars in the process.

Shadows ebbed and flowed around me. Had more basilisks come? Was my final battle before me? The goblin blade slept in my trembling hand.

The shaking in my limbs from the poison coursing through me increased until I collapsed and landed hard next to Grandma. I reached for her hand and locked my fingers with hers, but she didn't squeeze mine back.

CHAPTER 23

Doubts smothered me, like a hand pressed against my nose and mouth and there was no breath to save me. Had I failed? Was Grandma alive? As I swam in and out of consciousness, I didn't want to wake up yet from the comfort of my bed.

The scents around me were familiar. Thorn had laid next to me and held me close, but I wasn't at the cottage.

You're not home. That's not a good sign.

Eventually, the clues came together—the ethereal scent of spring sunshine to the soft womanly skin that rubbed my cheek to offer comfort. I was at my brother's home with the nymphs.

Why hadn't the pack healer taken care of me?

No one spoke when I was fed. Family prodded me to open my mouth and accept broth. They floated in and out, from my father's heavy footsteps to my mother's soft ones. Murmurs floated through the walls, but I couldn't make out the speaker or what was said.

But I wasn't in pain. Just a sense of being utterly and

completely drained. I urged my limbs to move, for my eyes to open, but my eyelids didn't so much as budge.

Time in bed can be a cruelty for a wolf. I longed for someone to open the window—if there was one.

I wasn't sure how much time had passed, but suddenly, I caught conversation coming from the hallway.

"Thank you for coming." It was Thorn. "I know you and I haven't been on the best terms, but I'm grateful you accepted my call."

Who was he addressing?

"Nothing has worked," I heard Aggie whisper. "It's been two days and the pack healer doesn't know what to do."

The door to the room opened. Thorn and Aggie approached me, their familiar scents enveloping me. Another set of footsteps approached, but this one didn't carry a scent. The hand that pressed against my shoulder was tentative, yet when he gripped me, I sensed his despair and urgency.

"I'm glad you contacted me," Nick's voice said firmly. "She's beyond your care now."

"Siphon strength from me, if necessary," Brenna said. So the earth witch had come to my aid, too.

"You don't need to do that..." Thorn murmured. "If you need power, you can take it from me."

"There's no need. Brenna and I will do what we can." Nick's healing magic flooded into me, tugging strength into me from my toes up to my ankles. He kept his hand on me as he grumbled, "She hasn't healed at all. She's merely existing right now. Nat, if you can hear me, wiggle your toes."

I wiggled my big toe under the blanket.

"Good job, Nat," he whispered.

"Do you detect anymore basilisk poison?" Brenna asked.

"A little," Nick said evenly.

"Let me draw it out." Brenna drew closer to me, her light citrus-scent filling my nostrils. Another hand touched my leg. The pain from the contact was brief and she released me. "There, I got it."

The warmth from Nick's healing continued upward until I finally managed to open my eyes to a slit. Nick kneeled beside my bed in the spare bedroom at my brother's home. Brenna stood behind him.

Not far from them, Aggie and Thorn waited with hopeful faces. My poor mate's shoulders sagged and his wrinkled clothes told me he hadn't been home in a long time.

My stubborn eyelids gave way. I opened my mouth and tried to produce sounds. A croak came out.

"You're still too weak," Nick said gently.

I mouthed one word in particular over and over again, but both of the spellcasters' faces scrunched in confusion. Brenna offered me a bit of water and I was able to whisper, "Grandma."

They glanced at each other as if considering what to say.

Was she dead? My heart collapsed like a supernova and I moaned in despair, but Nick patted my hand.

"She's alive—but, like you, she's not responding."

Brenna gave me a soft, reassuring smile. "Nick and I will go see her after we take care of you."

I tried to push Nick's hand off my shoulder so he could attend to Grandma, but I was far too weak.

"Still stubborn as always. I promise I will heal her." A sheen of sweat formed on Nick's brow and his lips paled. How much had he taxed himself to help me?

"Stop," I managed to say. "Rest."

He let go of me. His gaze jumped from my face to my

abdomen, exactly where I'd felt a piece of myself taken as the price of using magic. "What did you do to yourself?" he asked. "What spell did you cast?"

"I'd like to know the answer to that question too," Thorn said with a growing frown.

"Does it matter?" I asked as Brenna gave me another sip of water.

"Yes, it matters." Nick's dark eyes bore into me with disapproval. "You could've died."

"She promised me she wouldn't do Old Magic anymore." Thorn eased into a nearby seat.

"Nat wouldn't have done it unless she didn't have a choice, right?" Aggie's voice rose. "None of us know what happened but, based on all the blood we found, whatever went down had to be really bad."

Memories of the pain and fire consuming the basilisks flashed before my eyes. I cringed.

Nick stood. "You're more stable now, but you can't avoid the conversation we need to have about Old Magic."

What happened the other night unfolded in my thoughts. Would I have survived if I'd held my ground with only the goblin blade? Not necessarily.

As Nick and Brenna left, presumably to heal Grandma, Aggie approached the bed and adjusted the covers up to my chest. Thorn rubbed his face and then rested his elbows on his knees.

"You hungry?" she asked.

"No," I mumbled. "I'm very tired."

"Then rest some more. I'll be back with some chow and you're going to eat that," she said firmly.

I managed a nod.

My friend left the room, and Thorn strode up to the bed. He curled up next to me and I about melted from the warmth of his embrace. I almost fell back asleep, but

Thorn's heartbeat was far too fast. His worry seeping from his pores.

"Did something bad happen?" I gasped.

He shifted so I could see his face. His brow furrowed and tension filled his shoulders.

"Thorn?" I whispered.

I said his name again.

"After you left the house to save your grandmother, the pack ran into some problems back at your parents' place."

"Oh God no, I should've—" My heart plummeted and he placed his finger over my mouth.

"You did the right thing," he said. "I would've saved her too if I had to make the choice you did." He sucked in a deep breath. "After you left the house, the basilisk broke out of the basement. The human neighbors next door were attacked, including a small child. Multiple humans witnessed the supernatural world."

Oh, no.

"Are they okay?" I croaked.

"They'll live. The warlocks came to clean up our mess."

A dull ache formed on the back of my head. The pack's situation had worsened.

"I should've stayed to help, but if I hadn't gone after Grandma—"

"—she might be dead right now," Thorn finished for me. "You did the right thing, wife."

Doubts flicked at me. Despite what Thorn said, I knew very well Grandma would've chosen protecting the pack over herself.

"I'm old," she'd said to me. *"I can take care of myself."*

Thorn swallowed deeply. "You need to heal so we can protect everyone again." He tilted my chin to force me to meet his eyes. "The pack is strongest when we're together. I have the power to *bring* them together. You do, too."

Thorn's words should've reassured me, but I felt torn in two. An *innocent* child was attacked. Even if I'd walked away to save my grandma, the citizens of South Toms River fell under my care, too. I had to reflect on that while I recovered.

~

I dozed off, only to wake up again an hour later. Thorn had left, but another person sat in the chair next to the bed: Mevelyn.

"How long have you been here?" I asked with a yawn.

"Long enough to watch over you and make progress on my little project," the older nymph presented what she held in the middle of her palm: a carving of a small fish.

I squinted. "What's that?"

"A beautiful minnow." She smiled and the wrinkles along her eyes softened. "Karey told me she saw fishing supplies in a corner at the cottage and I thought I'd make a simple gift for you. Are you planning a trip soon?"

With a groan, I tried to ease into a sitting position and failed. Mevelyn helped me add two pillows behind me. Now that I was sitting up a little, I could see someone had left my goblin blade on a nearby dresser. I didn't have the strength to use it right now, but knowing it was nearby gave me relief.

A bit breathless, I managed to say, "Not any time soon." I told her about how Thorn and I wanted to go fly fishing in Maine. Maybe relax for a couple of days while fishing along the Kennebago River.

"Sounds amazing. I love to travel and see my sisters to the north." She retrieved her carving knife from the end table next to the bed and worked on the minnow.

The *flick-flick* sounds soothed me. My eyes drooped from fatigue, but I spoke so I wouldn't fall asleep again.

"How many sisters do you have?" I asked.

"Far too many," Mevelyn replied with a chuckle. "Nymphs guard clusters of trees and there are more glens, bogs, swamps than I can count. I used to be able to remember all my sisters' names, but time has a way of making you remember what's important." She paused to smile. "The people closest to you, right here and right now, should matter."

"Yes," I agreed. "They should."

"I know you're troubled right now, Sister Wolf, but have faith in yourself. I believe in you." She resumed her whittling. "With time, you'll find your way and see what's most important."

I nodded, praying for that clarity to come.

~

The day stretched out. After Mevelyn left, I rested, feeling as broken as that fairy tale character Humpty-Dumpty.

I'd survived my fight with the Basilisk King, but my heart hurt from the aftermath. Was I strong enough to get the pack through this troublesome time?

Five years ago, I had a similar feeling—despair and doubt. After college, Thorn and I had been dating for a while and things were going great. Then he disappeared. He vanished off the face of the Earth, and I was left with a broken heart. At the time, I had a comfy job in New York City, but my sadness made it impossible for me to function.

After I didn't answer any phone calls, my parents got

worried. They found me sitting in my apartment and brought me back to South Toms River.

Once back home, I tried to put myself back together again—like Humpty-Dumpty. Grandma kept me company, trying to cheer me up when she could. At the time, she'd given me the first piece of my holiday collection: a papier-mâché farmer boy holding a Christmas wreath. His face was beautifully painted with a bright smile. A smile full of hope.

"My child," Grandma had said, "hold onto him. He represents love. My beloved Pyotr fixed him for me after your aunt Olga tried to break him in half."

Over the springtime into the summer, I'd begun adding more and more to my collection while helping Aunt Olga care for Grandma. That summer should've healed my old wounds, but during that fateful season, my parents took me out to a pack picnic at Hope Park. Surrounded by pack members, they pushed Rex at me and expected me to forget about Thorn.

Wouldn't a new man help? they must've thought.

But I didn't want a new man. I needed time to be happy by myself. That horrible day, the pack witnessed my worst moment of shame: I had a panic attack in front of *everyone*. The scene was far too vivid in my mind, and every time I recalled it, I wanted to cry.

I could still see myself backing away from Rex, screeching out, "No! Don't touch me. Stay away from me!"

I continued to step backwards until I fell on the kids table. I collapsed on the children's plates of food, knocking everything to the ground. At the time, I couldn't control myself. I couldn't apologize or explain my actions. I only felt the need to flee. And anyone in my way, including my mother and father, would be pushed aside.

My father tried to placate me and hold my arms as I

flailed and jerked, but I was past that point. The whole moment felt surreal, as if I stood to the side and watched another person fall over the edge and plunge into the depths of darkness.

Soon enough, I calmed down, but the damage was done. From that moment forward, the pack saw me as weak. A mentally ill pariah incapable of functioning as a pack member.

But that darkness didn't prevail forever. Instead of sitting ignored at my parents' house, I escaped to one flea market then another. Just like my usual routine even now, shopping made everything better. Finding one treasured thing—that one diamond in the rough—had a way of lifting my spirits.

Then one day, I came upon a flea market I always passed. The place appeared dated and rundown on the outside. I mean, c'mon, would I find anything good at a place called The Bend of the River Flea Market?

Yet I went inside.

Instead of finding another collectible for my hoard, I found a job. A purpose.

For a girl like me, that was more valuable than anything.

CHAPTER 24

When Thorn said the dog shit had hit the fan and blasted everyone so badly that the spellcasters showed up, he wasn't kidding.

The next day, I heard many voices in the living room so I ambled out of bed to the bathroom—only to pass by a living room full of spellcasters. Two middle-aged men and a woman in casual clothes whispered to each other on the couch. My brother's ranch home had an open floor plan. Beyond the chatting spellcasters, the nymphs gathered in the kitchen. Before I disappeared into the bathroom, Mevelyn glanced my way in concern.

Good God, how long had they been sitting in there?

In the bathroom, I took my sweet time. The trip drained what little energy I had, so I washed my hands once rather than the usual twice. All the while, I strained to hear what the spellcasters were saying. Just how bad were things?

I knew damn well why they were here: now that I was feeling better, they wanted to hear what I knew about the

Basilisk King. Fatigue tugged at me. I was so not ready to face the Spanish Inquisition.

On the way back from the bathroom, I tried to resist a second peek into the living room, but this time, I caught the most delightful sight. My niece Sveta scampered like a marathon runner across the gray carpeted floor.

And she beamed with a cheesy toddler grin when she saw me.

My escape was thwarted, but I didn't mind and gingerly stooped down to her level. I doubt I had the strength to hold her, but she climbed into my lap, nonetheless.

"Oh, my *Printsessa!*" I leaned in and kissed her cheeks. Then I made fart noises in her neck like any proper aunt would. The toddler giggled. "My little princess has gotten so big."

"Goodness, Nat." Karey was breathless. "She's so fast."

"Yeah, pups develop faster than humans," I replied.

From behind Karey, I noticed the spellcasters looking our way.

Karey reached for Sveta, but her adventurous daughter shook her head and clung to me.

"Aren't you hungry, sweetheart?" Karey asked. Then she turned to me. "Your brother said I don't feed her enough."

"I think she looks healthy."

"She caught a mole outside." Karey shuddered. "I'm so glad she didn't eat it."

That got a laugh out of me. "That's my girl." I rubbed my nose against Sveta's, and the baby giggled again.

One of the warlocks, a short, dark-haired man with a sharp nose and eyes stepped forward. "I'm sorry for intruding, but we need to speak with Mrs. Grantham."

Fear curled in the back of my throat. This man could've been anyone—he smelled like cheap aftershave and your average office—but I'd learned from my time with Nick that appearances are deceiving. Able spellcasters masked their scent and appearance. The only thing I trusted was my intuition, and that gift from the wolf often stumbled about like a fool searching through a trap-filled dark room.

After kissing my niece's forehead, I said a silent prayer and handed her off to her mom. I'd be fine. My pack was here. My family, too, if I counted Karey and her kin. All I had to do was tell the truth and face their words as the alpha female.

Standing took far more effort and time than I wanted, but the warlock didn't interfere—nor did he offer to help. Rude. I wrapped my robe's sash tightly around my waist and shuffled to the nearest seat. A floral-printed La-Z-Boy threatened to swallow me, but the overstuffed seat gave me an optimal position to face the spellcasters.

The dark-haired warlock nodded to me. "Mrs. Stravin-sky-Grantham, we'd—"

My hand rose. "You can call me Mrs. Grantham. Can I get your names, please?"

That made the woman frown, but I didn't care. We wouldn't ever hang out together for drinks on the veranda, but if these guys posed a problem later, I needed their names now.

"I'm Sedgewick McGalleon," the dark-hair warlock said. "Other members from the various guilds joined me today." He pointed to his taller, brown-haired counterpart. "Crandall is from the Wizard's Guild."

"Good morning." Crandall gave me an informal nod, and his shoulder-length, curly hair flopped with the movement.

Sedgewick gestured to the final spellcaster, the very short, raven-haired witch with a cherub face and volup-tuous hips. "This is Angela Ambleberry, the representative from the Witch's Guild."

"Mrs. Grantham," the witch said sternly from between thin, heavily rouged lips. The way the witch pursed her mouth and sighed meant business.

I tried to straighten my back, even in a seat that only Alice in Wonderland could appreciate.

"Now that we've introduced ourselves," Crandall said, "We'd like to get down to business. How long have you been aware of the Basilisk King in your territory?"

"Exactly eleven days, ten hours," I glanced at the wall clock, "and twenty minutes."

That response got a sour look from the witch. "Thanks," she said.

"During that time, were there any human casualties?" Sedgewick asked.

Now this question made me want to squirm, but I held hard. Thorn was likely asked the same questions and would be honest in the interest of the pack.

I nodded. "A human died in the parking lot of The Bend of the River Flea Market, my work. You can speak to Bill, the owner, for more information."

Crandall harrumphed. "That goblin..."

I added, "Bill handled the situation and performed clean-up as you would call it. No authorities visited the site."

Sedgewick's thick black eyebrows rose. "What's to stop the human's family from investigating?"

"I don't know—but the incident occurred on Bill's grounds. It was his responsibility. Don't complain to me." My voice had weakened, but not my resolve.

Sedgewick sighed. "We're still investigating as to why the Basilisk King veered off course—"

The witch stepped forward, briefly revealing a whiff of her power through the stench of cinnamon. "That's privileged information the wolf doesn't need to know."

Sedgewick and Angela exchanged a hard look. "She's confronted him already. She should at least know we have unanswered questions. We expect her to comply and answer."

Angela then asked, "What happened to you after you went into Double Trouble State Park?"

I took a deep breath and considered the sequence of events. No humans were involved, and while the pack wouldn't be harmed, only a fool would reveal why he wanted Grandma and me. "The Basilisk King is searching for particular prey. He drained a shapeshifter at the Bashful Brownies Baking Company. I can only conclude he's looking for other shapeshifters in general, such as werewolves. He kidnapped my grandmother to lure our pack to her position. I didn't want the others to get hurt and made a leadership decision to face him alone."

They exchanged glances before Sedgewick prodded me. "And?"

His question begged to know what powers the Basilisk King possessed. What did he look like? Did I even harm him? I spilled as many details as I could without revealing my skills in Old Magic.

"That goblin blade sounds handy," Angela said. "Are you authorized to wield such a dangerous weapon?"

I snorted. "I didn't know Jersey had a magical concealed carry law."

"Please don't compare this to human firearm laws, but like the humans' weapons, you could unknowingly cause damage if you aren't properly trained to use it." Angela smirked. "We had to wipe the memories of five people, and a small child was attacked. The South Toms River Pack has been noticeably rowdy lately. Didn't a rival pack attack you last year?"

"Rowdy?" Had she lost her damn mind? She was lucky I

wasn't in my peak condition. "We defended ourselves. What were we supposed to do? Put out a welcome mat for other packs as they invaded our territory?"

My raised voice made the nymphs appear. Grace and Dione flitted near the door and headed outside while Mevelyn and Karey stood in observance next to me.

"Nat, is there a problem?" Mevelyn asked softly.

"None." I pasted a smile on my face. "Just answering their questions."

Angela pursed her lips. Her face was gonna stay like that if she wasn't careful.

I took the moment to ask, "Have you found the Basilisk King?"

"We're searching for him," Angela replied, "and we will determine whether he'll continue to be a problem."

Translation: they hadn't found a damn thing.

Angela added, "You must understand that no one in any of the Guilds has faced him before and lived to provide information."

"Until me," I finished.

"Until you," she conceded. "You're not a spellcaster nor are you the most reliable source of information, but you're all we have."

"Exactly." Nick materialized in the middle of the room.

The other spellcasters frowned. Looked like Nick had been waiting outside and the nymphs fetched him when they scurried out.

"We're conducting an interview, Fenton," Crandall said crisply.

"And Mrs. Grantham is my patient," Nick replied just as tartly.

"Patient?" Crandall glanced Nick over. "Last I heard you didn't even finish the first semester—"

Power flared in the room, and a white light flashed from where Nick stood. In less than a breath, the light disappeared yet all the spellcasters in the room no longer stood in the same spots. Angela sat on the couch, her legs crossed under her black skirt. Exasperation filled her face. From across the room, Crandell scratched his head. Sedgewick, on the other hand, fumed from where he stood closest to me.

What the hell did I just miss?

"Mrs. Grantham, let's wrap up this interview, shall we?" Sedgewick said sternly.

I cut a glance at Mevelyn, and she appeared equally confused, her mouth slightly open and brow knotted.

"Did something happen?" I whispered.

"The spellcasters had a brief...discussion and we resolved an internal matter," Sedgewick replied.

"About me?" I asked.

"You weren't the primary topic of the discussion, but Mr. Fenton told us you are a patient of Dr. Gustav Frankenstein and we should treat you with respect."

I hadn't heard Dr. Frank's true name in a while.

Nick stood like stone, but his hardened expression directed at Crandall seemed like a dare, *"Don't cross the line, Houdini."*

"The matter regarding all human interaction with the basilisk has been handled," Sedgewick declared. "A warning has been issued to the South Toms River Pack. We'll be watching you and observing how you conduct yourselves in the future. Members from the Warlock's Guild will be responsible for enforcing this observation."

My heart fell. This was bad. Very bad.

One would think having warlocks around to protect us from the Basilisk King might be a good thing, but I knew very well that not all warlocks had great intentions. Many of them used shapeshifters as power sources for malicious spells.

"Can we appeal this decision?" I managed to ask.

Nick slowly shook his head.

Sedgewick stood. "I spoke with your alpha, and he asked the same question—in a not-so-polite manner, I might add—but the answer is the same. For the well-being and protection of the humans from the supernatural world, we must intervene." He nodded as if such a decision had great weight. "We don't know whether the Basilisk King will return or if he's still following the fairy path's southward trajectory."

I could bet half my hoarded stash that bastard wasn't done with us yet. There weren't too many Old Magic practitioners, and if the Basilisk King was as hungry as he claimed, he'd line up at the buffet line again.

The rest of the spellcasters stood and vanished with a shimmer of dancing lights. They didn't even bother to say goodbye or thank me for my time, but then again, there was no reason to say goodbye when it was likely I'd see them again sooner rather than later.

CHAPTER 25

After my little chit-chat with the Guild representatives, I asked about seeing Grandma, but I was herded back to bed, fed broth, and forced to take a nap. The way Karey eyed me as she shut the door told me Sveta got similar treatment during nap time.

"I checked on Grandma and she's sleeping right now," Karey said. "You'll see her soon enough."

"Fine."

"I don't want to hear a peep," the nymph said.

"Gladly," I murmured.

A few hours later, I was refreshed and restless. A quick peek out my window showed four cars parked near the house. Two of them I knew belonged to pack members. Looked like we had plenty of guards around.

Karey left me some clothes, and though I wouldn't have chosen the bright yellow maxi dress, this outfit hit a home run compared to the Juicy ensemble I wore the other day. I slipped the garment over my head and paused. What was that earthy smell? I pressed the clothes to my face and took a deep breath. Oh, the clothes were made from hemp, but I detected an underlying scent within the folds.

Marijuana?

I snorted then giggled. *To each their own.* If the nymphs were hitting the chronic, that was their business, not mine. Surely, their use was medicinal.

Once I was dressed, I donned some flip-flops. Then I straightened my shoulders and placed the goblin blade in my pocket. The letter opener slipped in with ease. Time to check on Grandma and then face the pack for an update on any Basilisk King sightings.

I plodded out of my room and headed down the hallway. The master bedroom and Sveta's nursery were empty. Where were they keeping Grandma? I closed my eyes and focused. Several people moved around the house, in particular two people in the kitchen. But if Grandma was resting, why would she be in the kitchen?

My heart fell as I entered the kitchen to find Mevelyn and Karey. Little Sveta sat in a high chair munching on crackers.

"Good to see you up," Karey said brightly. "You hungry? I'm making vegan fettuccine alfredo with almond milk and stinkhorn mushrooms."

So that was the *ghastly* smell.

"Sounds lovely." I nuzzled the top of Sveta's head. "Where's Grandma?"

"After the wizard healed her," Mevelyn explained, "she was in much better shape so your family picked her up. Your mom wanted me to call her if your health improved."

I sighed in relief. At least Grandma was well. "I'm better now. Can someone give me a ride over there?"

"Are you sure you're up for it?" the nymph asked with concern.

"It doesn't matter whether I'm up for it or not," I said. "I need to see for myself if Grandma is doing better."

Reluctantly, Karey drove me to my parents' house. After we pulled up to the quiet Colonial, I shuffled up to the house. All this walking had drained me a bit, but I was much stronger than this morning.

I took in the street. The neighborhood was quaint and suburban. Sprinklers sprayed arcs of water in two yards, and a pair of middle-schoolers laughed as they rode their bikes down the road. All was well, but a couple of nights ago, terror and blood saturated the air. I closed my eyes and briefly gave in to experience their agony. I couldn't shove the feelings into a box and pretend the attack didn't happen. I had a town to protect now and their home was my home.

In a way, that meant the humans in the borough of South Toms River were my pack members too.

I made my way to the door, took three deep cleansing breaths, and knocked.

Mom answered the door, wearing a shawl and a soft smile. "Why didn't you call me to come get you?"

"Karey gave me a ride. I came to see Grandma," was all I said in Russian.

"She's awake and sitting with your auntie," Mom said, pulling me into a brief hug. "It's good to see you up and moving."

"Thanks, Mama."

I walked into the living room, and the ladies in the room hushed. My heart fell to see Aunt Olga still covered in bruises and scratches. Her body was also taking overly long to heal from the basilisk poison. Why hadn't Nick healed her, too? Grandma sat in her usual spot with an afghan covering her legs. She appeared small before, but this time, somehow the seat was far too big for her little frame. Had she shrunk in size or had the attack taken what few years she had left to live?

Mom picked up some empty cups of tea from the end table and carried them into the kitchen while I sat down across from my grandmother and aunt.

"Are you both well?" I asked softly.

Aunt Olga gave a ladylike giggle, immediately lifting my mood. "I've had better days, but you won't see me in Shop-Rite looking like this." She extended her hand to the couch to encourage me to come closer. "You're still recovering, Natalya. A harsh wind from the Baltic would blow you over, dear."

"I'm better." I sat next to my aunt. My throat dried, and I blinked hard to push back tears of relief. "I had to see if you're okay."

Grandma tsked, yet her voice was a thin whisper. "Lasovskaya blood is strong. My mother and the women before her survived worst."

Aunt Olga nodded sagely. "One man and his fat, ugly *kuritsa* won't get the best of me."

I chuckled. *Fat, ugly chickens, indeed.*

A question about what happened that night still hung in the air while we chatted about Grandma's life back in Russia. Once the reminiscing ended, I had to speak.

"*Babushka*, why did you leave the house to fight the Basilisk King?"

"You need to give me some credit, girl," Grandma said with a wheeze. "While I have strength in these hands, I will fight. That tyrant will want to face me again, and I don't want you involved."

"I don't want you involved either!" I blurted.

"Yes, but I did what I did for a reason, child. In the old times, you either struck first or you waited to be struck down in your bed. Before his scaly children subdued me, I hurt him—but in a way I hadn't expected."

Aunt Olga and I leaned forward.

"That smart-mouthed Sumerian can be wounded," Grandma said, "but you must get past his guards and he can summon hundreds of them. That's far too many for us to fight, and he's a demigod, after all."

My aunt asked, "So how can the pack win?"

"We can't," I said simply.

"Any creature that bleeds will heal over time," Grandma surmised. "He'll need to feed soon on better prey than a shapeshifter."

"And his source is either Old Magic practitioners or he'll have to return to drink from the wake of She Who Always Walks the Path," I said.

"Who's that?" Aunt Olga asked.

I explained my late-night journey north and the details about my encounter with the mysterious being. I didn't reveal her name—I had enough problems with the Basilisk King and didn't need to drag her into it as well.

Aunt Olga harrumphed. "Then he'll come again and again like a bad boyfriend with crabs."

Grandma and I frowned. Eww.

"Which means we need to hold the fort and wait for him to pass," Auntie added with flourish.

Grandma laughed, low and rich. "Starve him out like our people did with that little pissant Napoleon in 1812! Those were wild times!"

Aunt Olga covered her mouth to laugh while Grandma guffawed.

I wasn't as amused. "Every shapeshifter will have to work with us, but I like this plan."

"I do, too," my aunt agreed. "But where do we hide if that horrible man can leave those trunks anywhere?"

"Nowhere is safe right now." I shifted to stand, but an idea came to mind. "However, we might have a fort."

~

Thorn briefly came home, only to sleep next to me for a few hours, then leave again. He had to be weary from guarding Grandma all the time. All I could do to support him was offer my love and affection.

Even though I was a bit tired, I still got up, dressed in my standard skirt-and-blouse uniform, and trudged to The Bends at seven in the morning.

Aggie drove me to work.

"Don't you have to open Barney's around ten?" I asked her.

"You can give me every excuse in the book," she replied. "I'm going to follow your ass everywhere until we get rid of that damn trunk hoarder."

I sighed. "I feel bad. Every time you show up on my doorstep, shit goes down."

She snorted and sipped some hazelnut coffee she stowed away in a travel mug. "I was *positioned*," she used air quotes for emphasis, "to be an alpha female someday. I was honestly bred for an ass-kicking once in a while."

She shrugged to show me it wasn't a big deal. "Par for the course."

We'd reached The Bends, but I didn't bother to get out of the car. It was rather early at seven-thirty AM, and Thursday morning traffic along the Parkway hadn't picked up to its usual frantic pace with rush hour.

"I can't imagine how your life would've been if you'd left to go to Las Vegas like you said you would when you first arrived."

She leaned her head against the driver's side window.

"Probably would've blown whatever cash I made on the casino buffets." Her eyes went dreamy. "They got the best buffets ever. European brunches to midnight Vietnamese takeout. Don't get me started on the breakfast offerings—"

"Thanks, Aggie," I said with a soft smile.

She glanced at me and the sun hit the back of her head, illuminating her hair into a fiery halo. After knowing my best friend for so long, I knew her halo wasn't angelic in the least. She could be hell's angel when necessary.

"Don't get sappy on me." She checked for danger in the parking lot. "Get your ass in there—wait, aren't you supposed to be working at the troll place?"

"Yeah, but after the basilisk attack, he told me I wasn't welcome for the time being."

"That's a good thing."

I opened the car door with a frown. "No, it isn't. That's the thing, like werewolves, the fairy folk don't forget debts. Once this shit is sorted out, Kramkar will come knocking on my door with orders for me to work."

"That sucks." She picked up her cup and finished her coffee with flourish. "I'll be back to drive you home. I'm doing a shorter shift today."

I grabbed my tote bag, a new one with a festive Christmas wreath on the side, and hurried into The Bends.

To my relief, the back office didn't have any trunks, but other unexpected guests were there: Quinton the janitor necromancer and a few of his friends.

I use the term *friends* loosely since the new folks shambling around the back office didn't have a pulse and stank like burritos stuffed with incense and herbs.

"Mornin', Quinton." I kept my tote bag tucked next to me. The last time I'd encountered his minions, things hadn't gone well. It turned out his friends were rather protective of their master.

"Good morning, Natalya," he said.

All I could do was stand there—believe me, there was plenty to do since I missed a couple of days of work. A pile of invoices sat untouched next to the computerized inventory system station. Boxes of unsorted merchandise, also known as cash waiting to be made, waited in unopened boxes. And, even worse of all, every employee passed through this room but not one bothered to toss out the rock-hard cream donuts the goblin left for us to eat.

And now we had zombies in the mix, too.

Five zombies, their faces pale and blank, milled about. Their clothes were wrinkled, but clean and tidy. Two shuffled in an apparent guard formation back and forth near the door while two more followed Quinton around. The last one held a broom upside-down.

Based on past experience, my OCD never fared well with zombies. I'd come far in terms of therapy, but my mind kept flinging a message at me on repeat: they're corpses. Walking Petri dishes full of decay and bacteria. And oh, look, one of them just lost a nose.

"Uh, Quinton…" I managed to blurt.

The minion nearly stepped on his lost appendage, but the nimble necromancer retrieved the part.

"You have to be careful, Norbert," Quinton said gently as he folded the nose in a handkerchief.

I couldn't take it anymore. "What are they doing here?"

"They're protection," a voice said behind me.

I turned around to see Bill sitting at one of the work desks. I hadn't been able to smell him beneath the zombie funk.

"You could've hired the pack or maybe even other goblins." I reached for more reasons, but perhaps I was still dumbfounded as I darted out of the way of the sweeping zombie. The business end of the broom had yet to hit the floor.

"Pay another goblin? Bah!" Bill's usual frown deepened. "I'd rather take a spear up the butt than deal with those conmen." He pointed to Quinton's workers. "These guys are great. They do what they're told, work for minimal pay —nothing—and they don't talk back. It's a win-win."

"Why would Quinton sacrifice his children?" I turned to Quinton. "No offense."

"None taken." The janitor hauled boxes into the office from the back dock while two zombies pushed heavy merchandise across the floor at a sloth's pace. It was hard to move heavy items when falling limbs were a work hazard.

"What's to sacrifice? Aren't they dead already?" Bill said with a smile this time.

I reached up to rub my face in exasperation, then I considered the situation, and applied hand sanitizer instead. "Well, I'm back from Kramkar's for now. Do you have a problem with me working here?"

"Money is money." He shrugged. "The Bends has seen worse enemies cross my doors, and I've fortified the property."

Now would be a good time to discuss that very thing. "Bill, this may seem forward, but my grandma and I aren't safe."

He crossed his arms. "So I've heard. I know what the Basilisk King wants."

I gathered strength to ask what I needed. The likelihood of him saying no was rather high. Okay, fine, make that damn near certain.

I continued. "You mentioned having powerful wards around here; I need to protect my grandmother and the safest place for her to be would be The Bends. In particular, the showroom."

Bill laughed so hard his glasses fell off.

"What's so funny?" I asked.

"Does The Bends look like a retirement home?" he grunted. "'Cause the last time I passed the sign outside, it said the place was open for business to sell antiques and not hand out bed pans."

Wow, I sometimes forgot how harsh he could be. A tart reply sat on the tip of my tongue, but I checked myself. Based on past experiences, I knew every creature had their price and Bill responded to the kind that folded and crinkled in his pocket.

"How about this: while my grandmother is here, what if I worked double shifts and took less pay until the Basilisk King situation is contained?" I made sure to give an endpoint to keep myself out of trouble.

Bill slowly picked up his glasses. "She'd have to stay put and not bother the customers."

"That's easy. She'll probably people watch or knit scarves for everybody."

His jaw twitched. "Give me a couple of hours to think about it. I'm taking a hit now to keep this place safe. Double the trouble means double the work on my end."

One of Quinton's zombies hauled a box too close to me and I got out of the way. When I turned to speak to Bill, the goblin had vanished again. He was likely still sitting there with a glamour covering him, but speaking into open space like a damn fool wouldn't fix the situation.

He'd reappear when he was good and ready to give me his verdict.

A half-hour later, the rest of the crew arrived and the zombies finished bringing in the new goods. They gathered on the back dock and gave me space to begin working on cataloging products. Falling into work soothed my frayed nerves. We had a dusty box from Argentina full of arrayán wind wands. The rare arrayán tree was found only in the higher elevations and our customers would be clamoring for such a rare—and expensive—find.

I was sorting out the inventory numbers for a set of possessed first edition encyclopedias when Erica approached me.

"Good to see you back at work." She watched as I glanced up from my work, my hands still moving to type and catalog. "How do you do that?"

"Muscle memory," I admitted. Seeing her up close after what happened at her apartment felt weird. "I cleaned your clothes and have them with me. Would you like them now?" I shifted to stop working, but she shook her head.

"I can get them at the end of the day." She sighed, and I realized why she kept glancing at the pile of papers. She was the one who was supposed to have finished the cataloging over the last couple of days.

"You can finish these if you want?" I offered.

"I don't feel like working the floor today so I've been hiding in the back office. Ever since the troll mart opened, we haven't had as many customers." She searched the room, likely unaware that Bill was probably still here. "Bill is fussier than usual."

I finished adding one of the products into the computer system and got up. Might as well see what kind of mess waited for me in the showroom. "Bill is always fussy. How about you finish this while I handle the front?"

I turned to her, but I couldn't read her face. She appeared impeccable as always, dressed in tailored pants and a red, chiffon blouse. Her blonde hair hung in loose waves. Even her nude makeup was flawless.

Our gazes connected, and she didn't look away.

"Is something wrong?" she asked. "Do you need more time off work?"

"No, I'm fine." I was fine enough to work, but I wasn't sure how long things would be awkward between us. I had to figure out how to meet her in the middle someday.

I smoothed my skirt and headed into the showroom to see what disasters I'd uncover. The first wasn't hard to spot. Right next to the front door, a spellcaster browsed. My gaze locked on Sedgewick McGalleon, and the casual salute he gave me sent a chill down my back.

There went the neighborhood.

CHAPTER 26

As I suspected, the state of The Bends showroom had fallen from my high standards. The fire witch left her cigarettes beside the register—not sure why she didn't toss them in the bin outside the door. The jewelry in the glass displays were scattered about as if a heist had occurred, and to my absolute displeasure, the selection of Amish gnome furniture was turned toward the aisle instead of angled so folks could walk by. (This was basic stuff, people.)

For most of the morning, I gave in to the compulsion to arrange, organize, and chastise my co-workers.

Instead of grumbling, Millicent grinned and said, "I missed having you around, Nat."

Not sure if she was genuine, but I'd take what compliments I could.

By lunchtime, I got a text message from Bill that my grandma could stay here. Great! After that good news, I was ready to take a break, so I wandered around The Bends outside in search of anything amiss. The wood building appeared like any other outlet along the road, but as I rounded each corner, the ground hummed beneath my feet. When I brushed my fingers against the grass, the fronds seemed to push back. How strange. Bill didn't bother with flowers or any of the flashy landscaping Kramkar employed, but what little flora that Bill had was vibrant and well-kept.

"Folks want to buy my wares, not sniff the foliage. I've sold goods out of dumps even more successful than this place," he'd said a couple years ago.

Honestly, I never bothered with the outside of The Bends. Keeping the inside tidy was hard enough, and besides, Quinton handled mowing the lawn from spring into fall.

On the way back to the loading dock, I gave into the urge to touch the store's exterior walls. Could this place truly protect us? The wood was warm to my palm, and as I lingered the warmth spread up to my wrist. Something murmured against my hand. Almost like a little girl whispering in a voice as thin as a thread.

I leaned toward the wall and pressed my ear to it. The whispering grew louder, speaking in a guttural tongue, maybe German.

Die Stärke des Meißels des Kobolds wird seine Feinde schlagen...

The words came to me in repeat. What did they mean?

"Nat, what are you doing?" Erica said from behind me.

"Just resting." My face heated in embarrassment.

Erica walked up to the wall and rubbed her palm against it. "Is there something wrong structurally? Maybe pests?"

If only our problems were the *size* of rodents.

"Well, I heard something strange, but it's gone now," I replied. It wasn't a lie.

We strolled to the back of the Bends where I sat on the

docks. I expected her to go inside, but she took a spot next to me. We stared at the cars passing along the Parkway until she ended the silence.

"You were acting strange this morning," she remarked. "Usually you're barking out orders."

"True, guess I'm still recovering." I picked at a non-existent snag in my skirt.

More silence.

"I know we're not the closest of co-workers," she said hesitantly, "but I am trying to get to know you better."

I bit my lower lip. "You really want to get to know me better after what happened between us?"

She drew in a deep breath. "Yeah, even after what happened between us."

"I have to work with you every day at The Bends, but that doesn't mean I've forgotten about how you treated me in the past or that little meeting you had with Rex ever since the Basilisk King showed up."

I even told her about the *zmee* mentioning a wolf helper.

Her eyes widened. "I'll address our past in a second, but what do you mean by my little *meeting* with Rex?"

"Rex used to never come to The Bends. He avoided this place like he might catch fleas from me, but the moment Basilisk King appears, he shows up to see you and wants to talk. Why?"

She rolled her eyes. "It's not what you think."

"Then educate me. I trust Rex to stay out of trouble as much as Bill."

"He does want power—I'll give you that. But he's never mentioned helping the Basilisk King." Her face hardened. "Wow, so you thought I was behind all this?" She slowly shook her head and waves of anger floated off her. "He's been hitting on me, but I'm not biting on that foul-tasting bait."

I didn't detect any lies as to her allegiance with the Basilisk King, and honestly, I was relieved. We'd exposed the foul circumstances of our past—might as well dig up the entire rotted tree, roots and all.

"When it comes to you, I have trust issues because of what you did to me that night," I confessed. "You not only broke my leg, but you burned me, too. It was cruel of you, Erica, and it's been hard to see you—to maybe even start to like you—and know you also did everything you could to hurt me. And you did it to punish me because Thorn loved me."

Erica stiffened, but her eyes searched the horizon before she spoke. "Months ago, I was so angry. I still get mad, but it's not the same. Honestly, I still don't understand why he loves you. What makes you so special?"

Wow, Erica Holden was a piece of work. Domesticated animals like her housecat got better treatment than I had. I opened my mouth to reply, but telling her Thorn's endearments—how my imperfections made me perfect to him— would be callous and pour acid on her wounds.

A thick and heavy silence slithered between us. The pain from the night she struck me had receded from my mind, but her harsh words remained in my head and festered. Even if she didn't like my relationship with Thorn, somebody had to be the grown up, and since I was the alpha female of our pack...

"Erica, I'm sorry I accused you—"

She lifted her hand but kept her head lower than mine. "Considering our history, I'm hardly the cleanest dog in the kennel."

She shifted as if she planned to get up from the docks but remained seated. Was she not done?

"After you left for Russia, I wanted a fresh start," she added. "I should've moved to Boston and moved in with one of my girlfriends from college, but my dad wasn't doing well after he lost all his money so I stayed and got a job at The Bends." She paused as if collecting her thoughts. "After seeing you standing around all the time, I thought it was an easy gig. I even asked Bill to give me the same enchantments he gave you. Can you guess what he said?"

Erica wanted to get something off her chest so I remained silent. She heard my side, and now I needed to give her the same courtesy.

She continued. "His whole face scrunched up like he'd eaten bad sushi, so I point-blank asked him why he didn't want me to be better at helping his customers. He told me I couldn't organize my way out of a luxury shopping bag, that he'd never seen anyone with passion for his business like *you*."

Yep, still time for me to shut up. It was getting harder now, but I kept my peace.

Her frown melded into a straight line. "...Maybe if I spend more time with you, I'll understand you better. And maybe I'll become a better person, too."

A smile tickled my lips. I hadn't received an apology for what she'd done to me, but had Erica Holden admitted she wanted to meet me halfway? I thought she had. Perhaps in time, Erica would apologize even if she wasn't there yet. Grandma often said St. Petersburg wasn't built in a day.

~

The workday ended, and I trudged outside with a heaviness to my gait. Talking to Erica helped me understand her, but it didn't take away the burden within me.

I waited patiently. Aggie hadn't arrived yet. Erica emerged a couple of minutes later.

"Aggie's late for the pick up?" she asked with chuckle.

"Yeah, she's probably handling business at work." Or maybe a drive-thru caravan ensnared her again. The enticing scent of fresh fries from McDonald's was the downfall of mankind.

"C'mon. I'll give you a ride," Erica offered.

I hurried after and we strolled up to a dated BMW coupe. "This isn't your car," I remarked.

Usually, Erica drove a sensible Kia Rio.

She'd once admitted that the payments were much cheaper than her pink convertible, but still, it took me by surprise. "My dad lent the Beamer to me for the day. The Kia is in the shop for repairs."

I nodded with sympathy. Werewolves had increased strength and senses, but we couldn't magically fix broken cars. Rather sad, actually.

She hit the unlock button on her key. "Get in. I need to grab something out of the trunk."

I slid into the passenger seat, and she popped the back open. I expected her to return to the driver's seat, but she stood there.

"Everything okay?" I called.

When she didn't answer, I got out and joined her—only to see what stopped her cold.

In the trunk of Oliver Holden's car was an open trash bag. Stones and bones from the *zmee*'s altars lay inside.

"What is this shit?" she whispered.

I reached for one of the rocks but stopped. Would touching them trigger an attack? I motioned for Erica to keep her hands away as well.

"What's your dad doing with these?" I hissed.

"I don't know. Really." The shocked look on her face and truth lining her words made me back off.

"Fine. We need to call Thorn and—"

"No." Her voice was brittle with fear.

I wanted to shake her. "If you're dad has been carrying these around, that means he's the wolf minion who's been helping the Basilisk King."

"He'd never do that," she replied, but the doubt in her voice only strengthened.

I tried to sound rational. "He has every reason to, Erica. If the Basilisk King gets rid of me, he's one step closer to placing someone else in the position of alpha female. Your dad would do anything for you."

Those actions included putting a target on my back and sending basilisks to trash my belongings. It was rather clever of him to kick me below the belt.

Erica gave me a hard look then her head sharply turned toward The Bends. "You're right. He would."

I pulled out my phone, and an ocean of emotions passed over Erica's face: anguish, anger, then fear.

She quickly spoke. "I know we're still working on trusting each other, but I need to ask you for a favor. The kind of favor I don't deserve." She swallowed and wiped away a tear. "Give me a couple of hours to speak with my father."

"Excuse me?" My voice went hollow. She had to be kidding. Oliver had to answer for what he did.

"You know what will happen if Thorn and the pack is involved," she pleaded. "They're either kill him or he'll be banished and marked as a rogue."

I saw her side. I really did, except what he did was very wrong. I asked, "Wouldn't he deserve at least banishment for what he did?"

She squeezed her eyes shut. "Yes, he does and he'll pay a price for what he's done."

What price does she mean?

I took a deep breath. "Okay, say you do ask him to leave. Would he be willing to go if you tell him to do it?"

She thought briefly. "Yes, he'll do it or I will *end* him for shaming my family."

So there it was, and it chilled me because, if push came to shove, would my family have decided to end me for shaming them?

Erica added with a nod, "He'll go because Dad only loves one thing more than he loves power. He loves *me*."

As a sign of good faith, Erica took me with her to her father's home. My hands itched to call Thorn so the pack could sort out this matter. Could I truly trust a man, like Erica's father, who was willing to let basilisks roam the streets and attack innocent bystanders?

The need to exact justice melted away as we pulled up to a tiny, dark blue and beige house off 12th Street. It was cozy, but without the stench of wealth. Oliver had lost his beautiful home with its manicured lawn, drove around in an old BMW to save face, and now he'd lost his only daughter.

I waited in the car, imagining the conversation taking place in the house. Would Oliver storm out demanding the pack listen to him? I watched the door, expecting the knob to turn and for the Holdens from the past to show up.

But the sun dipped below the horizon and the only roar was from a TV through the open windows of a house across the street. After a while, the door opened, and only Erica trudged outside. Her eyes were red and her face puffy. She didn't speak until she got in the car.

"Thank you," she said thickly. "He'll be gone by midnight."

"And if he tries to return?"

I lowered my gaze to my purse in my lap to give her privacy as she broke into hard sobs.

For a brief time she didn't speak. Finally, she said, "Then I'll kill him myself."

CHAPTER 27

After a somber trip with Erica to her dad's home, she dropped me off at Barney's to wait for Aggie. I asked her to drop me off at home, but she didn't want me to be alone.

"The Basilisk King is still out there and you're a target," she whispered. "Don't worry about the rocks. I'm going to bury them in Double Trouble."

I merely nodded and watched her pull away.

Seeing the crowd at Barney's—with everyone going about their Thursday evening as if nothing was wrong, didn't settle my rattled thoughts. Was I wrong for not telling Thorn about this?

No, if there was one thing I could trust about Erica, she cared about the pack as much as she loved her Dad.

Aggie plodded over to me and offered me some chow. She wore khaki slacks and a business polo shirt. Her normally thick hair was tamed into a respectable bun.

"You doing okay?" she asked. "You look so sad."

"I could use some food." And a stiff drink, but Barney's didn't serve any liquor.

Aggie gave me a complimentary sandwich, as well as an oversized pickle, and I let my thoughts wander. On the one hand, I mused, at least no one would be setting traps with the pebbles, but the Basilisk King still threatened my grandma and me.

I considered my next step and remembered I had an unanswered question today: the foreign words I'd heard The Bends' wall utter.

I pulled out my smartphone and checked the words through a translation app. I got these results: *The strength of the goblin's chisel will strike his enemies.*

Whoa. I had no idea what those words meant and now wasn't the time to interrogate the goblin. The Bends still had secrets and I'd uncover them sooner or later.

Time passed. The early evening sun beat down on the asphalt and heat radiated toward the windows. The heat didn't hinder a mated pair of Cooper's hawks from hunting rodents along the Parkway. I focused on them to take my mind off my troubles.

Across the street from Barney's, an acreage lot left plenty of room for trees and wildlife. A female with a speckled beige and white breast scoped out her prey from the top of nearby oak and elm trees. Young rabbits skirted from one hiding place to another, unaware that they were being tracked. One rather plump cottontail in particular ventured toward the fence away from the tree's shade and the thicker clusters of fresh grass.

I took a sip of my drink, not wanting to look away. This was gonna be good. These birds didn't play when it came to hunting.

The closer the rabbit headed out in the open, the faster my heart sped. My fingers tingled from anticipation.

From above, the hawk's head lowered. The female's wings fluttered and she took flight, swooping left only to dive hard toward the rabbit. The female's prey flinched, calculating the safest path. The rabbit darted toward the tree line—only to stop hard as another hawk, the male, appeared from the other direction and flushed it back toward the fence.

With a shriek, the female swooped down and snatched the rabbit.

I pumped my fist and took a bite of my sandwich.

Well done, birds.

While I finished my meal, feeling a bit more at ease as I enjoyed the warmth of the wheat bread and turkey with Swiss cheese, the sequence of events played through my mind again and again. Werewolves often steered their prey into traps. Would such a plan work for prey such as the Basilisk King? But how?

And what kind of trap could hold a dude that could dematerialize at will?

Aggie slumped into the seat across from me. "You still look deep in thought."

I wanted to tell Aggie about what happened with Erica and Oliver, but I decided to deal with protecting my family.

"I asked Bill about letting me keep Grandma in his store room since he has powerful wards covering the whole place."

"I'm sure he said no."

I inhaled a homemade chip. "Actually, he agreed."

"Be careful, Nat. He's gonna want something out of this."

"Already considered that."

Aggie crossed her arms. "I'm proud of you."

"Huh?"

"Since you faced the Basilisk King, you're a lot more flexible and on the defensive. That's good."

"Every good defense requires offense though."

She slowly nodded. "Last I recall, the basilisks dragged your football team's ass up and down the field."

I swallowed past the fear welling in my stomach. The feeling of the basilisks overwhelming me rose, but I drop-kicked the feeling away.

"The magic I used to dispatch them worked well—but the execution was flawed," I surmised.

Aggie stole one of my chips. "I thought magic wasn't an option."

My gaze flicked away from the street to Aggie. "Magic is a double-bladed knife, but perhaps I can learn to wield it properly."

"From who? Are you still in contact with the chick who taught you in the first place?"

"No, I haven't heard from Tamara in months." I shook my head vehemently. "Tamara was willing to sacrifice herself to get what she wanted. She played in deadly magic, and I don't vibe well with that."

Aggie nodded. "What options do you have left?"

I opened my cell phone and shot a text to the one person who might have an answer.

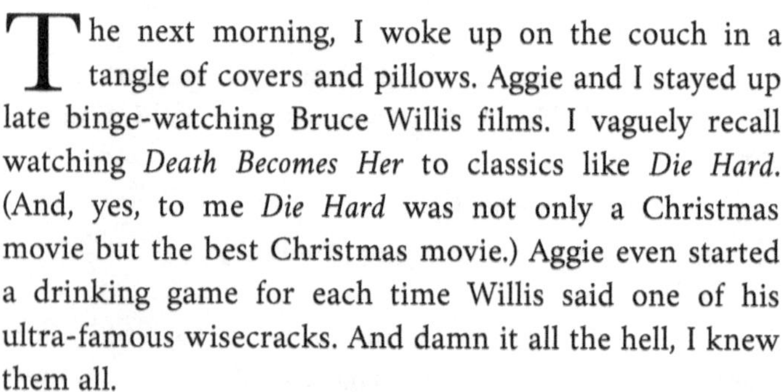

The next morning, I woke up on the couch in a tangle of covers and pillows. Aggie and I stayed up late binge-watching Bruce Willis films. I vaguely recall watching *Death Becomes Her* to classics like *Die Hard*. (And, yes, to me *Die Hard* was not only a Christmas movie but the best Christmas movie.) Aggie even started a drinking game for each time Willis said one of his ultra-famous wisecracks. And damn it all the hell, I knew them all.

Now that I thought about it, she did it on purpose to make me forget my troubles.

I still hadn't told anyone about Oliver's actions and I missed Thorn, but I understood why he remained at my grandmother's house. He loved her as much as I did.

My phone dinged and I unfurled myself from my covers to pick up the phone.

Looked like I got my reply to my question last night: *Meet me at the Four Winds Roadside Eatery at ten.*

"Who's that?" Aggie asked from underneath her blankets. She had a tiny hole for air.

"I asked for help and I got it." My phone read a few minutes past eight AM. "Want some breakfast?"

She peeked from under the covers. "You know how to make a girl happy with pillow talk."

I laughed and threw a pillow at her. "Here's some pillow talk for ya. You got an hour to wash your hair and get dressed."

"Ugh, if food didn't complete me, I wouldn't bother washing my hair for you."

A little over an hour later, we arrived at the Four Winds Roadside Eatery. The place was a supernatural, family-owned business run by wind witches. As I'd grown up, I never enjoyed the Eatery's "rustic" charm, but my family loved the generous portion sizes. The unusual and under-cooked meals made me cross this place off my tolerable list a long time ago.

Burn the bacteria away, I say.

We entered the restaurant, weaving around the tables of humans and supernaturals eating their chow. With its worn white tables and mix of red and green seats, the décor in the Eatery bordered on eclectic. Enchanted paintings lined the walls for the supernatural customers. The old television in the far corner wasn't as appealing as the painting of the Viking raid on the village to my right. The rest of the wall space had questionable shelves that held jars, vases, and containers full of who-knew-what.

Aggie spotted the person I wanted to meet: Brenna.

"Where's Nick?" Aggie asked.

"I didn't contact Nick. I texted her directly," I explained.

Her mouth formed an "oh" as we headed up to the counter.

"Want to eat first?" Brenna asked.

"Sure, let's get a table and we can chat while we wait for our grub," I said.

Brenna directed us to a four-seater table in the far corner. From an enchanted pocket in her purse, she withdrew a beautiful wand and tapped the edge of the table.

"What did you do?" Aggie asked.

Brenna slid into the closest seat. "I masked us from the human ears nearby."

"Perfect." I took the seat next to her and Aggie sat across from me.

A gray-haired waitress with a generous waist sidled up to us with a grin. "Well, good morning, you rays of sunshine!"

"Hey, Gertie!" Aggie said, clutching the menu with glee. "Your kitchen is cooking up the good stuff."

Gray-Haired Gertie, the eldest of the three sisters who owned the Eatery, returned a grin. "You want the usual, hon? Three Hairy Navel specials?"

Just hearing the words *hairy* and *navel* together never seemed appetizing. Even when I was a kid. I couldn't shake the image of picking bellybutton lint from my teeth.

My hand rose. "None for me. I'll take a stack of bacon—burn it beyond recognition."

Gertie pulled out her notepad. "Okay, one Hairy Navel and some charred piggies. And you?" she asked Brenna.

The earth witch took in the menu quickly. "A hot bowl of root vegetable soup sounds good. What kind of tea do you have?"

"Sweet tea?" Gertie supplied.

Brenna made a sour face. "Sacrilege. That's not the tea my mama makes."

The wind witch clicked her tongue and winked at us. "We got packets of herbal tea from the sampler set at Shop-Rite. One of those should work."

Brenna opened her mouth and shut it again. I shrugged and the earth witch shook her head with amusement.

With our orders done and Gertie gone, Aggie crossed her arms and glanced at both of us. "So why are we meeting?" she asked.

"I sent Nick a text last night and asked him for Brenna's information," I offered. "I have questions and she's the best one to answer them."

"About what? I know as much about the Basilisk King as Nick," Brenna replied.

I drew in a deep breath and considered my words before I spoke. "I've faced the Basilisk King once, and another confrontation is coming soon."

I told them about my tentative plan to deal with the Basilisk King, and I definitely piqued their interest.

I continued with, "I was hoping you'd be kind enough to help me master the fundamental exchange."

Aggie's head cocked to the side. "Master the what?"

Brenna slowly nodded. "You're asking about a thing even great spellcasters haven't mastered." She regarded Aggie with patience. "Magic in many ways is like the law for the conservation of energy. You can't pull the stuff out of nowhere. There has to be a source."

Not far from me, the earth witch wand on the table shifted. Was something wrong?

Brenna kept talking. "If you want to protect yourself again, I suggest you find a power source to tap into—other than using yourself."

"Where does she find those?" Aggie asked.

"Good question." The witch rested her head on her hand. "You need a relic that emanates power and those are rare. Like Hotep's Rod, Caprini's Grand Crown, and—"

"—I work at a supernatural flea market," I said with a chuckle. "I might have one of those if you had some extra time to help me find one at the flea market."

"We need to get rid of the Basilisk King before more people are hurt," Brenna said. "And well, I've got nothing else better to do since I'm job hunting."

Aggie jumped into the conversation. "You got cashier skills?"

"I don't think Brenna wants to drive all the way from New York to our small town for a job—"

"How much is the pay?" She cocked a grin, and I gave up. Seemed like everybody wanted to hang out in Jersey.

Gertie brought our food while Aggie talked about the open positions at Barney's. Somehow, with a mouth full of food, she gabbed about the benefits and the family-like team she wanted to build.

From between the salt and pepper shakers, the oak wand twitched again then shifted a couple of inches closer to me. I couldn't resist staring. When Brenna brushed her fingers against the wood, the weapon quivered.

"That's not a standard wand," I breathed.

"No, it's custom," she said. "I made it myself."

I nodded, quite impressed. Most spellcasters acquired their wands from a seller, but an adept witch could craft their own.

She must've caught my interest and grinned. "This one is crafted from an oak tree on my family's farm outside of

Charleston. It lost a branch in a storm years ago, and the wood called to me to make it useful again." She plucked the wand and offered it to me. Before I took it, I hesitated.

Wow, she trusts me. That was a lot, considering she barely knew me.

"You handle it with respect," she said with approval. "My daddy taught me how to use a wood burner and craft wands. One of my fondest gifts was an ancient carving set."

"It's gorgeous." I ran my fingers against the wand, marveling the bare wood. Brenna's loving hand had scraped off the bark and she'd wrapped dried ivy and twine from one end to the other. Nothing about it was brittle though, it melded perfectly into my palm the same way it must have fit hers. Unable to resist, I drew the wand to my nose and inhaled. A cacophony of scents crossed my nose—wind fluttering through ivy scaling up a brick house toward the sky to vibrant peppermint leaves ready for plucking. The earth rose to greet me and a smile broke out on my face.

"How come you don't use this as your day-to-day wand?" I asked, recalling that she carried a much plainer one when she'd helped us a couple of days ago.

Brenna said, "It's precious and I'd hate to have this wand damaged during spellcasting. Tapping into the earth is difficult."

"Yes, magic is beautiful, but it's also frightening." I returned her wand. "There's a harmonious symphony here and you play the notes with ease."

"I have a wand, but you're an instrument capable of playing any symphony." The seriousness in Brenna's gaze made me pause. "If you're serious, you'll learn to play. But each time you cast a spell, it might be your final performance."

She took a sip of her tea, made a face, and pushed the

cup away. I supposed the wind witches' idea of tea didn't fit her Southern standards. "We'll find you a source. Even if you have to drag Fulcrum's Arm Chair into battle."

I didn't like any of this but resigned myself to doing what I had to do.

~

After breakfast, we split up to get as much done as possible. Aggie hurried to my parents' house to fetch Grandma while I accompanied Brenna to find a power source. When the earth witch pulled up to my place to pick me up, I wasn't surprised to see she drove a sunshine-yellow, electric-powered VW bug.

"This is quite a car," I remarked as I settled into the comfortable cloth seat.

"It's my mom's car. After I got back from overseas, I needed a new ride, but everything on the lots near my parents' farm spewed noxious fumes all over the damn place." She started the car. "Let's get to business, shall we?"

She pulled out her beautiful oak wand, brought the glorious twig up to her lips and whispered to it—so low even I couldn't hear. Then she placed the wand on the dashboard underneath the rearview mirror. The wand shimmied as a gust of cinnamon swept through the car. Then like a dial on a compass, the wand swayed to the right, pointing south.

"Southward we go then, my love," she sang to the wand.

I quirked a smile.

We drove south along the Parkway, back toward South Toms River. Flea markets, stores, and shops dotted our path. A majority of them, like Elizabeth's Finer Things and McCormick's Antiques, belonged to humans. The wand continued to navigate us to keep going. More shops appeared, including a truck stop and Dollar Mart. I wanted to ask her if we'd have to go all the way to Boston, but the wand suddenly jerked to the right.

"There's something that way?" I asked.

"You better believe it. Hold on."

We almost passed a tiny store off a shopping complex, but Brenna pulled hard to the right to hit the next exit off the Parkway. The car's tires shrieked on the sharp curve, but we managed to veer onto a street that led us back to the shop.

Once we arrived, I peered closer, having passed this place countless times. Yet I'd never noticed this shop. Wouldn't I have raided this joint during one of my shopping binges? The rest of the shopping center was nondescript. Just another outlet on the Parkway. The outside was updated with a fresh coat of clay-colored beige and sandstone added an upscale touch to the walkway between the stores. A few cars filled the lot in front of a coffee spot and floral shop, but there weren't any cars near the dated storefront at the far end.

I picked up my phone and searched for the address for the shop in question. "1692. 1694. 1696. And…" I squinted. "1701." I harrumphed. "An odd-numbered shop on the even side of the road."

"Odd indeed," Brenna said with a cheesy grin. "The place is enchanted."

"How come I never saw it before?"

"Some places aren't meant to be found unless you seek them."

I nodded, recalling how the *zmee* had said something similar about the *Huldrefolk* bells.

We got out of the car, and I said, "Bill's gonna be irked we got more competition down the street."

"There will always be competition on well-travelled

roads," she replied. "Vendors go where they find the customers."

I nodded. Recalling what Mevelyn had said about the fairy path having the same effect.

The storefront was barely as wide as my stretched-out arms. Chipped red bricks lined the walls of a single-story building with a cornerstone that was too faded to read. Brenna opened the heavy wooden door, causing the bells attached to ring. A thick haze of bergamot and lavender crossed my nose. What kind of place was this?

I stepped into the shop and paused on the threshold, my breath caught in my lungs.

"Whoa," I murmured as I took in a shop full of feathers. Next to the door, five-foot-long obsidian feathers were arranged in a fan-like formation for display. The sunshine's rays hit the feathers and the light speckled across the floor.

The store wasn't well lit, but a few lamps here and there illuminated the space. Beyond the entrance, other shelves held more feathers, each individual one placed on a wooden stand to prop up the merchandise. I took in everything in awe. Every color imaginable filled the shop: jade-green feathers, rainbow, another dotted with black to burnt-orange.

A highlighted, white-hot feather in a small display case smoldered and wisps of smoke rose from the top. While to my right, another feather in a small, gilded cage wiggled about as if still attached to its owner.

Should I have called this place a "feathery?"

"C'mon, Nat!" Brenna urged me from deeper in the store. "What you want is back here."

I weaved around the circular display case in the middle of the store to head toward the back. More tall shelves gave the shop a maze-like feel as I passed by zebra-striped feathers and others that glowed with an unnatural radium green. (Were those radioactive?)

"Where are you?" I called.

"Keep going." She chuckled.

Beyond the point that any normal store should've ended, I finally reached the sales counter in the back. The counter was covered in a stone surface, polished so that it gleamed. Above the counter, a shiny metal sign read: *Gray Folk Feathers*. There wasn't much room for a cash register—there wasn't one—with all the clutter of small boxes, wrapping materials, and stacks of papers. Behind the counter, a spindly gentleman, with large, caved-in eyes and wide shoulders stared back at me. His clean-shaven face shimmered from a glamour and a shiver passed over me as light gray feathers danced behind the magical mask.

Beyond him, a single doorway headed into blackness.

"Natalya, this is Oswald, the shop clerk." Brenna leaned against the corner as if she'd spent the last couple of hours chatting away with him.

Probably did with an establishment as big as this one.

"She's shorter than I expected," Oswald said in a reed-thin voice. "How can someone so tall on the inside be so insignificant on the outside?"

My eyebrow rose. If this dude wanted repeat business, he needed to work on his customer service skills.

"Like I told you a bit ago, Nat is looking for a power source. A relic."

He nodded sagely and shuffled to the right, then he stooped and reached for something below the counter. His glamour weakened and the creature behind the counter resembled a human-sized griffin. The bird's black beak fluttered, making a faint *click-clack* sound. When Oswald caught me staring too closely, his obsidian eyes narrowed in my direction.

I really needed to mind my own business.

"Here's three possibilities you might like." The griffin arranged three feathers in front of two piles of rolled-up parchment.

The peacock feather on the far left appeared ordinary and insignificant, but a peculiar odor of fermented seafood wafted from it. I turned to the one in the middle, an iridescent, curved feather from a quetzal. Blots of a brilliant ultramarine formed a gradient to a tip with flecks of yellow and green. I had to tear my gaze away from the large feather to take in the third—a tiny one from a black hummingbird wing with streaks of dark-green and brown. The minuscule feather could fit in the middle of my palm.

"How much for the small one?" I asked. I could stick it in my pocket and be done with it.

"Overpriced and powerful. Good choice." Oswald named a price with too many zeros and I managed to keep a straight face.

I even glanced at Brenna and she shrugged.

"Do you know how much I get paid—never mind. How about the one that doesn't smell like fish left out too long?" I asked Oswald.

"That one is more reasonably priced at a hundred dollars!" he said proudly.

Sure, reasonable in an alternate universe where I could print cold hard cash.

"I'll take the quetzal feather, then." Might as well resign myself to curbing my compulsive shopping habits anyway. An emptier pocketbook helped.

To my surprise, the griffin rang up my order using a smartphone with a credit card dongle attached. He offered to put the feather in a knapsack, but I declined.

As I picked up the vibrant quetzal feather, my purchase briefly zapped me with a static electricity charge.

"Will it always do that?" I asked him.

"Yes, you should get used to that. The best tools aren't the easiest to use."

"Umm, okay."

We left the store and emerged outside to a bright afternoon sun.

"Wow, he's a peach," I couldn't resist saying.

Brenna said, "The Gray Feather Folk never lie—which also means they say the first thing on their mind."

"Maybe that's why the parking lot's so empty." I snorted. "He should hire some goblins and trolls as clerks. Most of my customers don't appreciate honesty."

"So you've got your power source now," Brenna said. "What's next?"

My small smile spread wider, and the feather in my hand shimmered under the summer sun. "We round up the troops and go basilisk hunting."

CHAPTER 28

A humid breeze fanned my face as I slid into Brenna's hot car. Icy fear sliced through me. I'd be facing the Basilisk King soon.

The prospects of not facing him alone still didn't lessen my fears. I would have to confront him again, and he'd probably be pissed.

"Do you want me to ask Nick to come help?" she asked.

"Not unless you know he's free. Nick has done enough for the pack." I rubbed the top of my phone, considering what I could do. Asking the pack for help wouldn't be easy.

"The power of the pack lies in its members working together," Thorn had said. He was right. I had to reach out and gather the people who made me want to fight harder. Be stronger.

And if they couldn't stand with me, I'd still stand with them if the time came.

After my little trip with Brenna to fetch the quetzal feather, I needed her help to make a couple more trips around town. Even with Sedgewick trailing after me in his car.

"Do you want me to get rid of him?" Brenna asked. "I

could curse him with poison oak on his privates. He'll be too busy scratching his balls to pay you any mind."

I shuddered, then said with as much seriousness as I could, "He might come in handy later. Let him play the enforcer for now."

We stopped at Archie's to warn Jake and Harold. The place was still under construction from the car crash.

"We're going to draw the Basilisk King out and corner him," I told Jake.

He listened to my plan then replied, "Just let me know where you need me to be and I'll be there."

Even Harold gave me a thumbs-up from the kitchen. I was grateful for their support.

I stopped at a couple more houses to face the pack members. A few didn't give me a warm welcome and others didn't answer the door when they spotted the warlock spying on me from his car. Sedgewick boldly waved to one family and they shut the door in my face.

So be it.

I still asked Brenna to take me from one house to the next.

"What does Sedgewick expect you to do?" Brenna asked, clearly more irritated by his presence than I was.

"He smells that we're planning a confrontation. He wants to keep the peace and I respect that," I said.

"So why doesn't he come right out and stop you?"

"He'll only do that if I show my hand, but the thing is, this card game hasn't started yet."

Some folks weren't home, so I stopped at a popular hangout, the Last Mark Bar and Grill off Dover Road. The likelihood of finding a couple pack members enjoying happy hour was high.

The parking lot was semi-full, typical for a Friday afternoon.

I hurried inside and ignored the bad smells. Underneath the layer of cheesy fries and over-cooked hot winds, this place was like any other tavern you'd encounter. Customers sat and drank at a long bar in the middle. Along the sides in the no-smoking area, not that it was really no-smoking since smoke spread everywhere, a werewolf here and there ate dinner at the small tables.

I scanned the crowd and spotted pack members. Many worked at the local mill. I walked past the bar and paused, seeing Rex and his younger brother Melvin in a booth in the back. Only Melvin sipped from a half-empty glass of beer.

"Hey, Rex!" Winston the owner sneered at him from behind the bar. "I'm not paying you on weekends to sit on your ass!"

With a glum expression, Rex slid out of the booth and headed behind the bar.

Even over the classic rock music, I could hear Winston chastising Rex. "You said you're low on cash and gotta take care of your own. Then act like it and scrub them toilets before the band comes at eight."

Damn, that was harsh.

The other patrons ignored the words, but the shame floating off Rex even hit me, too. I sighed and retreated. Was Rex's foul attitude due to his family's plight? I had no idea they were in bad shape. The pack took care of its own, but I knew Rex would never accept our charity.

He'd rather vent his frustrations on the rest of us.

By midafternoon, I finished notifying pack members and Brenna took me back to The Bends. I had one last person to contact on my list. The phone rang twice before the call went through.

"Hey, I didn't expect to hear from you so soon," Jocelyn

said. "What's up?" The sounds of customers around her faded as she moved to a quieter location.

"The pack will be making a move on the Basilisk King. Out of courtesy, I wanted you to know so you'll stay indoors. Also, you should batten down the hatches since there might be basilisks running around."

"Hmmm. How soon is this going down?" she asked.

"Tonight. Tomorrow. This guy isn't reliable—but we'll do everything we can to clean house tonight."

"Understood. We'll lock up tight then."

Jocelyn ended the call, then Brenna and I headed to the back dock of The Bends. A few pack members had showed up.

I greeted everyone. "Everything good?"

They nodded and their hesitation bounced against my skull. Time to rally the troops.

"Like Thorn told you in the group text," I said, "the Basilisk King will be coming to this spot. We're gathering the pack to end this tonight. Any questions?"

No one had any so Brenna and I headed inside. The rest of the Stravinskys waited inside The Bends. Grandma sat in one of the work chairs, knitting a pair of pink, child-size mittens while Aggie sat at her feet.

I approached them. "Any problems?"

"There's been nothing all day," Aggie reported. "Just Bill complaining about your grandma waving at the customers."

I chuckled.

Aggie drew her errant hair back into a ponytail. "I thought it was cute. Who doesn't want free adoration?"

"Apparently, not Bill." I glanced around, not seeing my mate. "Where's Thorn?"

"He's outside. Grandma wanted some fresh air so he

wanted to be a sentry. Now he's running the perimeter to see if he can spot that bastard first."

A swallow got stuck in my throat. "I don't believe we'll see the Basilisk King coming, but the best defense is a good offense."

The afternoon turned to evening. Soon, the sun dipped below the horizon and the employees left. Not long after, Bill waltzed into the back office.

"I should be charging you folks to mill about on my property," he belted out. "One of my chairs is broken."

"It was broken already, Bill," I groaned.

He stood in the middle of the room, and everyone ignored him. "Now it's even more broken."

"You deal with this every day?" Brenna mouthed to me.

I shrugged half-heartedly and left the back office. This time, I found Thorn in the backyard. A large tawny wolf faced the trees, his gaze focused on any movement in the forest beyond the market. I strolled to him and sat. A breeze rustled the trees and Thorn's fur swayed with the wind. If our enemies weren't chasing after us, today would've been a great day for a picnic. I leaned against him and he did the same.

After Thorn disappeared five years ago, I was left alone, but eventually, he did return and now we faced mortal danger again.

"Are we doing the right thing?" I whispered.

He chuffed in response and nudged me with his nose.

"I wish I was as confident as you are." I took a deep breath, and pressed my face to his flank to inhale everything that was *him*. He was alive and I'd fight the Basilisk King a thousand times to make sure he stayed that way.

The shadows deepened, and I left his side to head to the dock. Erica joined me there.

"You okay?" I whispered to her.

"No," she admitted, "I won't be okay for a long time, but I'm better than I could be."

I drew a deep sigh. "I wish I knew when that bastard is gonna make an appearance," I whispered.

"You and me both. I gotta pee sooner or later."

I laughed and the sound felt good, almost making me forget that we were waiting for someone who was quite likely going to try to kill us.

After a while, the clock ticked past eight o'clock. The others chatted in hushed voices in the back office while we stared into the deepening gloom. Would the Basilisk King unleash his minions in hordes? Would they surround us like before or draw us out with a trunk? It was hard not to dwell on all the possible ways things could go badly.

My nerves skittered back and forth between settled and frayed. The Stravinskys grew louder, their laughter over Aunt Olga losing a hand of bridge filtering to the dock where I sat with my back against the wall.

The goblin blade lay near my feet, silent and unmoving. I brushed my fingertips from one end to the other. Now that I had an idea of what I'd face, hopefully, I wouldn't drain the feather and kill myself in the process.

Suddenly, Grandma Lasovskaya appeared on the dock. Mom trailed after her along with Dad and Aggie.

"What's she doing?" I asked.

"She said she wanted some fresh air." Mom clasped her hands together with worry.

Others clustered onto the dock as Grandma shuffled up to me. "May I borrow the feather?" she asked.

"Umm, sure." How did she know I had it? Could she sense it? And most importantly, why did she want it?

I plucked the feather from underneath my blouse. With my feather in hand, she ambled down the steps and headed to the backyard. Thorn immediately rose from his guarding spot and trotted over to her. He circled her twice and whimpered.

She gently rubbed the top of his massive head. "You've done well," she said gently in Russian.

All around me, others held their breath, while Mom lingered on the staircase.

I stood and hurried to the staircase.

"Nat, wait…" Brenna whispered.

I ran up to Grandma but paused when she stooped over, murmuring magical words as she tapped a purple wildflower.

The strangest sight occurred. The harsh scent of ozone filled the air as the wildflower darkened to deep maroon before the petals glowed vibrant white. Then another nearby flower, closer to the tree line lit up, then another into the woods. I took in the path of glowing wildflowers as far as I could see until the trees obscured their lights.

I marveled at my grandmother's wit. Someday she'd have to share her secrets with me.

With her job done, Grandma shuffled back to The Bends and returned the feather to me.

"The mouse is hungry and wants cheese. Now, he'll come," she said to me with a mischievous wink.

Now that Grandma tossed a proverbial flare into the air, everyone scrambled to a better place to fight. Will jumped into Thorn's SUV while Karey waited in my Nissan with Mevelyn, Grace, and Dione. The Stravinsky clan and pack members disappeared into The Bends—only to emerge minutes later in their true form, beautiful wolves with coats ranging from midnight-black to deep brown. Nick passed by the wolves and joined Thorn on the lawn. He didn't bother changing his attire this time.

I should've warned the wizard he might want protection from all the goo that was about to fly everywhere.

The last one to leave the back door was Brenna. The earth witch came out wearing a shimmering golden robe, her chin-length hair slicked back.

The goblin blade trembled in my hand. Was it time? At the farthest point in the woods, a wildflower winked out. Then another. Closer.

The wolves assembled a loose formation in the backyard while my friends stood their ground on the back dock. Nick's grand white staff glowed brilliant red.

The wolves crept forward, their claws digging into the hard soil. Father's back hunched and the muscles in his back legs tensed. Near the front of the formation, Erica bared her teeth and growled.

The wolf within me strained to fight. If I didn't have weapons of my own, I would've joined them.

Yes, come play with us, you son-of-a-bitch.

I glanced around. Everyone was ready. Bill was nowhere to be seen, but he was the least of my problems. Let him hide. As long as he kept Grandma safe inside, protected by his wards.

Not far from me, Brenna shut the back door to The Bends and whispered, "May Mother Earth continue to bless us with breath."

With a nod, I said a prayer of my own. I didn't want God *suffocating* anybody today. The goblin blade grew heavy. The letter opener's head lengthened to form a lance.

I turned to see Brenna grinning with glee as she extended her wand to the sky. Fireflies shot from the tip like tiny missiles and the fluttering streaks rained down on the trees, illuminating the forest floor.

"Incoming!" she yelled. "I'll slow them down."

Dark figures approached. Bird-like shrieks and squawks grew louder. The treetops shook, then branches shot down, spearing basilisks as they sped through. The wolves shifted to the oncoming attack.

Suddenly, the basilisks spilled through the trees like muddied flood waters. Thorn and the rest of the pack slammed into the brunt of the wave. They tore at the basilisks' throats with their razorlike fangs. I entered the melee swinging hard. Bright lights blossomed across the space. But there were far too many. The basilisks gushed from the trees, creeping out of the bushes and clamoring down from the branches. Many of them were speared along the upper branches, but more and more came.

A plague of basilisks.

I never had a chance to catch my breath. When I cleaved an oncoming basilisk in two, another pair took its place. I caught the whiff of one trying to leap onto my back, but Thorn snatched it by the leg and flung the creature against The Bends. Instead of falling to the ground with a hard thud, the wood siding groaned and sucked the attacker inside with an audible slurp.

Now that wasn't expected. How The Bends didn't have trouble digesting them.

More basilisks spilled past us and the wolves gave chase. The Bends held the line. When basilisks tried to scamper up the walls toward the glass windows, shutters slammed over the openings. Approaching basilisks were sucked into the place like ships sinking into turbulent waters.

The number of basilisks far outnumbered us. I whistled hard. Time for phase two. The pack concentrated their efforts from the frontal assault to clearing a path for me to reach the cars.

In the parking lot, the headlights for the SUV and Nissan turned on. I broke out into a hard run, leaping over basilisks to race toward the cars. Basilisks danced about, scratching and nipping at my heels. I extended the lance in front of me, stabbing and flicking at any bird-snake daring to get in my way.

At the edge of the parking lot, I pivoted to glance back at the battlefield. In the middle of the fray, I caught a glimpse of Thorn. He paused and watched me leave.

"I love you," I whispered.

Whether he heard me or not didn't matter. I had a job to do, and Thorn would stay behind to protect Grandma just as Nick would do whatever he could to protect me for the second part of the plan.

A herd of basilisks jumped in front of me, forcing me back into the moment. The ground opened up. Brenna materialized on top of the truck and jerked her hands to the right. The ground turned to mud and the basilisks sank deep into a boggy pit.

I made it to the SUV and hurried to the passenger's side. Immediately, I realized the lance wouldn't fit in the front seat. Nick and Brenna materialized in the backseat—right as a boulder smashed into the side of the Nissan.

Shit, I'm gonna be eating TV dinners for a while.

Nick rolled down the window. "Give me that."

I passed him the lance, and he took hold, guiding it in through the window in a seemingly impossible feat. He'd probably find a place for the weapon in that super coat of his.

I jumped in the car and cringed as more boulders—the size of big screen TVs—rained down and slammed into my enemies.

"Was that you guys?" I yelled into the backseat.

"Definitely not me," Brenna said with wide eyes. "Those rocks...they're alive."

Will peeled out of the parking lot, darting out of the

way from a large rock that rolled eastward and headed back to the troll mart across the Parkway.

Looked like Kramkar wanted to kick some slimy basilisk ass, too.

As we roared northbound up the Parkway, I bumped my fist and roared, "Get 'em, Kramkar!"

This early on a Friday night, there was traffic on the Parkway and I didn't want to stay here for long. As expected, the unceasing current of basilisks stuck to our tails and formed a rip-tide of goo down the highway. Cars swerved and honked to dodge the obstacles.

From behind us, a vermillion light blossomed and grew brighter.

"What's that?" Will breathed. The car engine roared as he leaned on the accelerator. "Is that the Basilisk King?"

Nick glanced back. "It's Sedgewick. He's mopping up our rears to keep the humans safe, but he won't be able to cover us forever."

"Yeah, I need you to gun it until we get to Highway 28. Then we need to head northwest," I ordered Will.

"Where are we going?" he asked. "Do the nymphs know in case we lose them?"

"They know where we're going," I said smoothly. "We're heading to Sourland Mountain Preserve."

∼

As we reached the outskirts of the wildlife preserve, my heart threatened to stop from beating so fast. But, then again, wasn't fear a good thing? Didn't that mean I was still alive?

I glanced out the window and recalled the unnatural chill from before. I didn't dare open myself to feel for the fairy path this time. She was closer now. I didn't have to go far.

We roared into the park through the southern entrance. The park closed about an hour ago, but the spellcasters in the car broke through the gates. We pulled into the empty parking lot and spilled out of the car.

"How much time do we have before they arrive?" Will asked. "I tried to pull ahead as far as I could."

"Not much," I said with a sigh. "He could've called them back to their trunks and brought them here."

The nymphs pulled up next to us. Mevelyn, Grace, and Dione jumped out.

"Get in the car with Karey," I said firmly to Will.

"What?" his mouth dropped.

Nick passed me the goblin blade from his coat. I didn't have long to get Will out of here. As I wrapped my fingers around my weapon, I told Will, "Karey's got a kid and you have to make sure she returns home."

"Thorn made me promise I'd protect you," he said firmly.

"And now I'm here and I'm your alpha. I'm ordering you to make sure Karey returns home to see my niece." I added a push to my words.

Will's jaw twitched, but he bowed his head and slid into the Nissan's passenger seat. I watched the car disappear back to the entrance.

Mevelyn approached me. "Time to hold the line, Sister Wolf?"

I nodded to her.

Sweat formed on my brow, but not from the June heat, but rather from panic threatening to crash through my bones.

She is close, the wolf within me whined.

I clutched the goblin blade, still in its lance form, as the breeze shifted from eastbound to westward.

"He's coming," Brenna warned. "Y'all ready?"

The nymphs ran to the trees. I'd yet to see them fight, but more than anything, I hoped they stayed safe.

"The wolves had a tough time." I glanced at the spellcasters. "You have enough gas in your tanks to help me drive them northward?"

Brenna's smile deepened and the sparkles in her hair glinted. "The Basilisk King isn't the only person affected by the fairy path. Get going, Nat. We'll be fine."

The basilisk horde emerged from the trees to the south and raced across the parking lot. I turned and sprinted to the north.

Behind me, great flashes of light and explosions filled the air. The spellcasters would hold them over, but I knew they wouldn't be able to hold the line for long. I ran as hard as I could. Up ahead, I spotted the nymphs. They'd enchanted the trees to create a living dam. As I approached, the trees dipped. I leaped over them and they stretched up again.

More time bought.

The rocks jutting from the ground and the upward incline hindered me, but I climbed from rock-to-rock, knowing that sooner or later the basilisks would catch up with me, and in turn the Basilisk King would have me within his reach.

Soon, I caught the distinct crunch of breaking branches. The basilisks' jubilant squawks and shrieks bounced among the trees. I paused and glanced over my shoulder—only to feel the strange sensation of someone brushing their hand down my cheek. The touch left a burn on my skin, and I growled in pain.

"Natalya…" a man's deep voice intoned.

The Basilisk King was near.

With a sense of urgency, I climbed higher up Sourland Mountain. The top wasn't steep. It wasn't even a quarter of a mile high, but my destination was there. The final confrontation wasn't far from where I stood.

I leaped up another rock, and the first basilisk caught my leg. I fell hard and they jumped in for the kill. Without hesitation this time, I clutched the feather under my shirt. I murmured the words to cast a spell, seeing the turbulent fires swirling in my head rise to reality. All around me, basilisks burned, many exploding before falling away. Covered in new scratches, I stood again and made my escape.

The spell only bought me a few precious seconds. Farther below, the Basilisk King walked toward me, flicking his hands to direct more trunks to appear and disappear. His movements were calm and precise.

Finally, I reached the summit. A flat area where I could see the rest of the preserve. The waning moon winked from behind thick clouds until my mother moon appeared again.

I took two steps before I was forced to my knees with a rush.

She Who Always Walked the Path had me now, but I wasn't the only one she'd snatched.

Behind me, the Basilisk King grunted, and I caught the sound of him falling and his head hitting the ground to kneel before her.

Relief filled me.

You're stuck with me now, I thought triumphantly.

It didn't take long for the sensations from that strange night to take my breath away. A great weight pressed my shoulders down and forced my forehead to the cold rock. In my mind, I retreated again to that dark place as the muscles in my legs tightened and my jaw hurt from biting down so hard.

But through the darkness, I laughed and laughed.

Who's the king now? I thought.

The essence of She Who Always Walks the Path called to the Basilisk King first.

You've culled too many prey, Erpetó Vasiliá, the paper-thin voice whispered. *How dare you soil my path? You will worship me until I see fit to release you.*

The lilting voice held me to the ground, but I caught the Basilisk King's footsteps as he was drawn to walk past me then he disappeared to the north.

I waited, knowing I was next.

The tug came fast and hard, dragging me up like a pup by the scruff. My feet shuffled forward, and I gasped for breath.

You will run in reverence, Wolf, the feminine voice whispered.

I shuddered as the wolf beneath my skin quaked. Fur burst along my backside and I hunched over as my bones broke and reshaped themselves. My true form emerged. I collapsed again amid the vice-like sensation of a heavy metal bracelet looping around my neck.

Sleep now, Wolf.

The last thing I heard before I fell into slumber was Diana the Huntress saying, *At the return of the full moon, you'll hunt with my dogs for all eternity.*

CHAPTER 29

I wasn't sure how long I dreamed or whether I dreamed at all. I only recalled the weight of the collar around my neck and the chill from rocks pushing into one side of my body while the sun warmed the other.

The limbo of time grew murky as I caught the sound of light footsteps. It was night again. Had the Huntress come for me again? Yet instead of rising to join her pack of dogs, I felt the collar on my neck give way. The force holding me against the ground lifted, and Mevelyn knelt beside me.

A gust of wind flowed through me, bringing the voice of the Huntress, *Your surrender is sacred and irrevocable.*

At first, I thought this message was for me, but as I blinked to stare at the woman beside me I realized Mevelyn was the recipient.

With a wistful smile, the old nymph pressed her fingertips on my eyes to close them.

The wind whispered, *May your sacrifice prove fruitful.*

As darkness folded over me again, Mevelyn replied, "It shall. Sister Wolf still has work to do."

When I came to again, it wasn't night but day. The

midday sun bathed my naked back where I lay in a field. The nearby rocks signaled I was still in the preserve, but what had happened to everyone? What about the nymph?

How much time had passed, and more importantly, what happened to Mevelyn? My thoughts were jumbled, but I had enough sense to notice someone left something next to me: a neatly folded pile of clothes with a letter opener on top. My goblin blade.

CHAPTER 30

Again and again, after my time in the clutches of She Who Always Walks the Path, I kept thinking about sacrifices and every time someone else had put their lives on the line for me.

My friends. My family. My grandma. Now I had a debt to Mevelyn, too.

No one could reach me for more than a week.

Thorn and the pack were kept from searching for me through Mevelyn's urgent instructions to Nick and Brenna.

"She didn't want the rest of our pack to be captured," Thorn explained to me that hazy Sunday. "Karey told me they reached you the first time through their pacification rituals. Mevelyn did it again by herself—and it looks like she was successful."

Successful how? I'm back home and she isn't.

Now that I was safe and sound, my mate followed me every where. Made sure I ate my meals—even when I stared at the food. I had no words to say. Not yet, anyway.

Pack members stopped by the house from afternoon

into the evening. Somber faces wished me well. But one face blended into the other. Until Grandma appeared. Neither of us spoke, and she merely held me close, whispering words from a Russian folk song I hadn't heard in a very long time: *Odnozvuchno gremit kolokolchik.* The Lonely Bell.

The song told of a coachman who left home and never returned. In her sweet soft voice, I could hear her sadness, how she feared I wouldn't return.

From across the room, I caught my father saying, "What's wrong with my daughter?"

Thorn replied, "A part of her is probably still on the mountain. We need to give her time…and love."

When twilight hit, my family left and Karey and her kin checked on me. I could smell them before they entered the cottage and anguish hit me like an ocean's unyielding waves. All of us were back home, but not her aunt.

Instead of sharing tears, Karey, Dione, and Grace sat with me, their expressions bittersweet and pensive.

"Oh, Nat." Karey hugged me again and again. "Auntie wouldn't want to see you like this." She placed the fly fishing lure her aunt crafted for me in my palm. The handcrafted wooden minnow had exquisite detail from its head down to its tail.

"Do you know," I managed to ask, "if she's okay?"

Dione shook her head. "Those who serve She Who Always Walks the Path are never heard from again. Knowing our aunt though, she's alive and making things more difficult for her new mistress. We hope."

Karey reached out to touch my knee. "We all make choices for the greater good," she said softly. "Some of them grand. Some of them small. My aunt wouldn't have taken your place unless she knew something we didn't. You're important to her. To everyone here."

Mevelyn's words echoed through me. *"Sister Wolf still has work to do."*

How I wished I knew what she wanted me to do. Was I supposed to save the world or something?

I spent the evening with my family, even enjoying a meal from my mom, but as night descended and Thorn made me go to bed, my anxiety crept in. Feeling my mate settled against my back should've eased my fears, but I couldn't stop thinking about the Huntress's collar around my neck. Or the monstrous strength of the leash that chained me to her.

"You're shaking," he whispered and clenched me tighter.

"Oh, Thorn. So much has happened." I spilled everything, telling him about my time with the Huntress. I even revealed how Erica's father was the one who helped the Basilisk King.

My mate listened and didn't interrupt me.

"Just rest now," he said when I finished. "You don't have to worry anymore." He stroked my arms. "Erica told me everything after we fought the Basilisk King."

"And?" I whispered.

"Oliver's gone and if he returns, he must face the *fury* of the pack."

Morning arrived and I'd barely slept. When I got up, Thorn tried to tug me back to bed, but I refused. Lying in bed would only allow me to dwell on what I'd lost.

I got dressed and Thorn prepared a hot breakfast of French toast covered in powdered sugar and strawberries. He even turned on the radio and switched to my favorite jazz station. My appetite hadn't improved, but I took a couple of bites to show my gratitude.

To help clear my head before I showed up at The Bends, I took the long way to work. I drove past Oliver Holden's house, taking in the somber For Sale sign, before I headed south down the Parkway. I weaved through the back roads around Double Trouble State Park. Heat rose off the concrete in waves, but the humid breeze swept through the car, bringing serenity.

I arrived at work, my thoughts less scattered, but heart no less heavy. Mevelyn said I had work to do. Not sure if living as an alpha female and working at The Bends was what she meant, but I might as well prepare for what was to come.

As I got out of the Nissan, I ignored the dented front fender. Thorn assured me our insurance would cover the damages, but our monthly payments sure as hell weren't going down.

In the back office, Erica nodded my way from one of the work desks. "Good to see you. The fire witch keeps sneezing and setting small fires. Bill sounded eager to have you back, too." She grimaced. "I'd take your time going in."

I shrugged. Might as well jump into the wolf's mouth.

I walked out onto the showroom floor and inhaled the familiar scents that steadied me: furniture polish, floor cleaner, and aged antiques. Bliss.

"About time you got here," Bill grumbled from behind me.

I glanced at my watch. "I came early to clean up any messes you guys left me. What is it this time?"

"I've got good news for you."

Bill never had good news for other people. The news was only good if he got a benefit out of it.

His mouth spread out in a full smile. "I spoke to Kramkar, and he was impressed you drove out the Basilisk King."

"Great—"

"And he told me you don't have to finish the week at his shop."

Now this was the kind of news I needed to hear.

Bill added, "You can work for the demons down the road for a couple of days. What do you think?"

I didn't answer the goblin and marched out the back door. I kept going until I reached my car. I'd need another lap around the state park again. Maybe two at this rate.

I sighed. Erica did warn me.

Guess I'd never learn.

The End

ACKNOWLEDGMENTS

My journey with Natalya Stravinsky has come a long way since 2011. Yep, you read that right. I came up with Natalya's character almost ten years ago. I was reading a medical journal and came upon an article about obsessive compulsive disorder and the treatment plans. Yeah, I know, light reading. My writer brain sparked and I asked myself the question: what if a werewolf had OCD?

Since that fateful first story sold to Del Rey and Random House, I have had many adventures with Nat. The one author who has been there since the beginning was Sarah Jude, my partner-in-crime who helped whip me into shape. You are *still* the best Grammar Chick ever, Sarah, and I hope to be as awesome as you someday. I also have to thank Yasmine Galenorn for her encouragement. You are a source of light in the dark, Yasmine.

Thanks also to Nam Nguyen, my content editor, and MK Books Editing for helping me craft a better story. I'm so grateful you joined me for the ride!

A smart, sexy, rip-roaring good time!

ANGIE FOX, NYT BESTSELLING AUTHOR

Coveted is odd, funny, original and not at all what you'd expect. The writing is excellent, the characters come off so realistic they should have their own reality show, and the story is authentic and original.

LYNN VIEHL, NYT BESTSELLING AUTHOR

Characters of all shapes, sizes and species abound in this new series from debut author Madison…How can you go wrong when your heroine is a werewolf with OCD? Madison tells her story with a lot of humor, and readers will be waiting with bated breath for her next story.

ROMANTIC TIMES BOOK REVIEWS

This is the start of a funny and touching new paranormal series, which may be dealing with supernatural creatures, but gives them all very human problems that make them very relatable. I loved this book and can't wait to see what's in store for Natalya next!

PARKERSBURG NEWS AND SENTINEL

Want to see how it all began?

COVETED

Prequel
Novella
0.5

Book
1

Book
2

Novella
2.5

Book
3

Short Story
Collection

Prequel feat.
Aggie
McClure

VALKYRIE
RISING
PRESS

ALSO BY SHAWNTELLE MADISON

Coveted Series

Collected (Prequel Novella) #0.5

Coveted #1

Kept #2

Pocketed (Novella) #2.5

Compelled #3

Cursed (Collection of Short Stories)

Flea Market Magic Series

Thrift Store Trolls

Heroes Run in Packs Series

Hadley Werewolves

Windham Werewolves

McGinnis Werewolves (Coming soon)

Urban Fantasy/Paranormal Romance

Bitter Disenchantment

Repossessed

Taming the Viking's Dragon

At Your Service Series

Bound to You

Surrender to You

ABOUT THE AUTHOR

Shawntelle Madison is a Web developer who loves to weave words as well as code. She'd be reluctant to admit it, but if pressed, she'd say that she covets and collects source code. After losing her first summer job detasseling corn, Madison performed various jobs, from fast-food clerk to grunt programmer to university webmaster. Writing eccentric characters is her favorite job of all. On any given day when she's not surgically attached to her computer, she can be found watching cheesy horror movies or the latest action-packed anime. Shawntelle Madison lives in Missouri with her husband and children.

www.ingramcontent.com/pod-product-compliance
Lightning Source LLC
Chambersburg PA
CBHW021109110726
47900CB00007B/2103